Textbook written according to revised syllabus of F.Y.B.Com.
prescribed by University of Pune from 2013-2014.
Also useful for other universities in Maharashtra.

Business Environment and Entrepreneurship

Prof. Ravindra Kothavade

M.Com., M.I.M.A.,
(Head of the Commerce Dept.)
C. T. Bora Collage, Shirur, Dist. Pune

Diamond Publication

Business Environment and Entrepreneurship

Prof. Ravindra Kothavade

First Edition : June 2013

ISBN 978-81-8483-536-6

© **Diamond Publications**

Cover Page :
Sham Bhalekar

Published by :
Diamond Publications
264/3 Shaniwar Peth, 302 Anugrah Apartment
Near Omkareshwar Temple, Pune - 411 030
☎ 020-24452387, 24466642

info@diamondbookspune.com
www.diamondbookspune.com

Sale Distributor :
Diamond Book Depot
661 Narayan Peth
Appa Balwant Chowk
Pune 411 030
Tel. - 24480677, 66020282

University of Pune
(2013 - 14)
F.Y.B.Com.
Optional Paper
Subject Name : Business Environment and Entrepreneurship

Objectives :
1. To make the students aware about the Business Environment.
2. To create entrepreneurial awareness among students,
3. To motivate students lo make their mind set for taking up entrepreneurship as career.

Term I

Unit No.	Topic
1.	Business Environment - Concept- Importance - Inter relationship between environment and entrepreneur, Types of Environment- Natural, Economic - Political - Social - Technical - Cultural - Educational - Legal - Cross-cultural - Geographical etc.
2	Environment Issues Protecting the Natural Environment – prevention of pollution and depletion of natural resources; conservation of natural resources, Opportunites in Environment.
3	Problems of growth Relevance to entrepreneurship - Unemployment- Poverty-Regional imbalance- Social injustice- Inflation - Parallel Economy- Lack of Technical knowledge and information.
4	The Entrepreneur- Evolution of the term entrepreneur-" Competencies of an entrepreneur - Distinction between entrepreneur and manager- Entrepreneur and enterprise - Entrepreneur and Intrapreneur. Entrepreneur and Entrepreneurship.

Unit No.	Topic
1	Entrepreneurial Behaviour - Comparison between entrepreneurial and non-entrepreneurial Personality-Habits of Entrepreneurs - Dynamics of Motivation
2	Entrepreneurship Importance of Entrepreneurship - Economic Development and Industrialization, Entrepreneurship in Economic Theory- Role of Entrepreneurship ~ Entrepreneur as a catalyst.
3	National Level Training Organizations in promoting entrepreneurship (1) Entrepreneurship Development Institute of India (EDII) State Level Training Organizations in promoting entrepreneurship (1) MCED (2) DIC (3) Maratha Chamber of Commerce and their role. (4) Local NGO's and their roles.
4	Biographical study of entrepreneurs i) Narayan R. Murthy ii) Cyruas Poonawala iii) Any successful Entrepreneur from your area (Milind Kamble)

Contents

Part I

Part II

Chapter 1
Business Environment

Introduction:

The process of starting up and developing a business is a real challenge. In order to help entrepreneurs with this, it is essential to create a favorable business environment. Ensuring easier access to funding, making legislation clearer and more effective and developing an entrepreneurial culture and support networks for businesses are all important in setting up and growth of businesses.

Business does not operate in a vacuum. Generally, business operates in a multifaceted environment which is subject to a large measure of change. There is a mutual relationship between business and its environment; that is, the environment exerts pressure on business while business, in turn, influences various aspects of its environment. Business also depends on its environment for the supply of all its input and at the same time to absorb its output. The environment provides opportunities or alternative avenues for investment which the business manager can exploit to his/her advantage. The business environment may also constitute a threat to business if changes in it are unfavorable to business operations. If the business must survive in the long run, it must be capable of responding and adapting to environmental conditions from time to time as these environmental factors are dynamic in nature. Therefore, the business manager must make his/her plans, take decisions and execute them within the limits imposed by the environment.

Concept:

Business environment can be defined as a series of factors or conditions that are external to the business but which have influence on the operations of the business enterprise. By 'external', it means that these factors or forces are not usually within the control of the business enterprise. Business environment forms the setting in which the firm makes its decisions. For the firm to succeed, it must take its environment into account in making its decisions.

A business firm is an open system. It gets resources from the environment and supplies its goods and services to the environment. There are different levels of environmental forces. Some are close and internal forces whereas others are external forces. External forces may be related to national level, regional level or international level. These environmental forces provide opportunities or threats to the business community.

Every business organization tries to grab the available opportunities and face the threats that emerge from the business environment. Business organizations cannot change the external environment but they can adjust accordingly. They change their internal environment to grab the external opportunities and face the external environmental threats.

It is, therefore, very important to analyze business environment to survive and to get success for a business in its industry. Hence managers play a vital role to analyze business environment so that they could pursue effective business strategy. A business firm gets human resources, capital, technology, information, energy, and raw materials from society. It follows government rules and regulations, social norms and cultural values, regional treaty and global alignment, economic rules and tax policies of the government. Thus, a business organization is a dynamic entity because it operates in a dynamic business environment.

The term 'business environment' is affected by external forces, factors and institutions that are beyond the control of the business. These include customers, competitors, suppliers, government, and the social, political, legal and technological factors etc. While some of these factors or forces may have direct influence over the business firm, others may operate indirectly. Thus, business environment may be defined as the total surroundings, which have a direct or indirect impact on the functioning of business. It may also be defined as the set of external factors, such as economic factors, social factors, political and legal factors, demographic factors, and technical factors etc., which are uncontrollable in nature and affects the business decisions of a firm.

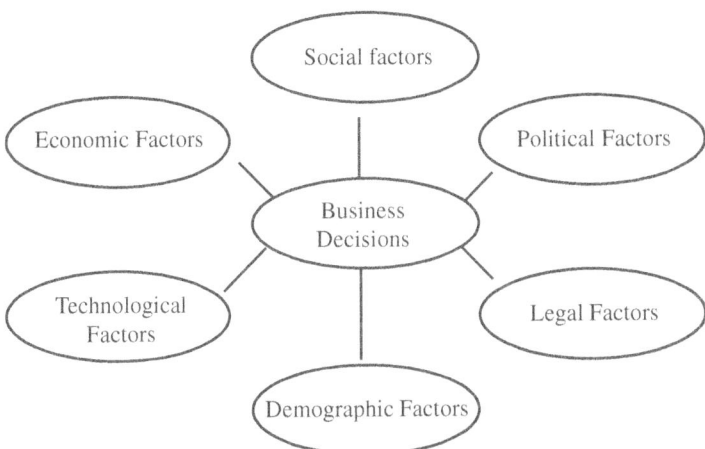

Thus following are the chief characteristics of the business environment:

1. Totality of External Forces:

Business environment is the sum totals of all those factors which are available outside the business and over which the business has no control.

2. Specific and General Forces:

Specific forces affect the firms of an industry separately, e.g., customers, suppliers, competitive firms, investors, etc. And General forces affect all the firms of an industry equally, e.g., social, political, legal and technical situations.

3. Interrelatedness:

The different factors of business environment are co-related. For example, let us suppose that there is a change in the import-export policy with the coming of a new government. In this case, the coming of new government to power and change in the import-export policy are political and economic changes respectively. Thus, a change in one factor affects the other factor.

4. Dynamic Nature:

As is clear that environment is a mixture of many factors and changes in some or the other factors continue to take place. Therefore, it is said that business environment is dynamic.

5. Uncertainty:

Nothing can be said with any amount of certainty about the factors of the business environment because they continue to change quickly. The professional people who determine the business strategy take into consideration the likely changes beforehand. But this is a risky job. For example, technical changes are very rapid. Nobody can anticipate the possibility of these swift technical changes. Anything can happen, anytime. The same is the situation of fashion.

6. Complexity:

Environment comprises of many factors. All these factors are related to each other. Therefore, their individual effect on the business cannot be recognized.

7. Relativity:

Business environment is related to the local conditions and this is the reason as to why the business environment happens to be different in different countries and different even in the same country at different places.

Importance:

As we know, business environment refers to the surrounding factors of business enterprise which affect its operation and determines its effectiveness. Now-a-days modern business is not independent. It cannot work in isolation. So to achieve its economic goal, it cannot ignore the interest of the society. The government of the country also has the interest in business affairs. It enacts legislation, formulates business policies and controls business in the best interest of people.

Thus we can say that business environment is a wide term as it has got two dimensional relationships with the environment. On the one hand it affects the social, political and economic environment and on the other hand it is affected by country's social, political, economic and legal environment.

An analysis of business environment helps to identify strength, weakness, opportunities & threats to the business enterprise. Analysis is very necessary for the survival and growth of the business enterprise. The importance of business environment can be briefly explained as below.

1. Identification of Strength:

The analysis of the internal environment helps to identify strength of the firm. For instance, if the company has good personal policies in respect of promotion, transfer, training, etc. then it indicates the strength of the firm in respect of personal policies. This strength can be identified through the job satisfaction and performance of the employees. After identifying the strengths the firm must try to consolidate its strengths by further improvement in its existing plans and policies.

2.Identification of Weakness:

The analysis of the internal environment indicates not only strengths but also the weakness of the firm. A firm may be strong in certain areas; whereas it may be weak in some other areas. The firm should identify such weaknesses so as to correct them as early as possible.

3.Identification of Opportunities:

An analysis of the external environment helps the business firm to identify the opportunities in the market. The business firm should make every possible effort to grab the opportunities as and when they come.

4.Identification of Threats:

Business may be subject to threats from competitors and others. Therefore environmental analysis helps to identify threats from the environment identification of threats at an earlier date is always beneficial to the firm as it helps to take preventive measures for the same.

5.Exploitation of Business Opportunities:

Environment opens new opportunities for the expansion of business activities. Study of environment is necessary in order to discover and exploit such opportunities fully.

6.Keeping Business Enterprise Alert:

Environment study is needed as it keeps the business unit alert in its approach and activities. In the absence of environmental changes, the business activities will be dull and lifeless. The problems and prospects of business can be understood properly through the study of business environment. This enables an enterprise to face the problems with confidence and secure the maximum benefits of business opportunities available.

7.Keeping Business Flexible and Dynamic:

Study of business environment is needed for keeping business flexible and dynamic as per the changes in the environmental forces. This will enable the development of business organization.

8.Understanding Future Problems and Prospects:

The study of business environment enables to understand future problems and prospects of business in advance. This enables business organizations to face the problems boldly and also take the benefit of favorable situation.

9. Making Business Socially Acceptable:

Environment study enables businessmen to expand the business and also make it acceptable to different social groups. Business organizations can make positive contribution for maintaining ecological balance by studying social environment.

10.Ensures Optimum Utilization of Resources:

The study of business environment is needed as it ensures optimum use of resources available. For this, the study of economic and technological environment is useful. Such study enables organization to take full benefit of government policies, concessions provided, and technological developments and so on.

11.Ensures Survival and Growth:

Study of Business environment informs about suitable changes to be affected in business policies. This helps the business organizations to grow & prosper.

12.Maintaining adaptability to changes:

Business environment guides the business organization about socio-economic changes & the organization must accordingly adapt these changes. This enables the business organization to survive for a longer period.

Interrelationship between Environment and Entrepreneur:

Every member of the society must work under the sphere of natural environment and therefore relationship with natural environment with that of an entrepreneur must be studied.

Environment:

The natural environment encompasses all living and non-living things occurring naturally on Earth or some region thereof. It is an environment that encompasses the interaction of all living species.

Entrepreneur:

The entrepreneur is an individual who, rather than working as an employee, runs a small business and assumes all the risk and reward of a given business venture, idea, or good or service offered for sale. The entrepreneur is commonly seen as a business leader and innovator of new ideas and business processes.

Environment brings certain threats as well as opportunities to the organization and every entrepreneur must look for them in order to succeed in achieving goals of the organization.

Interrelationship between environment and entrepreneur can be stated in a following manner:

a) Environment is an outer sphere in which entrepreneur must work for the organizational benefit. Opportunities and threats from the environment must be studied and evaluated accordingly.

b) In India three legislations are active for industries to remain within the pollution control standards set by Government.

    1)   Water (Prevention and Control of Pollution) Act, 1974, with amendments made in 1988

    2)   Air (Prevention and Control of Pollution) Act, 1981, with 1987 amendments

    3)   Environment (Protection) Act1986

Every entrepreneur must study these legislations in detail and work out business plans accordingly. Provisions of these laws are very crucial for the implementation of business plans. Care must be taken while formulating strategies and those must be made in light of these three laws.

c) Raw material procurement is an important issue which needs attention from today's entrepreneurs because shortage of raw material is increasing rapidly and hence raw material wastage must be looked for and audit must be planned for raw material management.

d) Global Warming: Scientists say that unless we reduce global warming emissions, average global temperatures could rise and lead to undesirable economic, climatic, biodiversity and public health consequences. Momentum to address global warming has undeniably accelerated in recent years, heightened by media and entertainment industry attention to the reality and impacts of global warming, as well as attitude changes in federal, state and local legislatures.

This critical issue must be taken in to consideration while managing business. Entrepreneur needs to be dynamic while reacting to the external environment forces.

Types of Environment:

There are mainly two types of business environment, internal and external. A business has absolute control in the internal environment, where as it has no control over the external environment. It is therefore, required by businesses, to modify their internal environment on the basis of pressures from external.

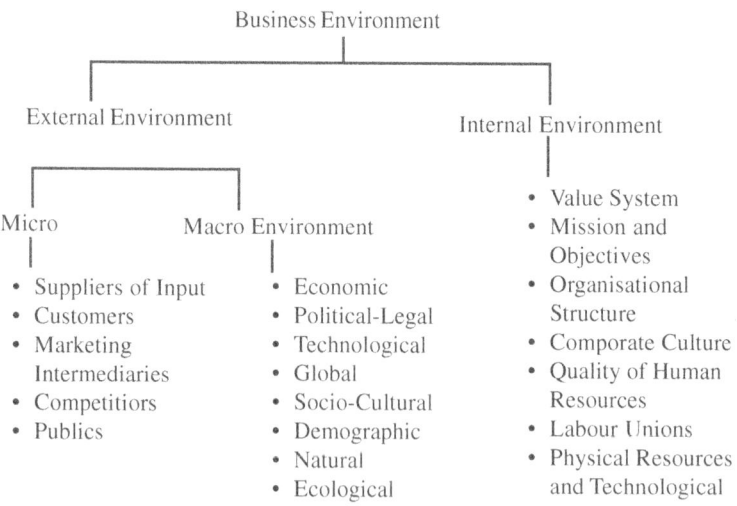

1. External Environment:

A) External Micro- Environment:

Micro environment includes those people whose decisions and actions have a direct impact on the company. Production and selling of commodities are the two important aspects of modern business. The various constituents of micro environment are as below:

a. Suppliers of inputs: An important factor in the external micro environment of a firm is the supplier of its inputs such as raw materials and components.

b. Customers: The people who buy and use a firm's product and services are an important part of external micro environment. Since sales of a product or service is critical for a firm's survival and growth, it is necessary to keep the customers satisfied.

c. Marketing intermediaries: In the firm's external micro environment, marketing intermediaries play an essential role of selling and distributing its products to the final customers. Marketing is an important link between a business firm and its ultimate customers.

d. Competitors: Different firms in an industry compete with each other for sale of their products. This competition may be on the basis of pricing of their products and also non- price competition through competitive advertising such as sponsoring some events to promote the sale of different varieties and models of their products.

e. Publics: Finally, publics are an important force in external micro environment. Public, according to Philip Kotler, "is any group that has an actual or potential interest in or impact on the company's ability to achieve its objective." Environmentalists, media groups, women's associations, consumer protection groups, local groups, citizens association are some important examples of publics which have an important bearing on the business decisions of the firm.

B) External macro environment:

Apart from micro environment, business firms face large external environmental forces. An important fact about external macro environmental forces is that they are uncontrollable by the management. Because of the uncontrollable nature of macro environment, it forces a firm to adjust or adapt to these external forces. These factors are:

a. Economic Environment: Economic environment includes all those forces which have an economic impact on business. Accordingly, total economic environment consists of agriculture, industrial production, infrastructure, and planning, basic economic philosophy, stages of economic development, trade cycles, national income, savings, money supply, price level and population.

b. Political-legal Environment: The political- legal environment includes the activities of three political institutions, namely, legislature, executive and judiciary which usually play a useful role in shaping, directing, developing and controlling business activities. In order to attain a meaningful business growth, a stable and dynamic political-legal environment is very important.

c. Technological Environment: Technology implies systematic application of scientific or other organized knowledge to practical tasks or activities. Business makes it possible for technology to reach the people in proper format. As technology is changing fast, businessmen should keep a close look on those technological changes for its adaptation in their business activities.

d. Global or International Environment: The Global environment plays an important role in shaping business activity. With the liberalization and globalization of the economy, business environment of an economy has become totally different wherein it has to bear all shocks and benefits arising out of global environment.

e. Socio-cultural Environment: The social and cultural environment also influences the business environment indirectly. These includes people's attitude to work and wealth, ethical issues, role of family, marriage, religion and education and also social responsiveness of business.

f. Demographic environment: The demographic environment includes the size and growth of population, life expectancy of the people, rural-urban distribution of population, the technological skills and educational levels of labor force. All these demographic features have an important bearing on the functioning of business firms.

g. Natural Environment: The Natural environment influences business in diverse ways. The natural environment is the ultimate source of many inputs such as raw materials and energy. In fact, the availability of natural resources in the region or country is the basic factor in determining business activity in it. The natural environment which includes geographical and ecological factors such as minerals and oil reserves, water and forest resources, weather and climatic conditions and port facilities are all highly significant for various business activities. For example, steel producing industries are set up near the coalmines to save cost of transporting coal to distant locations. The natural environment also affects the demand for goods. For example, in places where temperatures are high the demand for coolers and air conditioners are high. Similarly, weather and climatic conditions influence the demand pattern for clothing, building materials for housing etc. Natural calamities like floods, droughts, earthquake etc. are devastating for business activities.

h. Ecological environment: Due to the efforts of environmentalists and international organizations such as the World Bank the people have now become conscious of the adverse effects of depletion of exhaustible natural resources and pollution of environment by business activity. Accordingly, laws have been passed for conservation of natural resources and prevention of environment pollution. These laws have imposed additional responsibilities and costs for business firms.

2) Internal Environment:

The factors in internal environment of business are to a certain extent controllable because the firm can change or modify these factors to improve its efficiency. However, the firm may not be able to change all the factors.

The various Internal Factors are:

a. **Value system:**

The value system of an organization means the ethical beliefs that guide the organization in achieving its mission and objectives. It is a widely acknowledged fact that the extent to which the value system is shared by all in the organization is an important factor contributing to its success.

b. **Mission and objectives:**

The business domain of the company, direction of development, business philosophy, business policy etc. are guided by the mission and objectives of the company. The objective of all firms is assumed to be maximization of profit. Mission is defined as the overall purpose or reason for its existence which guides and influences its business decision and economic activities.

c. **Organization Structure:**

The organizational structure, the composition of the board of directors, the professionalism of management etc. are important factors influencing business decisions. An efficient working of a business organization requires that the organization structure should be conducive for quick decision-making.

d. **Corporate culture:**

Corporate culture is an important factor for determining the internal environment of any company. In a closed and threatening type of corporate culture the business decisions are taken by top level managers while the middle level and lower level managers have no say in business decision making. This leads to lack of trust and confidence among subordinate officials of the company. This results in a sense of separation among the lower level managers and workers of the company. In an open and participating culture, business decisions are taken by the lower level managers and top management has a high degree of confidence in the subordinates.

e. **Quality of human resources:**

Quality of employees that is of human resources of a firm is an important factor of internal environment of a firm. The characteristics of the human resources like skill, quality, capabilities, attitude and commitment of its employees etc. could contribute to the strength and weaknesses of an organization. Some organizations find it difficult to carry out restructuring or modernization plans because of resistance by its employees.

f. **Labor Unions:**

Labor unions collectively bargains with the managers for better wages and better working conditions of the different categories of workers etc. For the smooth working of business firm good relations between management and labor unions is required.

g. **Physical resources and technological capabilities:**

Physical resources such as plant and equipment and technological capabilities of a firm determine its competitive strength which is an important factor for determining its efficiency and unit cost of production. Research and development capabilities of a company determine its ability to introduce innovations which enhances productivity of workers.

We will now concentrate more deeply on Macro environment viz. Natural, Economic, Political, Social, Technical, Cultural, Educational, Legal, Cross-cultural and Geographical.

1) Natural Environment:

As mentioned earlier the natural environment is the source of many inputs such as raw materials and energy. Availability of natural resources affects most of the business activity. The natural environment which includes geographical and ecological factors such as minerals and oil reserves, water and forest resources, weather and climatic conditions and port facilities are all highly significant for various business activities. The Natural Environment also affects the demand from the customers.

So the Natural Environmental Factors that affect business are:

Companies in the industrial or manufacturing industry often work with different kinds of equipment, machinery and chemical-producing agents. In effect, a business' day-to-day operations can have an impact on the natural environment. To reduce the likelihood of damage to the environment, federal and state regulations require businesses consider certain natural environmental factors in their overall operations plans.

1. Environmental Regulations:

Regulating business activities is one way government agencies protect the environment. Businesses must meet certain standards that help to reduce any adverse effects a company's activities have on the environment. As a result, natural environmental factors, such as clean water and clean air, dictate how companies conduct their day-to-day operations.

2. Permit Requirements:

Companies involved in activities that impact their surrounding environment typically have to file for operating permits through a local, state or federal government agency. Business permit requirements enable government agencies to regulate and keep track of business activities. These permits serve different purposes, some of which include setting minimal standards for any air emissions, dictating certain procedures for handling waste and hazardous materials and regulating how a company's day-to-day operations interact with nearby water supplies. In effect, natural environmental factors determine the types of operations a company can engage in within a particular locale or region.

3. Compliance Requirements:

Natural environmental factors affect a business' operations as well as its ability to expand or take on new operations. In effect, companies must comply with environmental regulations in all stages of a business' development. Companies considering purchasing a building should ensure the building conforms to environmental regulations or risk paying penalties for noncompliance. Building expansions must also meet regulatory requirements. Companies that have a record of noncompliance may risk having their operations shut down on a permanent basis. Ultimately, natural environmental factors affect a company's overall costs in terms of ensuring equipment and procedures meet regulatory requirements.

4. Environmental Contaminants:

Businesses that work with hazardous materials on a regular basis have certain responsibilities when it comes to ensuring contaminants don't reach or affect the natural environment. There are laws which hold business owners liable for activities that contaminate surrounding air, soil or water supplies. These laws even apply to new business owners who unknowingly purchase a contaminated site or purchase an operation that fails to meet compliance standards. Ultimately, owners, both old and new, must cover cleanup costs as well as the costs of restoring a property to required environmental standards.

Natural Environment is again important to businesses that directly rely on the environment, e.g. tourism or mining industries. So the benefits derived from Natural environments are.

Benefit	Meaning
Provisioning	Providing goods such as fuel, energy, water, food, timber/paper etc.
Regulatory	Providing regulation in the climate, disease, flooding, etc.
Cultural	Meeting recreational, spiritual, aesthetic, inspirational needs etc.
Supporting	Supporting the above 3 benefits, for example, soil formation, nutrient recycling, etc.

2) Economic Environment:

The economic environment of a business refers to the broad characteristics of the economic system in which a business firm operates. The present day economic environment of business is a complex phenomenon. The business sector has economic relations with the Government, the capital market, the household sector and the foreign sector. These different sectors, together, influence the trends and structure of the economy. The form and functioning of the economy varies from country to country. The design and structure of an economic system is conditioned by socio-political arrangements. Such arrangements are relevant from the standpoint of macro-economic decision-making.

For example, in a democratic set up, people exercise an influence, direct or indirect, through the system of casting votes, on the nature of the decisions taken by the Government. In a parliamentary system, most decisions are processed by Cabinet ministers, whereas under a presidential form of Government the President acts as the real manager of the state: It is he who takes or makes decisions. Similarly, Marco-decision-making is more decentralized in a federal form of Government than in unitary form of Government. You may argue that the decisions being referred to are political decisions. True, but it must be emphasized that political decisions have far-reaching economic implications. After all, the Government is the manger of the economy.

The nature of Government ownership, control and regulation of the economic activities of a country provides form and shape to the nature of economic organizations. In a capitalist society, the private sector induced by the profit motive and led by the free market, takes the major economic decisions of investment, production and distribution. In a socialist society, most of the economic decisions are taken by the Government which is guided by the social welfare motive and central planning. In a communist society, economic decisions, including those of consumption, are taken by the state in the interest of the community as a whole. In a mixed economy, the private, public and joint sectors and the like all have some say in the major decisions that influence the functioning of an economy.

All modern economics, whether capitalist, socialized, communist or missed, have certain fundamental economic problems to deal with. In each and every economy, including the so-called "affluent society", some or many resources are scarce. Consequently, choices concerning the resource use have to be made together by individuals, by business corporations, and by society. It is the social choice and community preferences which give substance to the question of macro-economic decisions. From the standpoint of resources, the basic economic problem of every economy is that of just allocation of resources and subsequent optimum production. There are many aspects to this problem: What to produce? How to produce? For whom to produce? When to produce?

Every economy has to decide on the quality and quantity of the goods and services to be produced. It has to decide on the nature of the technology and technique of production in view of factor endowment. It has to decide on the course and pattern of distribution of goods and services produced. It has to decide on the timing of production. The process of decision-making differs depending on how these problems are solved in different economies. This is what constitutes the functioning of the economy, or the nature of the economic environment.

So some of the points which can be made about the organization and functioning of modern economics are:

1. In most economies, both "free market mechanism" and "Centralized planning" exist in different degrees even today. By "free market mechanism" or "price mechanism", it means a free play of the market forces of demand and supply to determine an equilibrium solution of the allocation problem. Market mechanism determines commodity prices, factor prices, and income distribution. By "planning", it means a program of action based upon consistency and feasibility of attaining a set of targets in view of a set of objectives through a set of instruments. Thus, the economy in which a business firm operates today is not an exclusively free economy making an indiscriminate use of prices and the markets. Rather, it is directed by a system of planning, control, regulation and coordination.

2. In most economies, positive intervention by the Government in day-to-day economic affairs has existed over several decades in the past. Planning is a form of Government intervention. Besides this, the Government can also intervene through a system of controls and regulations. The government enforces minimum wages, commodity controls, fair trade practices, etc, through legislation. The basic objectives of such economic legislations and policies are : growth, efficiency and equity. However, intervention by the Government is now on the decrease. Many economics have relaxed regulations and controls through economic reforms, and are allowing a free play of market forces.

3. Modern economies are not "closed" and "open"; they are actively engaged in international trade and cooperation. So, the international transmission effect today is stronger than ever before. The maintenance of steady growth and enveloped countries dependent on the acceleration of growth in underdeveloped countries. This idea has given new dimensions to issues like the role of multinational corporations, the ecological balance and the

transfer of technology. The technological revolution is making a prominent effect. In order to keep their dynamism, the economics are determined to develop science and technology.

These facts define the environment and set the constraints within which modern business firms must operate. The managements cannot overlook the environment, whether market or non-market. No management can ignore the functioning of markets, the objectives of national planning, the polices of the Government or their social responsibilities, or the rate, pattern and structure of economic changes, or the forms of international cooperation. Progressive managements must keep themselves continuously informed about the magnitude and direction of changes in the national as well as international economic environment. Of course, both economic and non-economic environment have an important bearing on managerial decisions.

So far we discussed the effect of Economic Environment on the business of a firm. So let's now discuss how the Indian economic environment is.

Indian Economic Environment:

India's is a mixed economy. In fact, Indian has a very complex mixed economic system.

A simple mixed economic system is characterized by the existence of the private and public sectors. India has a multiplicity of sectors: private and public sectors. India has a multiplicity of sectors: (dominant undertakings, foreign companies, etc.), public, joint, co-operative, workers' sectors and also "tiny sector".

Secondly, a simple mixed economy is characterized by complementarily between central planning and pricing. India has a multiplicity of mechanisms at work: five-year plans, annual plans during plan holidays, economic reforms and reconstruction programs during and after plan vacations, a system of controls and regulatory measures, attempts towards streamlining and simplification of procedures, private traders and public distributors for the same product and hence a system of dual prices, ceiling prices, floor prices, subsidized prices, statutory prices, retention prices, procurement prices, levy prices, and free market prices; concretionary monetary policies and expansionary fiscal policies, etc. In India there is a complex system of liberal rules, strict regulations, control mechanisms, planning and a host of price regulations.

The social welfare function in India is defined by the multiplicity of objectives which are sometimes conflicting in nature. For example, in terms of our five-year plans, India is aiming at efficiency, justice and stability. A progressive tax system is used as a means to reduce income inequalities, but the same tax policy hampers private incentives to invest and to generate the growth forces thereby.

The present day mixed economy of India has evolved through a series of policy formulations and legislations.

There are a few critical elements of the economic environment. These critical elements are relevant from the standpoint of both corporate business management and national economic management in India.

The critical elements of macro-economic environment are :
• Economic system
• Nature of the economy
• Anatomy of the economy
• Functioning of the economy
• Economic planning and programs
• Economic policy statements and proposals
• Economic controls and regulations
• Economic legislations
• Economic trends and structure, and
• Economic problems and prospects

3) Political Environment:

The political environment in a country affects business organizations and could introduce a risk factor that could cause them to suffer a loss. Businesses need to be prepared to deal with the fallouts of government politics.

Impact on the Economy:

The political environment in a country affects its economic environment. The economic environment, in turn, affects the performance of a business organization.

Changes in Regulation:

Governments could change their rules and regulations, and this could have an effect on a business.

Political Stability:

Particularly for businesses that operate internationally, a lack of political stability in any country has an effect on its operations. Such disruptions have occurred in Sri Lanka, which went through a protracted civil war, and in Egypt and Syria, which have been subject to disturbances as people agitate for certain rights.

Mitigation of Risk:

One way to manage political risk is to buy political risk insurance. Organizations that have international operations use this type of insurance to mitigate their risk exposure as a result of political instability. Government actions which affects the operations of a company or business. These actions may be on local, regional, national or international level. Business owners and managers pay close attention to the political environment to gauge how government actions will affect their company.

No matter how attractive the economic prospects of a particular country or region are, doing business there might prove to be financially disastrous if the host government inflicts heavy financial penalties on a company or if unanticipated events in the political arena lead to the loss of income-generating assets.

The political environment in which the firm operates will have a significant impact on a company's international marketing activities. The greater the level of involvement in a foreign markets, the greater is the need to monitor the political climate of the country. Changes in government often result in changes in policy and attitudes towards foreign business. Bearing in mind that a foreign company operates in a host country at the discretion of the government concerned, the government can either encourage foreign activities by offering attractive opportunities for investment and trade, or discourage its activities by imposing restrictions. An exporter that is continuously aware of shifts in government attitude, will be able to adapt its marketing strategies accordingly.

Nearly all governments today play active roles in their countries' economies. Government ownership of economic activities is still prevalent in the developed economies, as well as in certain developing countries which lack a sufficiently well developed private sector to support a free market system.

The primary concern to an exporter should be the stability of the target country's political environment. A loss of confidence in this respect could lead to a company having to reduce its operations in the market or to withdraw from the market altogether. One of the surest indicators of political instability is a frequent change in regime. Although a change in government need not be accompanied by violence, it often leads to a change in policy towards business, particularly international business. Such a development could impact harshly on a firms long-term international marketing program.

Products considered by a government to be non-essential, undesirable, or a threat to local industry are frequently subjected to a variety of import restrictions such as quotas and tariffs. It is also important to be aware of the nature of the relationship between your country and the foreign target market.

The political environment is connected to the international business environment through the concept of political risk.

Political risk:

Political risk is determined differently for different companies, as not all of them will be equally affected by political changes. For example, industries requiring heavy capital investment are generally considered to be more vulnerable to political risk than those requiring less capital investment.

Political risk is of a macro nature when politically inspired environmental changes affect all foreign investment. It is of a micro nature when the environmental changes are intended to affect only selected fields of business activity or foreign firms with specific characteristics.

When business is conducted in developing countries, the risks of greatest concern are civil disorder, war and expropriation. When business is conducted in industrialized countries, labor disruptions and price controls are generally seen to pose the greatest threats to a company's profitability.

All organizations doing business abroad should be aware of the fact that what they do could be the object of some political action. Hence, they need to recognize that their success or failure could depend on how well they cope with political decisions, and how well they anticipate changes in political attitudes and policies.

Businesses can be affected by many aspects of government policy. In particular, all businesses must comply with the law. They must also consider the impact of any forthcoming legislation on their operations. This may require taking action before the legislation comes into effect.

Legislation and regulations:

One issue that affects manufacturers and retailers of electronic goods is the disposal of these products at the end of their life. Recycling is high on the public agenda. There are government initiatives to promote more recycling. Businesses must obey these environmental laws. However, a company that goes further by taking other measures to minimize its environmental impact will be seen more favorably by consumers.

Government initiatives:

Businesses also have to take into account the more general political ambitions of the government. The current government may be looking at cutting jobs from the public sector and give more importance to the private sector and attract foreign investment.

Impact of Political environment on doing business in India:

As in any part of the world, political influence is highly essential to start a business in India. Not only for safeguarding the interest of the company but even to begin the process of getting the required sanctions, one requires hold in the politics and administrative circles.

India is the biggest democracy in the world with multi party political system. In population, India is second to China, with nearly 120 crores of people. This is the most important consumer market in the world. It is a fast developing world. India is the third largest economy in the world and second fast growing economy in Asia. With all these advantages and the huge market potential, world entrepreneurs are looking for business establishments in India. With the overcrowded population and the millions of hard working and qualified personals, India offers a very cheap work force to the world. Many have realized the business potential in India, started exploring the unique opportunities of investments.

During the last couple of decades, India has opened its market to world. It has absolutely become an open global market. Banking sector, insurance sector and all fields of industrial and business and reatil are now open for multinational investment.

India has a plural political system. With numerous political parties, national level and state level, it is very difficult to get a consensus among all parties for starting any business. Also these political parties have patronage of many factors, caste, creed and ideologies.

4) Social Environment:

Business includes social factors like customs, traditions, values, beliefs, poverty, literacy, life expectancy rate etc. The social structure and the values that a Society includes, have a considerable influence on the functioning of business firms. For example, during festive seasons there is an increase in the demand for new clothes, sweets, fruits, flower, etc. Due to increase in literacy rate the consumers are becoming more conscious of the quality of the products. Organisations are at the centre of changes taking place in the social environment therefore organization must be aware of the culture, needs , preferences, purchasing patterns of consumers. Management must be fully aware of the social composition for both its consumers and its labor force in order to establish the best advantage for its customers and employees.

The social environment of a business can be integral to its success or failure. Employees are often influenced by the context in which they work and this can have implications for productivity. Some effects of the social environment are easier to measure than others. Employers who take the necessary strides to create a positive and harmonious social environment in the workplace can set themselves up for future success.

When we discuss business environment; the social factors and their impact on business must be given due consideration. The Social change is when the people in the community adjust their attitudes to the way they live. The business also needs to be aware of their social responsibilities. A lot of variables should be taken into account if one should decide to do a business in a certain location. One variable to consider is to what degree a social environment of the business is conducive to the business success. Business will accumulate wealth only if the business ecosystem supports the growth of business.

Social Environment and Responsibility:

Social change is when the people in the community adjust their attitudes to way they live. Businesses will need to adjust their products to meet these changes, e.g. taking sugar out of children's drinks, because parents feel their children are having too much sugar in their diets. The business also needs to be aware of their social responsibilities. These are the way they act towards the different parts of society that they come into contact with. It is also important to consider the effects a business can have on the local community. These are known as the social benefits and social costs.

A social benefit is where a business action leads to benefits above and beyond the direct benefits to the business and/or customer. For example, the building of an attractive new factory provides employment opportunities to the local community.

A social cost is where the action has the reverse effect - there are costs imposed on the rest of society, for instance pollution. These extra benefits and costs are distinguished from the private benefits and costs directly attributable to the business. These extra cost and benefits are known as externalities - external costs and benefits. Governments encourage social benefits through the use of subsidies and grants (e.g. regional assistance for undeveloped areas). They also discourage social costs with fines, taxes and legislation.

5)Technical Environment:

Changes in technology affect how a company will do business. A business may have to dramatically change their operating strategy as a result of changes in the technological environment.

Technology can be defined as the method or technique for converting inputs to outputs in accomplishing a specific task. Thus, the terms 'method' and 'technique' refer not only to the knowledge but also to the skills and the means for accomplishing a task. Technological innovation, then, refers to the increase in knowledge, the improvement in skills, or the discovery of a new or improved means that extends people's ability to achieve a given task.

Technology can be classified in several ways. For example, blueprints, machinery, equipment and other capital goods are sometimes referred to as hard technology while soft technology includes management know-how, finance, marketing and administrative techniques. When a relatively primitive technology is used in the production process, the technology is usually referred to as labor-intensive. A highly advanced technology, on the other hand, is generally termed capital-intensive.

Changes in the technological environment have had some of the most dramatic effects on business. A company may be thoroughly committed to a particular type of technology, and may have made major investments in equipment and training only to see a new, more innovative and cost-effective technology emerge.

Indeed, the managing director of multinational organization manufacturing heavy machinery once said that the hardest part of his job had nothing to do with unions, pay or products, but with whether or not to spend money on the latest technologically improved equipment. Computer technology has had an enormous impact on education and health care, to name but two areas affected. The advancements in medical technology, for example, have contributed to longevity in many societies. In addition, the introduction of robots in many factories has reduced the need for labor, and the use of VCR's and microcomputers has become commonplace in many homes and businesses.

Unfortunately, there is a negative side to technological progress. The introduction of nuclear weapons, for example, has made the destruction of the human race a frightening possibility. In addition, factories using modern technologies have polluted both air and water and contributed to various environmental and health-related problems.

Technology is a critical factor in economic development. Because of the advances of international communication, the increasing economic interdependence of nations, and the serious scarcity of vital natural resources, the transfer of technology has become an important preoccupation of both industrialized and developing countries. For many industrialized countries, the changes in the technological environment over the last 30 years have been immense particularly in such areas as chemicals, drugs, and electronics. It is vital that organizations stay abreast of these changes - not only because this will allow them to incorporate new and innovative designs into their products, but also because it will give them a firmer base from which to anticipate and counteract competition from other organizations.

When the Gillette company developed a superior stainless steel razor blade, it feared that such a superior product might mean fewer replacements and sales. Thus, the company decided not to market it. Instead, Gillette sold the technology to Wilkinson, a British garden tool manufacturer, thinking that Wilkinson would use the technology only in the production of garden tools. When Wilkinson Sword Blades were introduced and sold quickly, Gillette understood the magnitude of its mistake.

The transfer of technology is essential for attaining a high level of industrial capability and competitiveness. Multinational corporations are playing an increasingly important role in technology transfer because they invest abroad to expand production, marketing and research activities. There is also a growing consciousness amongst governments of the need to increase technology transfer to the developing countries to help stabilize their economic and social conditions.

In spite of the many differences in social, political, cultural, geographic and economic conditions, there are some common characteristics in the technological environments of developing countries. The most common technology transfer from industrialized to developing countries has been in agriculture and health care. As a result of improved health care systems, infant mortality rates have been cut while the incidence of once common diseases such as malaria and typhoid has been reduced in Latin America, south-east Asia and Africa (although the incidents of the AIDS virus has increased alarmingly). Similarly, agricultural technology has increased agricultural productivity in Brazil, India and elsewhere. However, in most developing countries, technology has made little impact on the productive systems, income distribution and living conditions of the majority of the population.

Technology transfer is a complex, time-consuming and costly process, and the successful implementation of such a process demands continuous communication and co-operation between the parties involved. Furthermore, technology transfer cannot be effective if it experiences conflict with the economic and social needs of the recipient country. The agricultural development of north-eastern Brazil, for example, was largely financed by international banks and financial organizations in the 1960's. Much of this region had been inhabited by Brazilian aborigines but it was owned by a small number of wealthy landowners. The introduction of large-scale mechanical agricultural technology in areas of the tropical rain forest of the Amazon has caused serious environmental damage such as erosion of tropical topsoil and the destruction of the natural environment of numerous birds and animals, and has displaced a large number of the local inhabitants of the forests. Technology transfer may become a serious source of conflict between donor and recipient countries. The recipient country may feel that the donor is trying to dominate it through technology, capital and production. Dependence on foreign technology can be viewed as a serious threat to economic independence. Countries that export technology may experience different problems. For the seller of technology, the technology transfer can result in unemployment in the home country and future loss of technological superiority. For example, Japan transferred modern steel production technology to South Korea in the early 1970's. As labor and production costs in Japan increased, the Korean steel industry began to take over a significant portion of the previously Japanese-controlled international market. Some Japanese executives are now complaining that the cost of technology transfer has been much greater than the income received through the sale of technology.

Technology can be transferred from person to person, industry to industry and government to government, although the government of any country generally plays the most important role in facilitating or impeding the transfer process. Contacts amongst students from different countries are also a means of technology transfer as are journals, books, technical and professional publications, trade magazines and product pamphlets. Furthermore, multinational corporations play an important role in technology transfer by transferring information and technology from the parent company to subsidiaries in other countries, training foreign employees, etc.

6) Cultural Environment:
What is culture

On the surface most countries of the world demonstrate cultural similarities; there are many differences, hidden below the surface. One can talk about "the West", but Italians and English, both belonging to the so called "West", are very different in outlook when one looks below the surface. The task of the global marketer is to find the similarities and differences in culture and account for these in designing and developing marketing plans. Failure to do so can be disastrous.

So the culture is defined as "The integrated sum total of learned behavioral traits that are manifest and shared by members of society" Culture, therefore, according to this definition, is not transmitted genealogically. It is not, also innate, but learned. Facets of culture are interrelated and it is shared by members of a group who define the boundaries. Often different cultures exist side by side within countries, especially in Africa. Culture also reveals itself in many ways and in preferences for colors, styles, religion, family ties and so on.

Culture, alongside economic factors, is probably one of the most important environmental variables to consider in global marketing. Culture is very often hidden from view and can be easily overlooked. Similarly, the need to overcome cultural myopia is paramount.

Approaches to the study of culture:
Keegan(1989) suggested a number of approaches to the study of culture including the anthropological approach, Maslow's approach, the Self- Reference Criterion (SRC), diffusion theory, high and low context cultures and perception. There are briefly reviewed here.

1. Anthropological approach:
Culture can be deep seated and, to the untrained can appear bizarre. The Moslem culture of covering the female form may be alien, to those

cultures which openly flaunt the female form. The anthropologist, though a time consuming process, considers behavior in the light of experiencing it at first hand. In order to understand beliefs, motives and values, the anthropologist studies the country in question anthropology and unearths the reasons for what, apparently, appears bizarre.

2. Maslow approach:

In searching for culture universals, Maslow's (1964) hierarchy of needs gives a useful analytical framework. Maslow hypothesized that people's desires can be arranged into a hierarchy of needs of relative potency. As soon as the "lower" needs are filled, other and higher needs emerge immediately to dominate the individual. When these higher needs are fulfilled, other new and still higher needs emerge. The hierarchy is illustrated in figure below.

Physiological needs are at the bottom of the hierarchy. These are basic needs to be satisfied like food, water, air, comfort. The next need is safety - a feeling of well being. Social needs are those related to developing love and relationships. Once these lower needs are fulfilled "higher" needs emerge like esteem - self respect - and the need for status improving goods. The highest order is self actualization where one can now afford to express oneself as all other needs have been met.

3. The self reference criterion (SRC):

Perception of market needs can be blocked by one's own cultural experience. Lee (1965) suggested a way, whereby one could systematically reduce this perception. He suggested a four point approach.

a) Define the problem or goal in terms of home country traits, habits and norms.

b) Define the problem or goal in terms of the foreign culture traits, habits and norms.

c) Isolate the SRC influence in the problem and examine it carefully to see how it complicates the pattern.

d) Redefine the problem without the SRC influence and solve for the foreign market situation.

The problem with this approach is that, as stated earlier, culture may be hidden or non apparent. Uneartherning the factors in b) may, therefore, be difficult. Nonetheless, the approach gives useful guidelines on the extent for the need of standardization or adaption in marketing planning.

4. Diffusion theory:

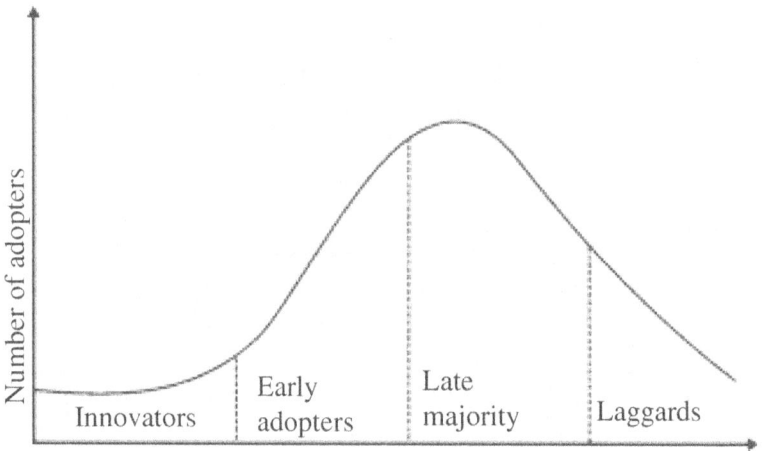

In this theory the innovators are small percentages who like to be seen to lead, and then the others, increasingly more conservative, take the innovation on. The adoption process itself is done in a series of stages from awareness of the product, through to interest, evaluation, trial and either adoption or rejection (in the case of non adopters). The speed of the adoption process depends on the relative advantage provided by the product, how compatible or not it is with current values or experiences, its complexity, divisibility (how quickly it can be tried) and how quickly it can be communicated to the potential market. In international marketing an assessment of the product or service in terms of these latter factors is very useful to the speed of its adoption. Most horticultural products, for example, have no problem in transfer from one culture to another, however specific types may have. It is unlikely that produce like "squash" would sell well in Europe, but it does in Zimbabwe.

5. High and low context cultures:

Hall (1977) has suggested the concept of high and low context cultures as a way of understanding different cultural orientations. In low context cultures messages have to be explicit, in high context cultures less information is required in the verbal message. In low context cultures, for example like Northern Europe, a person's word is not to be relied on, things must be written. On the other hand, in high context cultures, like Japan and the Middle East, a person's word is their bond. It is primarily a question of trust.

6. Perception:

Perception is the ability to see what is in culture. The SRC can be a very powerful negative force. High perceptual skills need to be developed so that no one misinterpret a situation, which could lead to negative consequences

Many of these theories and approaches have been "borrowed" from other contexts themselves, but they do give a useful insight into how one might avoid a number of pitfalls of culture in doing business overseas.

Consumer products are likely to be more culturally sensitive than business to business products, primarily because technology can be universally learned. However there are dangers in over generalizations. For example, drink can be very universal and yet culture bound. Whilst appealing to a very universal physiological need - thirst - different drink can satiate the same need. Tea is a very English habit, coffee American but neither are universals in African culture. However, Coca Cola may be acceptable in all three cultures, with even the same advertising appeal.

7. Nationalism:

Nationalism is a cultural trait which is increasingly surfacing. In Western, developed countries a high degree of interdependence exists, so it is not so easy to be all that independent. In fact, blocs like NAFTA and the EU are, if anything, becoming more economically independent. However, less developed countries do not yet have the same interdependence in general, and so organizations need to reassess their contribution to the development of nations to make sure that they are not holding them "to hostage".

Culture is a very powerful variable and cannot be ignored. Whilst "universals" are sought there is still a need to understand local customs and attitudes. These are usually no better understood than by the making use of in country personnel.

The elements of culture:

The major elements of culture are material culture, language, aesthetics, education, religion, attitudes and values and social organization.

1. Material culture:

Material culture refers to tools, artifacts and technology. Before marketing in a foreign culture it is important to assess the material culture like transportation, power, communications and so on. Input-output tables may be useful in assessing this. All aspects of marketing are affected by material culture like sources of power for products, media availability and distribution. For example, refrigerated transport does not exist in many African countries. Material culture introductions into a country may bring about cultural changes which may or may not be desirable.

2. Language:

Language reflects the nature and values of society. There may be many sub-cultural languages like dialects which may have to be accounted for. Some countries like India have many languages with numerous dialects. Language can cause communication problems - especially in the use of media or written material. It is best to learn the language or engage someone who understands it well.

3. Aesthetics:

Aesthetics refer to the ideas in a culture concerning beauty and good taste as expressed in the arts -music, art, drama and dancing and the particular appreciation of colour and form. African music is different in form to Western music. Aesthetic differences affect design, colours, packaging, brand names and media messages. For cxample, unless explained, the brand name FAVCO would mean nothing to Western importers, in Zimbabwe most people would instantly recognise FAVCO as the brand of horticultural produce.

4. Education:

Education refers to the transmission of skills, ideas and attitudes as well as training in particular disciplines. Education can transmit cultural ideas or be used for change, for example the local university can build up an economy's performance.

Education levels, or lack of it, affect marketers in a number of ways:
- · Advertising programs and labeling
- · Girls and women excluded from formal education (literacy rates)
- · Conducting market research
- · Complex products with instructions
- · Relations with distributors and,
- · Support sources - finance, advancing agencies etc.

5. Religion:

Religion provides the best insight into a society's behavior and helps answer the question why people behave rather than how they behave.

Religion can affect marketing in a number of ways:

· Religious holidays - Most shops will be closed during religious holidays.

· Consumption patterns - No non-vegetarian food during festivals or fasting etc.

· Economic role of women - Islam

· Caste systems - difficulty in getting to different costs for segmentation/ niche marketing

· Joint and extended families - Hinduism and organizational structures;

· Institution of the church - Iran and its effect on advertising, "Western" images

· Market segments - Malaysia - Malay, Chinese and Indian cultures making market segmentation

· Sensitivity is needed to be alert to religious differences.

6. Attitudes and values:

Values often have a religious foundation, and attitudes relate to economic activities. It is essential to ascertain attitudes towards marketing activities which lead to wealth or material gain.Also "change" may not be needed, or even wanted, and it may be better to relate products to traditional values rather than just new ones. Many African societies are risk averse; therefore, entrepreneurialism may not always be relevant. Attitudes are always precursors of human behavior and so it is essential that research is done carefully on these.

7. Social organization:
Refers to the way people relate to each other, for example, extended families, units, kinship. In some countries kinship may be a tribe and so segmentation may have to be based on this. Other forms of groups may be religious or political, age, caste and so on. All these groups may affect the marketer in his planning.

There are other aspects of culture, but the above covers the main ingredients. In one form or another have to be taken account of when marketing internationally.

"Power distance" - Society's endorsement of inequality, and its inverse as the expectation of relative equality in organizations and institutions.

In conclusion, therefore, "better" economic growth can be explained more by culture than structural or material changes. Economic power, from this study, comes from "dynamism" - the acceptance of the legitimacy of hierarchy and the valuing of perseverance and thrift, all without undue emphasis on tradition and social obligations which could impede business initiative; "individualism" - the tendency of individuals primarily to look after themselves and their immediate families and finally a tendency towards competitiveness at the expense of friendship and harmony.

Culture has both a pervasive and changing influence on each national market environment. Marketers must either respond or change to it. While internationalism in itself may go some way to changing cultural values, it will not change values to such a degree that true international standardization can exist. The world would be a poorer place if it ever happened.

7) Educational Environment:
Education, entrepreneurship and development are interrelated. Education is the best means of developing man's resourcefulness which

encompasses different dimensions of entrepreneurship. Thus, formal education is always considered an important asset of an individual in building an occupational career. It makes available more skills necessary to entrepreneurial endeavor.

As generally found in empirical studies, success of entrepreneurship increases with education but this might stem from the fact that more talented individuals are both more successful and more educated.

Schooling is an endogenous decision and unobserved variables such as individual skills and talents might drive the results leading to biased estimates of returns to schooling.

Education influences the selection to become an entrepreneur through various mechanisms. More education is generally correlated with higher wealth and consequently lower start-up costs for enterprise activities. The direct impact of education might also differ across occupations and therefore influence the initial choice of occupation. If education has a higher impact on the productivity in business activities compared to other occupational choices, more talented persons become entrepreneurs. When education improves the entrepreneurial ability, but not the productivity of an individual employee - education will increase both the likelihood of becoming an entrepreneur and the performance of the entrepreneur.

Hence education plays key role in molding an ordinary man into the entrepreneur. Education motivates person to become an entrepreneur. However in India education system is degraded and every education system nowadays look for job oriented curriculum rather than entrepreneurship development.

8) Legal Environment:

Governments control the business activities is many ways both direct and indirect. We have already covered government's economic policies. However, government can control business activities in a more direct way. These are as follows:

1. Controlling what to produce:

In order to safeguard the interest of the community government may ban or limit the production of certain goods and services. For example, selling of guns, explosive and dangerous drugs are illegal in many countries. Moreover, Goods which harm the environment are also totally banned or strictly controlled in many countries, e.g. aerosol cans that use CFCs which has been banned because of their damaging effect on the ozone layer.

2. Employees Protection legislations:

Government may pass laws to protect the interest of employees such as Laws against unfair discrimination at work and when applying for jobs. There is no unfair discrimination on the basis of Race, religion, sex, age, or color.

3. Legislations for health and Safety at work:

- To protect workers from dangerous machinery.
- Workers should be provided with proper safety equipments and clothing.
- A reasonable workforce temperature is maintained for workers.
- Proper hygienic conditions and washing facilities are provided.
- Workers get adequate breaks between shifts.
  Protect employees against unfair dismissal

Business can not dismiss the workers because they have joined a trade union or for being pregnant. There should be proper warning before dismissing a worker otherwise it will be treated as unfair dismissal.

4. Ensure fair wages for the employees:

In many countries, government makes it mandatory to have a written contract of employment. It contains the details of the wage rate; working hours, deductions (if any) and other necessary details regarding working conditions. Minimum wages paid to different types of workers are also determined by the government.

Consumer Protection legislations:

Most of the countries have consumer protection laws aimed at making sure that businesses act fairly towards their consumers: A few examples are

Weight and Measures Act:

Goods sold should not be underweight. Standard weighting equipments should be used to measure goods.

Trade Description Act:

Deliberately giving misleading impression about the product is illegal.

Consumer Credit Act:

According to this act consumers should be given a copy of the credit agreement and should be aware of the interest rates, length of loan while taking a loan.

Sale of Goods Act:

It is illegal to sell products with serious flaws or problems and goods sold should conform to the description provided.

Firms involved in global business must be familiar with and obey the laws of their home country, the local laws of each country in which they do business, and international laws. Some specific examples of differing local laws which can have a major impact on international business are as follows.

Local content:

It is not unusual to face with local laws that stipulate that a certain amount of a good or service is supposed to be supplied by local producers; this is referred to as local content requirement. Under such laws, companies are required to use locally available raw materials, local labor resources, or purchase parts from local suppliers. The purpose of such a measure is to foster greater local economic activities that spur more jobs for the citizens of the host country. However, among many complexities that may arise, multinational firms need to watch for two potential problems in adhering to local content rule.

The quality of local raw materials: A lot of companies rely on the quality of their products in order to retain the loyalty of their customer base or maintain or increase market share. With that said, it is imperative to obtain quality parts and quality raw materials to use in assembling a final product to satisfy customers Hence, if the requirements of local content laws mean purchasing lower quality, local raw materials or parts this may affect the quality of the final product and that will, in turn, diminish market share.

The low-skilled labor force: By the same token, when multinational corporations are forced to use the local labor force, they may face a problem if that workforce is low-skilled. The low-skilled labor force may cost less, but it may also translate into a low-quality product or defective product. In the case of low-quality product, market share can be lost to competitors with better products. As for defective products, the company and its officials can be held liable for damages resulting from product use. The other option may be to train the local employees to bring them to a productive level. However, the training can be costly, the learning curve may be steep, and once the employees are well trained, there is no guarantee that they will stay as your employees. Consequently, this requirement may hamper efficiency, as well as the quality of the product, resulting in loss of revenue for the company involved.

Product safety:

Product liability allows consumers to hold manufacturers, sellers, even some company officials liable for death, personal damage or injury caused by defective products. Countries usually enact product safety laws to protect their citizens and set up the standards to manufacture the products. In order to avoid retaliation and lawsuits, it is of crucial importance to familiarize the enforcement of local product liability laws.

Taxation:

Countries always have some sort of system for tax collection purposes. Governments levy taxes for various reasons. For instance, a tax can be levied on imported products to make the products more expensive than similar products manufactured locally, this is referred to as an import tax. Taxes are also a great source of revenue for governments to pay their employees and to finance and maintain specific projects. In addition, many governments collect a value added tax(VAT). The VAT system works by charging a tax at each stage a value is added to a product.

Legal Considerations - International:

Businesses must also follow those international laws which govern international trade. For example, dumping which is a practice of selling exported products at a very low price, in some instance, lower than the cost of production with the ultimate intention to drive local competitors out of the market. Under the pressure of local companies, governments may find it necessary to intervene to prevent such practice by adopting antidumping laws and regulations.

Cross-Cultural Environment:

A society's culture can tremendously affect its economic activities and its culture is in turn affected by its economic activities. Culture is characterized by the acceptable ways in terms of behaviors, customs, and values of a specific society. Hence, a good understanding of the culture of a nation will enhance greatly the chances of your business succeeding. It is important, therefore, to acknowledge and take into consideration the main cultural and social factors such behaviors, education, language, values, customs, as well as religion when conducting international business.

Culture:

Set of values, beliefs, rules, and institutions held by a specific group of people

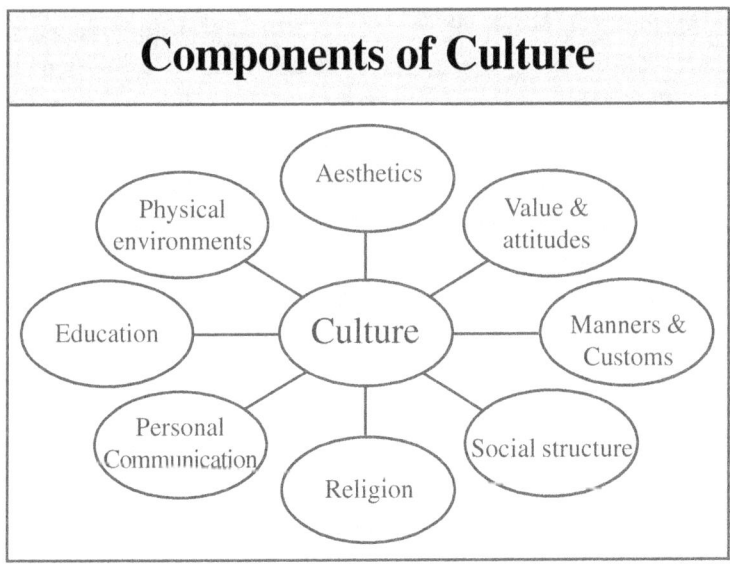

Hofstede Framework

This framework compares cultures along five dimensions:

Individualism versus Collectivism. Individualist cultures value hard work, entrepreneurial risk-taking, and freedom to focus on personal goals. Collectivist cultures emphasize a strong association with family and work groups to maintain harmony and to work toward collective goals.

Power Distance:

Large power distance means greater inequality between superiors and subordinates, more hierarchical organizations, and power derived from prestige, force, and inheritance. Small power distance implies greater equality, more equally shared prestige and rewards, and power derived from hard work and is often considered more legitimate.

Cultures having large uncertainty avoidance tend to value security, systems of rules/procedures, low employee turnover, and relatively slower change. Those with low uncertainty avoidance are more open to change and new ideas.

Achievement versus Nurturing:

Cultures with high achievement versus nurturing scores emphasize assertiveness, the accumulation of wealth, and an entrepreneurial drive. Cultures rating low on achievement versus nurturing value relaxed lifestyles and are more concerned for others than they are with material gain.

Long-term Orientation:

Cultures scoring high (strong) on long-term orientation place value on respect for tradition, thrift, perseverance, and a sense of personal shame. Cultures scoring low (weak) on long-term orientation tend to value individual stability and reputation, fulfilling social obligations, and reciprocation of greetings and gifts.

Geographical Environment:

The Geographic environment includes

1) Weather and the effect on agriculture, travel, building design
2) Distance, distance to travel, time zones
3) Topography - mountains, flat land and the effect on transportation systems
4) Latitude, is it tropical or arctic, number of days and hours of sunshine

Geography has a big place in e-commerce, especially when you think about the influences of distance to ship products sold online, and when you think about how geography influences the social-cultural environment (language, customs, etc.)

Geography also effects weather and weather has an effect on the internet from a technological point of view. Weather situations can cause disruption of communication lines which means the "web is down" in parts of the world effected by a crisis. In some places affected by an earthquake, or tsunami, it can takes days or weeks for telecomm services to be restored and in that time period web based services cannot be accessed in the effected region.

The geographical environment also includes topographical challenges and advantages. Challenges apply when the land is very steep, which limits the available acreage of arable land so you cannot grow enough crops (like the sides of steep hills or old volcanoes as in the case of Japan). Advantages take place when the land is flat, and the soil is rich in nutrients. Countries that have geographic environmental limitations have to import massive quantities of food which is expensive and, to some extent, affects the national sovereignty.

While the Competitive Environment is perhaps the most powerful environment in terms of influencing whether we do, or don't do certain things, it should be understood that the Geographic environment is also powerful in the sense that negative things effecting the planet can have long term negative consequences for the ability of companies to sustain their activity - examples include New Orleans and the time spent recovering from the hurricane and as well as regions in South Asia effected by the massive tsunami in December 2004.

Climate:

One of the most important factors in geography is, where the country is in the world, and climate. It's no coincidence that the poorest countries are in the tropics, where it is hot, the land is less fertile, and water is scarcer, where diseases flourish. Conversely, Europe and North America profit from huge tracts of very fertile land, a temperate climate, and good rainfall.

Location:

Secondly, geographical location plays a part in access to markets. All the great empires have been based around trade routes. Many of the world's poorest countries are severely hindered because they are situated in high mountain ranges; or lack navigable rivers, long coastlines, or good natural harbors.

Resources:

Thirdly, every country has been dealt a hand in natural resources. It takes infrastructure to capitalize on these, but some places have a distinct advantage over others. Oil is the most obvious. Nobody any doubt about how Saudi Arabia or UAE make their money. Among other advantages, gold and diamonds have helped South Africa build the most successful economy on the continent. These are all non-renewable resources - once they're gone, they're gone, but while stocks last there is wealth to be made.

Besides these there are renewable resources - forests, fish, stocks that, if correctly managed, will refresh themselves. Much South American development has been based on the Amazon rainforest, in natural rubber and then timber.

Finally, there are what are sometimes called 'flow resources'. These are renewable that need no management, wind, tide and solar resources.

Stability:

Finally, environmental stability can be a factor in development. Some countries are more stable than others. In some countries, there may be the annual cyclone season regularly sweeping away roads and bridges, damaging railways and refineries, and taking the roofs of houses and hotels. How do you build and sustain infrastructure in those conditions? It's not impossible, but these are problems most countries don't have to face.

Chapter 2
Environmental Issues

Introduction:

It is important to study and understand the Natural environment in a book of business environment. Natural environment exert significant influence on business activities. Man is said to have achieved independence from nature because of modern technology and zeal for achieving more and more in limited resources available from nature. This opposition towards natural forces made him think that he can sustain without natural environment and thus made him rather ignorant. Infertile soil and erosion of soil no more destruct his potential of getting crop and food. Failure of rains may not worry him because he knows how to extract water from ground and divert water from river and streams for irrigating crops.

His search for new areas of mineral deposits and substitutes and new uses for resources under exploitation have given him courage and confidence to launch giant manufacturing plants, consuming resources on an unprecedented scale. Mountains, deserts, oceans and distances are no barriers to him to reach any part of the globe to sell his products. Thus man's technological progress during last 150 years has been so great , his insight into nature so deep that his ingenuity has finally given him the whip hand out and that the natural environment is something secondary importance, something essentially passive, existing to serve him as he sees fit.

Natural Environment hardly finds a mention in literature on economic development or development planning. Some years before, thousands of development economists from different parts of the world met in New Delhi for world Congress of the International Economic

Association. The subject of the association was the appropriate balance between industry and agriculture in resources development activity. Currently natural resources have not entered the agenda of analysis in development economics and national planning. Though man thinks that he is independent of nature but he cannot still hold control over the natural calamities like tsunami. Tsunami which hit several parts of Asia, including India on Dec 26.2004, further demonstrates the supremacy of nature.

Therefore it can be concluded that man has not become completely independent of Nature. His activities are directly or indirectly guided by his natural or physical environment.

Following picture shows the way environment is getting disturbed with metropolitan cities and other so called development elements.

We shall now discussing following key issues regarding Natural Environment:
1) Protection of Natural Environment
2) Prevention of pollution and depletion natural resources
3) Conservation of Natural resources, Opportunities in Environment

1) Protection of Natural Environment:

As we have seen in the introduction, how natural environment is overlooked by modern man because of false belief of self reliance and independency. In this part we are more concerned with the protection of Natural Environment , ways of protecting Natural Environment, preserving important minerals and environmental elements.

First task is to understand the need of protection of our Natural Environment.

Environmental protection is a practice of protecting the natural environment on individual, organizational or governmental levels, for the benefit of the natural environment and humans. Due to the pressures of population and technology, the biophysical environment is being degraded, sometimes permanently. This has been recognized, and governments have begun placing restraints on activities that cause environmental degradation. Since the 1960's, activity of environmental movements has created awareness of the various environmental issues. There is no agreement on the extent of the environmental impact of human activity, and protection measures are occasionally criticized.

Academic institutions now offer courses, such as environmental studies, environmental management and environmental engineering, that teach the history and methods of environment protection. Protection of the environment is needed due to various human activities. Waste production, air pollution, and loss of biodiversity (resulting from the introduction of invasive species and species extinction) are some of the issues related to environmental protection.

Environmental protection is influenced by three interwoven factors: environmental legislation, ethics and education. Each of these factors plays its part in influencing national-level environmental decisions and personal-level environmental values and behaviors. For environmental protection to become a reality, it is important for societies to develop each of these areas that, together, will inform and drive environmental decisions.

Overview of the Natural Environment Protection scenario:

The natural environment is being degraded in many ways. Rural tranquility is becoming increasingly difficult to find and the facility for the natural landscape to provide restorative leisure for people is being diminished. Urban open spaces are being lost or damaged. Noise and light pollution are getting worse and, in some areas, transport and other emissions are a hazard to health. Soil fertility and its ability to capture and store carbon are being lost. The marine environment is being damaged by aggregate extraction, inappropriate fishing methods, and rubbish dumped at sea.

The land use planning system provides one key to protecting the environment. However, it currently operates without any clear context for the overall effect of decisions on the natural environment. Basing substantive spatial decisions for development on the environmental capacity of the competing sites could greatly enhance the ability to protect environmental resources. However, a lack of data - especially in commercial waste and biodiversity - currently inhibits informed decision making.

With the introduction of the draft Marine Bill, the government is at last recognizing the need for action in this area. While the proposal to set up a Marine Management Organization (MMO) and enable the designation of Marine Conservation Zones are welcome, there is no provision for coastal communities to play a role within the MMO and no clarity about how the extent of the conservation zones is to be designated or timescales for action.

Soil quality is essential to conserve biodiversity and ensure sustainable agriculture and forestry and healthy urban green spaces. In 2004, Defra produced the first Soil Action Plan for England. Although weak in certain key areas, implementing the Plan would begin to provide the framework necessary to protect soil quality. An alternative approach is the use of voluntary land care partnerships between farmers, local authorities, government agencies and advisers; however, concern has been expressed by the Parliamentary Office of Science and Technology that these lack the necessary rigor to address the fundamental causes of long-turn soil degradation and inappropriate land use.

There is also a need for action to urgently reverse the destruction of the world's rainforests, which is being driven by the global market for timber, meat and bio fuels. The damage is immense, for the rainforests are home to the world's richest biodiversity, as well as being a significant carbon sink. Controlling the demands that lead to rainforest destruction and rewarding local people for conserving their environments require international action.

Flooding is an issue both inland and on the coast. The frequency and severity of flash floods is likely to increase. Hard defenses that try to drain water away are likely to be overwhelmed and there is a need to switch back to using the natural environment to absorb storm water and then allow it to flow away slowly. This means that flood plains and wetlands must be protected and, in some cases, reinstated. Sustainable urban drainage systems must become the norm for new developments and, where possible, be retrofitted in vulnerable areas. Planning policies also need to concentrate more on enabling people to live with higher summer temperatures. Building regulations and planning policies must ensure that buildings have sufficient thermal mass, shading, and natural ventilation to keep them cool during the day.

Government Actions:

Over the years Government of India have enacted various laws and regulative bodies for the protection of Natural Environment. It must be a long term initiative and patience must be maintained throughout the implementation procedure. Many times laws and legislature are enacted but its implementation is not monitored so the result is always a failure. We shall see the actions taken by Government in following part of this chapter.

In the Constitution of India it is clearly stated that it is the duty of the state to 'protect and improve the environment and to safeguard the forests and wildlife of the country'. It imposes a duty on every citizen 'to protect and improve the natural environment including forests, lakes, rivers, and wildlife'. Reference to the environment has also been made in the Directive Principles of State Policy as well as the Fundamental Rights.

The Department of Environment was established in India in 1980 to ensure a healthy environment for the country. This later became the Ministry of Environment and Forests in 1985.

The constitutional provisions are supported by a number of laws – acts, rules, and notifications. The EPA (Environment Protection Act), 1986 came into force soon after the Bhopal Gas Tragedy and is considered an umbrella legislation as it fills many gaps in the existing laws. Thereafter a large number of laws came into existence as the problems began arising, for example, Handling and Management of Hazardous Waste Rules in 1989.

Following is a list of the environmental legislations that have come into effect:
1) **General**
2) **Forest and wildlife**
3) **Water**
4) **Air**

1) **General:**
1) 1986:
The Environment (Protection) Act authorizes the central government to protect and improve environmental quality, control and reduce pollution

from all sources, and prohibit or restrict the setting and /or operation of any industrial facility on environmental grounds.

2)1986:

The Environment (Protection) Rules lay down procedures for setting standards of emission or discharge of environmental pollutants.

3) 1989:

The objective of Hazardous Waste (Management and Handling) Rules is to control the generation, collection, treatment, import, storage, and handling of hazardous waste.

4)1989:

The Manufacture, Storage, and Import of Hazardous Rules define the terms used in this context, and sets up an authority to inspect, once a year, the industrial activity connected with hazardous chemicals and isolated storage facilities.

5) 1989 :

The Manufacture, Use, Import, Export, and Storage of hazardous Micro-organisms/ Genetically Engineered Organisms or Cells Rules were introduced with a view to protect the environment, nature, and health, in connection with the application of gene technology and microorganisms.

6) 1991:

The Public Liability Insurance Act and Rules and Amendment, 1992 was drawn up to provide for public liability insurance for the purpose of providing immediate relief to the persons affected by accident while handling any hazardous substance.

7) 1995:

The National Environmental Tribunal Act has been created to award compensation for damages to persons, property, and the environment arising from any activity involving hazardous substances.

8) 1997:

The National Environment Appellate Authority Act has been created to hear appeals with respect to restrictions of areas in which classes of industries etc. are carried out or prescribed subject to certain safeguards under the EPA.

9) 1998:

The Biomedical waste (Management and Handling) Rules is a legal binding on the health care institutions to streamline the process of proper handling of hospital waste such as segregation, disposal, collection, and treatment.

10) 1999:

The Environment (Sitting for Industrial Projects) Rules, 1999 lay down detailed provisions relating to areas to be avoided for sitting of industries, precautionary measures to be taken for site selecting as also the aspects of environmental protection which should have been incorporated during the implementation of the industrial development projects.

11) 2000:

The Municipal Solid Wastes (Management and Handling) Rules, 2000 apply to every municipal authority responsible for the collection, segregation, storage, transportation, processing, and disposal of municipal solid wastes.

12) 2000:

The Ozone Depleting Substances (Regulation and Control) Rules have been laid down for the regulation of production and consumption of ozone depleting substances.

13) 2001:

The Batteries (Management and Handling) Rules, 2001 rules shall apply to every manufacturer, importer, re-conditioner, assembler, dealer, auctioneer, consumer, and bulk consumer involved in the manufacture, processing, sale, purchase, and use of batteries or components so as to regulate and ensure the environmentally safe disposal of used batteries.

14) 2002 :

The Noise Pollution (Regulation and Control) (Amendment) Rules lay down such terms and conditions as are necessary to reduce noise pollution, permit use of loud speakers or public address systems during night hours (between 10:00 p.m. to 12:00 midnight) on or during any cultural or religious festive occasion

15) 2002 :

The Biological Diversity Act is an act to provide for the conservation of biological diversity, sustainable use of its components, and fair and equitable sharing of the benefits arising out of the use of biological resources and knowledge associated with it

2) Forest and wildlife:

1) 1927:

The Indian Forest Act and Amendment, 1984, is one of the many surviving colonial statutes. It was enacted to 'consolidate the law related to forest, the transit of forest produce, and the duty leviable on timber and other forest produce'.

2) 1972 :

The Wildlife Protection Act, Rules 1973 and Amendment 1991 provides for the protection of birds and animals and for all matters that are connected to it whether it be their habitat or the waterhole or the forests that sustain them.

3) 1980:

The Forest (Conservation) Act and Rules, 1981, provides for the protection of and the conservation of the forests.

3) Water:

1) 1882:

The Easement Act allows private rights to use a resource that is, groundwater, by viewing it as an attachment to the land. It also states that all surface water belongs to the state and is a state property.

2) 1897:

The Indian Fisheries Act establishes two sets of penal offences whereby the government can sue any person who uses dynamite or other explosive substance in any way (whether coastal or inland) with intent to catch or destroy any fish or poisonous fish in order to kill.

3) 1956:

The River Boards Act enables the states to enroll the central government in setting up an Advisory River Board to resolve issues in inter-state cooperation.

4) 1970:

The Merchant Shipping Act aims to deal with waste arising from ships along the coastal areas within a specified radius.

5) 1974 :

The Water (Prevention and Control of Pollution) Act establishes an institutional structure for preventing and abating water pollution. It establishes standards for water quality and effluent. Polluting industries must seek permission to discharge waste into effluent bodies. The CPCB (Central Pollution Control Board) was constituted under this act.

6) 1977:

The Water (Prevention and Control of Pollution) Cess Act provides for the levy and collection of cess or fees on water consuming industries and local authorities.

7) 1978:

The Water (Prevention and Control of Pollution) Cess Rules contains the standard definitions and indicate the kind of and location of meters that every consumer of water is required to affix.

8) 1991:

The Coastal Regulation Zone Notification puts regulations on various activities, including construction, are regulated. It gives some protection to the backwaters and estuaries.

4) Air:

1) 1948:

The Factories Act and Amendment in 1987 was the first to express concern for the working environment of the workers. The amendment of 1987 has sharpened its environmental focus and expanded its application to hazardous processes.

2) 1981:

The Air (Prevention and Control of Pollution) Act provides for the control and abatement of air pollution. It entrusts the power of enforcing this act to the CPCB.

3) 1982:

The Air (Prevention and Control of Pollution) Rules defines the procedures of the meetings of the Boards and the powers entrusted to them.

4) 1982:

The Atomic Energy Act deals with the radioactive waste.

5) 1987:

The Air (Prevention and Control of Pollution) Amendment Act empowers the central and state pollution control boards to meet with grave emergencies of air pollution.

6) 1988:

The Motor Vehicles Act states that all hazardous waste is to be properly packaged, labeled, and transported.

[The above laws have been sourced from: Environmental policy-making in India – The process and its pressure, TERI report. Indian Environmental Legislations, list from the MOEF web site.

Strengthening Environmental Legislations in India, document by Centre for Environmental Law, WWF.]

2) Prevention of pollution and depletion of natural resources:

a) Pollution :

"Pollution is nothing but the resources we are not harvesting. We allow them to disperse because we've been ignorant of their value" – Richard Buckminster, Fuller

Pollution is releasing harmful contaminants in to the environment causing instability and harm to the eco system. Pollution is defined as "An unwanted change in the environment which involves the physical, biological and chemical changes involving air, water and land which affects the human life in one way or the other". Pollution is in any form like noise, water and air. Pollution has become a serious issue after World War II in developing countries due to rapid industrialization and lack of regulations. Pollution is the root cause of many diseases that kill and disable living organisms.

Current scenario:

The environmental pollution affect the health of more than 100 million people worldwide. Pollution is the contaminant into a natural environment, usually by humans. The specific types of pollution are Land pollution, Air Pollution, Water pollution (Oceans, rivers, ground water) , Plastic pollution, Noise pollution, Light pollution, space Ozone layer and many more.

In India the increasing economic development and a rapidly

growing population that has taken the country from 300 million people in 1947 to more than one billion people today is putting a strain on the environment, infrastructure, and the country's natural resources. Industrial pollution, soil erosion, deforestation, rapid industrialization, urbanization, and land degradation are all worsening problems. Overexploitation of the country's resources be it land or water and the industrialization process has resulted environmental degradation of resources. Environmental pollution is one of the most serious problems facing humanity and other life forms on our planet today.

India's per capita carbon dioxide emissions were roughly 3,000 pounds (1,360 kilograms) in 2007, according to the study. That's small compared to China and the U.S., with 10,500 pounds (4,763 kilograms) and 42,500 pounds (19,278 kilograms) respectively that year. The study said European Union and Russia also have more emissions than India.

India is among the world's worst performers when it comes to the overall environment. We rank 125 of 132 countries. Even Pakistan and Bangladesh are less polluted than we are. A study released earlier this year by the environmental research centers of Columbia and Yale showed that India was at the bottom of the heap when it came to air pollution. Following are some of the primary causes of pollution in India:

1) Air Pollution:

Discharge of chemicals and particulates like carbon monoxide, sulfur dioxide, chlorofluorocarbons and Nitrogen oxides produced by industries and motor vehicles in to the environment.

India has the worst air pollution in the entire world, beating China, Pakistan, Nepal and Bangladesh, according to a study released during this year's World Economic Forum in Davos. Of 132 countries whose environments were surveyed, India ranks dead last in the 'Air (effects on human health)' ranking. The annual study, the Environmental Performance Index, is conducted and written by environmental research centers at Yale and Columbia university's with assistance from dozens of outside scientists. The study uses satellite data to measure air pollution concentrations.

Indian air pollution has been blamed for its dry monsoon season, but a scientist has revealed that European pollution may also play a part in it. The volume of the summer monsoon has been weakening since the 1950s. And Yi Ming of Princeton University in New Jersey claimed his experimental models suggest that the effect of European aerosol pollution accounts for about half the drop in the volume of monsoon rainfall – the other half is down to pollution over south Asia.

2) Coal pollution:

India's environmental problems are exacerbated by its heavy reliance on coal for power generation. "More than 80 per cent of energy is produced from coal, a fuel that emits a high amount of carbon and greenhouse gases." said one thinker. According to IMF chief Christine Lagarde on July 10, 2012 said pollution from coal generation plants causes about 70,000 premature deaths every year in India. Andhra Pradesh, the coastal state of eastern India is experiencing a coal-plant construction boom, including the 4,000-MW Krishnapatnam Ultra Mega Power Project, one of nine such massive projects in planning or under construction in country.

On August 23, 2011 the Jharkhand State Pollution Control Board has ordered the closure of 22 BCCL mines in the underground fire zone of Jharia. BCCL had taken over most of the 103 mines from private owners. Hence, none of them had got environmental clearances. Most of the coal mines under the JSPCB's scanner were located in Jharia.

The 2,640-MW Sompeta plant proposed by Nagarjuna Construction Company and the 2,640-MW Bhavanapadu plant proposed by East Coast Energy have both provoked large nonviolent protests that have ended in police attacks, including four deaths of local residents. As of May 2011, the Sompeta plant had been cancelled and the Bhavanapadu plant had been placed on hold by officials, with corruption investigations continuing.

On April 12, 2011 the Ministry of Environment and Forests (MoEF) has tightened pollution monitoring norms for power projects with a generation capacity of 500 Mw and above, integrated steel plants with a capacity of 1 million tons per annum and cement plants with a capacity of 3 million tons per annum.

Polluting industrial units: On May 26, 2011 the Haryana State Pollution Control Board has ordered closure of 639 polluting industrial units in 2010-11 and directed the highly polluting industries to set up continuous online monitoring stations to ensure compliance of standards of air emissions. The Government has launched prosecution against 151 polluting units in the Special Environment Courts in Faridabad and Kurukshetra, install 9,239 units   pollution control devices.

3) Water Pollution:

Release or discharge of commercial and industrial wastewater into surface waters; discharge of untreated domestic sewage, and chemical contaminants, such as chlorine, from treated sewage; release of waste and contaminants into surface runoff flowing to surface waters, waste disposal and leaching into groundwater; eutrophication and littering is a water pollution.

Above diagram show how water is polluted with dangerous material like plastic bottles and trash which cannot be degraded and remains as it is until burned.

Contaminated and polluted water now kills more people than all forms of violence including wars, according to a United Nations report released on March 22, 2010 on World Water Day that calls for turning unsanitary wastewater into an environmentally safe economic resource. According to the report — titled "Sick Water?" — 90 percent of wastewater discharged daily in developing countries is untreated, contributing to the deaths of some 2.2 million people a year from diarrheal diseases caused by unsafe drinking water and poor hygiene. At least 1.8 million children younger than 5 die every year from water-related diseases.

Fully 80 percent of urban waste in India ends up in the country's rivers, and unchecked urban growth across the country combined with poor government oversight means the problem is only getting worse. A growing number of bodies of water in India are unfit for human use, and in the River Ganga, holy to the country's 82 percent Hindu majority, is dying slowly due to unchecked pollution. Ganga river

New Delhi's body of water is little more than a flowing garbage dump, with fully 57 percent of the city's waste finding its way to the Yamuna. It is that three billion liters of waste are pumped into Delhi's Yamuna (River Yamuna)each day. Only 55 percent of the 15 million Delhi residents are connected to the city's sewage system. The remainder flush their bath water, waste water and just about everything else down pipes and into drains, most of them empty into the Yamuna. According to the Centre for Science and Environment, between 75 and 80 percent of the river's pollution is the result of raw sewage. Combined with industrial runoff, the garbage thrown into the river and it totals over 3 billion liters of waste per day. Nearly 20 billion rupees, or almost US $500 million, has been spent on various clean up efforts. Much of the river pollution problem in India comes from untreated sewage. Samples taken recently from the Ganges River near Varanasi show that levels of fecal coli form, a dangerous bacterium that comes from untreated sewage, were some 3,000 percent higher than what is considered safe for bathing.

4) Plastic Pollution:

Plastic bags, plastic thin sheets and plastic waste is also a major source of pollution. A division bench of Allahabad High Court, comprising Justice Ashok Bhushan and Justice Arun Tandon, in May 03, 2010 had directed the Ganga Basin Authority and the state government to take appropriate action to ban the use of polythene in the vicinity of Ganga in the entire state. Also Plastic Bag Pollution in the country is the biggest hazards. On August 2, 2010, seeking to know whether a fine should be imposed on pan masala or gutkha packet manufacturers for polluting and choking the drainage systems, the Supreme Court has directed the Union government to file its reply in six weeks.

From January 20, 2011 sale of plastic or polythene bags has been banned in the vicinity of rivers or any other water body after Uttar Pradesh Governor B L Joshi gave his assent to an ordinance in this regard. "The Governor has given his assent to UP Plastic and Bio-Degradable Garbage and Waste (Use and Disposal) Ordinance which makes areas around river and water bodies no-polythene zone," he said.

5) Mining Pollution:

New Delhi-based Center for Science and Environment (CSE) on December 29, 2007 said mining was causing displacement, pollution, forest degradation and social unrest. According to the Centre for Science and Environment (CSE) report the top 50 mineral producing districts, as many as 34 fall under the 150 most backward districts identified in the country.

The CSE report has made extensive analysis of environment degradation and pollution due to mining, wherein it has said, in 2005-06 alone 1.6 billion tonnes of waste and overburden from coal, iron ore, limestone and bauxite have added to environment pollution. With the annual growth of mining at 10.7 per cent and 500-odd mines awaiting approval of the Centre, the pollution would increase manifold in the coming years.

The Supreme Court on February 25, 2011 ordered a probe by its committee into alleged illegal mining in Bellary and other forest areas of Karnataka. A bench headed by Chief Justice S.H. Kapadia asked the apex court- appointed Central Empowered Committee to conduct the probe and file its report within six weeks. The explosive report of Lokayukta on July 28, 2011 uncovered major violations and systemic corruption in mining in Bellary Environmental degradation in this region in terms of plundering forest land and complete violation of air and water pollution standards have been devastating. Due to illegal mining in Bellary tanks and natural streams are polluted. There is evidence of perennial rivers drying up and complete devastation of roads and other infrastructure due to transportation of iron ore.

Other Types of Pollution:

1) Light Pollution:
It is caused due to over illumination and astronomical interference.

2) Noise Pollution:
This occurs due to roadway noise, aircraft noise, industrial noise as well as high-intensity sonar.
This is increased even in festive seasons throughout the country.

3) Soil Contamination:
It occurs due to releasing of chemicals through underground leakage. Among the most significant soil contaminants are hydrocarbons, heavy metals, MTBE, herbicides, pesticides and chlorinated hydrocarbons.

4) Radioactive Contamination:
It occurs due to radioactive activities like nuclear power generation and nuclear weapons research, manufacture and deployment.

5) Thermal Pollution:
It occurs due to change in temperature and natural water bodies due to coolant in a power plant.

6) Visual Pollution:
It occurs due to overhead power lines, motorway billboards, and scarred landforms, open storage of trash or municipal solid waste.

Following measures must be adopted in order to control and stabilize pollution:

1) World Bank Cooperation on India's Green Agenda:
India and the World Bank agreed on January 13, 2011 to further strengthen their partnership to advance India's green-growth agenda. The Bank will now support to strengthen Indian capacity of Central Pollution Controls Board, State Pollution Control Boards and biodiversity conservation in addition to other various projects for which financial support have already been given.

2) India to build advanced coal-fired power plant :
Indian scientists aim to built an advanced ultra-super critical coal-fired power plant in the next six years. Once realized, the plant is expected

to put India in a very select group of nations having the technology which would reduce the amount of pollution when compared with the current thermal power plants.

3) Green Court launched:

India launched a "green" court on October 19, 2010 to make polluters pay damages as it steps up its policing of the country's environmental laws. Environment Minister Jairam Ramesh said India was only the third country in the world after Australia and New Zealand to set up such a tribunal. "This is the first body of its kind (in India) to apply the polluter pays principle and the principle of sustainable development," Jairam Ramesh told reporters in New Delhi.

4) National Action Plan on Climate Change:

The Centre has made a provision of Rs. 25,000 crore to mitigate the effects of climate change, a serious problem that India will face in the coming decades, Minister of State for Environment and Forests Jairam Ramesh told the Rajya Sabha on August 21, 2010. Besides, the Finance Ministry has also sanctioned Rs. 5,000 crore as recommended by the 13th Finance Commission to tackle this serious problem," Mr. Ramesh said About 220 scientists from 120 research institutions were working on assessing the impact of climate change on agriculture, water, health and forests.

5) National Clean Energy Fund (NCEF):

For funding research and innovative projects in clean energy technology. Allocation for National Ganga River Basin Authority has been doubled in 2010-11 to Rs.500 crore. The "Mission Clean Ganga 2020" under the National Ganga River Basin Authority (NGRBA) with the objective that no untreated municipal sewage or industrial influent will be discharged into the National river has already been initiated.

b) Depletion of natural resources:

Natural resources are useful materials from the Earth, such as coal, oil, natural gas, and trees.

People use natural resources as raw materials to manufacture or create a range of modern conveniences. Water and food provide humans with sustenance and energy, for example, and fossil fuels generate heat as well as energy for transportation and industrial production. Many of the same natural resources used by people are important to plants and wildlife for survival as well.

Types of Natural Resources:
Natural resources can be categorized on the basis of renewability:

a) Renewable resources :

Renewable resources, such as forests and fisheries, can be replenished or reproduced relatively quickly. The highest rate at which a resource can be used sustainably is the sustainable yield. Some resources, like sunlight, air, and wind, are called perpetual resources because they are available continuously, though at a limited rate. Their quantity is not affected by human consumption. Many renewable resources can be depleted by human use, but may also be replenished, thus maintaining a flow. Some of these, like agricultural crops, take a short time for renewal; others, like water, take a comparatively longer time, while still others, like forests, take even longer.

b) Non-renewable Resources:

are formed over very long geological periods. Minerals and fossils are included in this category. Since their rate of formation is extremely slow, they cannot be replenished once they are depleted. Out of these, the metallic minerals can be re-used by recycling them, but coal and petroleum cannot be recycled.

Dependent upon the speed and quantity of consumption, overconsumption can lead to depletion or total and everlasting destruction of a resource. Important examples are agricultural areas, fish and other animals, forests, healthy water and soil, cultivated and natural landscapes. Such conditionally renewable resources are sometimes classified as a third kind of resource, or as a subtype of renewable resources. Conditionally renewable resources are presently subject to excess human consumption and the only sustainable long term use of such resources is within the so-called zero ecological footprint, wherein human use less than the Earth's ecological capacity to regenerate.

Depletion of Natural Resources:

Resource depletion is the exhaustion of raw materials within a region. Resources are commonly divided between renewable resources and non-renewable resources. Use of either of these forms of resources beyond their rate of replacement is considered to be resource depletion. Resource depletion is most commonly used in reference to farming, fishing, mining, water, and fossil fuels.

A good example of resource depletion is the growing use of petroleum, which is a finite resource which takes millions of years to create. At the rate we are using up petroleum we could be facing depletion within the next five generations. With growing population and land degradation we are also facing a situation where the Earth can no longer feed the vast amount of people on the planet.

Between 1850 and 2010, people on Earth used about half of the world's estimated 2 trillion barrels of petroleum. Currently the world's population uses about 30 billion barrels of oil annually. Some analysts predict that by the year 2030, oil production will be down to about half of that amount.

The declining production of fresh, clean water is making this resource even more valuable than fossil fuels in some locations. The United Nations' Global Environment Outlook 4 report estimates that nearly 2 billion people – a third of the world's current population – will live in regions with water scarcity by 2025, while the remaining two-thirds are expected to be under "water stress."

In a major development, a High Power Committee established by the state government of Kerala in India has recommended today that Coca-Cola be held liable for Indian Rupees 216 crore (US$ 48 million) for damages caused as a result of the company's bottling operations in Plachimada. The Committee thus has compelling evidence to conclude that the HCBPL has caused serious depletion of the water resources of Plachimada, and has severely contaminated the water and soil. HCBPL is the Hindustan Coca-Cola Beverages Private Limited, a subsidiary of Atlanta based Coca-Cola Company.

Added to an increasing decline of arable land for food production, the future of the world looks bleak from a global resource depletion viewpoint. The increased public and political focus on global warming has diverted discussion away from world resource depletion, particularly the depletion of fossil fuel energy with its potentially disastrous impact on world food production, points out Emeritus Professor R A Leng, University of New England, Australia.

Humankind has consumed more natural resources over the past century than over all earlier centuries put together. Planet Earth struggles to reproduce these precious resources, which are sometimes taken away too quickly to be made again. The depletion of natural resources caused by humans requires immediate and intelligent solutions for the benefit of our world.

Resources, such as forests, fish, fossil fuels, and healthy soils are rapidly being depleted, and these valuable gifts of nature are in danger of vanishing from the planet. For example, statistics show that 1.5 acres of forest are lost every second, which adds up to an area the size of Germany being cleared each year. Forty percent of forests worldwide have been depleted since the 1700s. Deforestation occurs when people want the land to grow crops or to obtain timber to make products. Only one quarter of the world's population disproportionally consumes fully three quarters of all processed paper and lumber, which are products generated from deforestation. Nearly twenty percent of climate warming greenhouse gas emissions are due to deforestation that releases stored carbon back into the atmosphere. As a natural resource, the planet's forests are being destroyed at an alarming rate with definite effects.

Another depleted resource involves various fish species. Ninety percent of large fish have been overfished in the seas. Fish species are becoming limited; in 2004, 156 million tons of seafood was eaten throughout the world. Many people rely on fish as a major food source and they are being depleted at record rates. Another resource that is being majorly affected is fossil fuels. Three quarters of all our energy comes from fossil fuels. In 2006, the world used 3.9 billion tons of oil for automobiles and powering machines. In 2005, the United States gave off over twenty-one percent of global carbon emissions from fossil fuel burning. Over the entire world, fossil fuel usage in 2005 produced 7.6 billion tons of carbon emission. Fossil fuels are largely being depleted but the Earth's land is also being affected greatly. A quarter of the planet's fertile soils have been destroyed by overuse and misuse. One-third of the world's cropland has been abandoned in the past forty years after erosion made it unusable and almost one-fifth of the world's cropland is characterized by desertification. Coral reefs provide an environment for more than a quarter of all marine life and close to one-third of coral reefs have been damaged or destroyed by humankind. Marine life has also been affected by the demand for fresh drinking water. In 2009, more than one in five people on earth lacked clean drinking water. Agriculture is one of the largest water consumers, consuming about seventy percent of global water use. Many valuable resources are tragically being affected.

The loss of resources puts people's livelihoods and food security at risk, and affects the world economy. Humans are using up the planet's raw materials about twenty percent faster than they are being replenished. One and a half billion people rely on forests for their life, and as much as forty percent of the world's population still relies on wood products for their energy source for cooking and heating. Fifty-four nations are already more than ninety percent deforested. Americans are estimated to waste nine hundred billion gallons of water each year, yet more than two billion people suffer due to water stress, or pollution of the water. Nearly three billion people rely on fish as a primary protein source which could be a problem in the future. Environmental issues largely affect national politics, and state and local politicians must convince voters that they will work to solve environmental problems in the area .

Humankind has consumed more natural resources over the past century than over all earlier centuries put together. As human populations continue to grow to over 6.7 billion, the rates of consumption and waste are increasing rapidly. As populations grow more rapidly, more people are forced to compete for resources. Developed countries, such as the U.S, consume thirty-two times the resources per person than countries still developing. Resources have been worn away because of people's greed. Increased wealth has spurred the demand for resources, like luxury foods. Humans in arid, populous regions, like the Middle East, demand more fresh water, which is endangering freshwater environments and species. In less developed countries, like some African countries, surprisingly more water is wasted and pollution is less carefully controlled than in more developed countries. People all over the world have been forced to focus more attention on consumption of resources and moving beyond individual action. In years to come, people may no longer have the luxury they have today. Humans may have to step up their commitment to environmentalism; they will have to find better solutions to save resources.

If we want to live sustainably, we need to reduce the size of our environmental footprint. Innovation has increased the productivity of natural resources over time. We will need to find new sources of energy to power our lives without hurting the air. Smart consumers can reduce the use of new materials by buying products without extra packaging and investing in longer lasting products. The Environmental Protection Agency (EPA) administers all the federal government's existing and future programs concerning the environment. The EPA was created by Richard Nixon and its headquarters are in Washington D.C. Many countries must begin cooperating with other nations immediately .Individual nations have passed thousands of laws to protect common resources. People all over the world have established more than 100,000 protected areas to protect natural resources from damage of development.

In many nations, a multitude of businesses have had to alter their business practices to obey environmental regulations. Some companies in America have provided consumers with eco-friendly goods to help the environment. Other companies are developing alternative fuels, such as biodiesel and ethanol. Companies are also developing other renewable energy sources, including solar and wind power, to combat global warming. People have had to alter the amount of resources they have been consuming. One way that people have had to change their lifestyles is by trading in their largely gas consumed cars to more fuel efficient cars, like hybrids, which only use electricity to run and are environmentally cleaner. Former governor of California, Arnold Schwarzenegger, pledged to cut fossil fuel emissions by thirty percent by 2020. To save electricity, it could be as easy as turning off lights and electrical appliances when not in use, or buying more energy efficient appliances. The use of compact fluorescent light bulbs is more common now instead of traditional light bulbs, which consume more energy. The state of California is expecting to create thirty-three percent of electricity from renewable resources by 2020. To produce energy, people all over the world use moving water and wind turbines to create electricity. By 2003, in the U.S, more than 8,000 curbside collection programs have served about 140 million people. Recycling was a requirement by local governments, but is now a daily habit for Americans. People will have to recycle and reuse on a very high scale to balance the convenience of consumption and the wisdom of conservation. If everyone in the United States recycled just one out of every ten

In conclusion, the depletion of natural resources caused by humans requires immediate and creative solutions for the benefit of our world. Planet Earth needs help in reducing the consumption of natural resources by people who need to create better solutions, for a path to an improved future. Humankind has consumed more natural resources over the past century than over all earlier centuries put together. If humankind consumes any more of these natural resources, there may not be any more for people in the next century.

3) Conserving Natural Resources:

Resources are features of environment that are important and value of to human in one form or the other. However, the advancement of modern civilization has had a great impact on our planet's natural resources. So, conserving natural resources is very essential today. There are many ways that one can conserve natural resources. All you need to do is to look around and see what natural resources you are using and find out ways to limit your usage. Most of the people use natural gas to heat their water and their home. You can monitor how much you are using this resource to minimize its usage. For conservation of natural resources like natural gas, one can get tank less water heater as it reduces the usage of natural gas. The other way to save natural gas is the use of another energy source for instance hydro, solar or wind power are all healthy and great alternatives to conserving natural resources. In fact these energy sources are clean and healthy for environment. Moreover, these energy sources do not emit or produced harmful gases or toxin into our environment like that of the burning fossil fuels at the same time they are renewable as well as are not easy to deplete. Today, most of the people are finding many ways for conserving natural resources.

One of the great option before is Hydro-power and solar power. Power can be generated from these sources and these are the best ways for natural resources conservation like fossil fuels. There is also way to conserve natural resource like trees. It can be conserve through recycling process. Many products come from the trees like papers, cups, cardboards and envelopes. By recycling these products you can reduce the number of trees cut down a year. One should make the most use of these paper products without being wasteful and then recycle them. This is one great way for conserving natural resources. Fossil fuels on Earth will not last forever; we need to conserve these fossil fuels. To conserve fossil fuels one can choose to buy a hybrid car. Some of these cars will run on electricity combined with using small amounts of gas. Some hybrid cars just run on electricity. Either way it is a great way for conserving natural resources when it is concern with fossil fuels.

Chapter 3
Problems of Growth

Introduction:

Economy faces many problems in the short run as well as in the long run. Many economical problems are so fatal that immediate attention is required from the finance department of a country so that these problems are analyzed and systematically solved in the long run. Developing economy is an open house for problems like, unemployment, poverty, inflation, black money etc.

Every country faces such problems and hence watches its growth declining in a long run.

Economic growth is, 'An increase in the capacity of an economy to produce goods and services, compared from one period of time to another. Economic growth can be measured in nominal terms, which include inflation, or in real terms, which are adjusted for inflation. For comparing one country's economic growth to another, GDP or GNP per capita should be used as these take into account population differences between countries.' The growth of an economy is thought of not only as an increase in productive capacity but also as an improvement in the quality of life to the people of that economy.

Therefore economic growth is a positive change in the level of production of goods and services by a country over a certain period of time. Nominal growth is defined as economic growth including inflation, while real growth is nominal growth minus inflation. Economic growth is usually brought about by technological innovation and positive external forces.

Economic growth affects employment, output, standard of living, per capita income, currency and finally whole country. There are certain hurdles which holds the economic growth of a country and which in turn gets affected by the changes in economic growth movement.

Following diagram shows the economic growth for 2012-13:

% Growth at constant 2004-05 Prices

GDP of Factor Cost	Q4 2011-12	Q4 2011-12	2011-12 (RE)	2011-12 (PE)
GDP of Factor Cost	**5.1**	**4.8**	**6.2**	**5.0**
Agriculture, Forestry and Fishing	2.0	1.4	3.6	1.9
Mining & Quarrying	5.2	-3.1	-0.6	-0.6
Manufacturing	0.1	2.6	2.7	1.0
Electricity, Gas & Water Supply	3.5	2.8	6.5	4.2
Construction	5.1	4.4	5.6	4.3
Trade, Hotels, Transport & Communication	5.1	6.2	7.0	6.4
Financing, Insurance, Real Estate & Business Services	11.3	9.1	11.7	8.6
Community, Social & Personal Services	6.8	4.0	6.0	6.6

Source :- Central Statistical Organization
RE : Revised Estimates
PE : Provisional Estimates.

In this chapter we are dealing with the problems of growth in detail.

1) Problem of Unemployment:

Introduction:

The problem of unemployment means the problem of providing work to those who are willing to work. A large number of educated and uneducated people, who are capable of work and are also willing to do it, roam here and there without any job. So the problem has assumed an acute form.There is a large number of people who are either partly employed or wholly unemployed. The lives of such people, as well as of their families, are extremely miserable. India cannot claim to be a welfare state so long as this problem remains unsolved. Before discussing the ways and means of solving this problem, unemployment was counted as a crime in modern society. Development of a country depends on its citizens. A developed country is that country which provides employment to its citizens.

India ,having large population suffers by unemployment problem. Here millions of youth are facing unemployment problem .

In society there is no respect for unemployed persons. society blame them lazy. Some unemployed persons are highly qualified but they don't get a platform to implement their knowledge .Relatives also cut relation with an unemployed person. As a result they are isolated from the society and habituated with bad habits. Jobs in India are shrinking at an alarming rate. Privatization and globalization have further aggravated the problem. Instead of generating employment, they have rendered millions of hands idle. American policies are effective there but not in India where the accursed ones are left to fend for themselves leading to frustration, disappointment, anger and violence. So this problem must be taken seriously and solved accordingly. Instead of this politician seems careless about the current scenario of distress and idleness. India knows one thing based on demographic trends, is that to keep the jobless rate from rising more, it must create some 60 million jobs in five years as more Indians enter the job market. More than 65 percent of the population is under 35. India expects economic growth of at least eight percent in the year ended March 2013. But economists say it's not enough to create 12 million jobs a year. For instance, the country's success in information technology and emerging areas such as retail and tourism is expected to adjust some 2.2 million jobs in the next few years, according to industry estimates. Government adviser Lahiri bristles at the suggestion this is a jobless recovery. "I don 't think the growth has been jobless is an overstatement" he said.

But economists say the trend threatens long-term prospects."If we fail to create more jobs it will lead to a lot of social tension which in turn will hurt the economy," said Saumitra Chaudhuri, economic adviser at ICRA "Large unemployment for a country like India is not something desirable," he said.

Some economists say the jobs problem stems from an economic liberalization program launched more than a decade ago. The country's huge public sector has shed thousands of jobs since it stepped on the road to privatization in the early 1990s. The Planning Commission, in a report on employment published last year, attributed rising joblessness to a policy of shedding excess labor in both the private and public sector. It said companies had stepped up investment in plants and machinery more than in labor-intensive industries. Economists add that a $53 billion fiscal deficit prevents the government from creating employment by spending more on social sectors such as health and education." We should be looking for a fiscal-led economic expansion based on the basic needs of the people which will have a much higher multiplier effect," says Jayati Ghosh, professor at New Delhi's Jawaharlal Nehru University.

In the light of this the task of harnessing the unemployed should be put on a war footing. Massive urban recruitment will be useless as the cities which have got along well enough without the recruits, can certainly continue to do so. Besides, massive urban recruitment will be. inflationary and hence is impracticable. The unemployed population should be mobilized for rural reconstruction, especially as the villages lack technical know-how and also that 70 per cent of India's population lives there. Stressing on agronomy will augment rural reconstruction, enlighten the farmers, raise agricultural production, conserve foreign exchange and above all be a step towards self-sufficiency and employment for ail.

Estimates of the total number of Indians unemployed or underemployed vary between 70 and 100 million. This figure can cause concern to any nation, but to a developing country like ours, it is the cause of great distress. A developing country must mobilize its manpower resources to the maximum possible extent and a developing country with such a large segment of its population unemployed or under-employed is a contradiction in terms. It is true that the future of a country depends on the ability and the mental attitudes of its young men and women then India has already lost the will to develop. If India allows her young men to be gripped by insecurity and frustration, she will have to pay for modernization and rapid advancement with several years of stagnation.

The major causes which have been responsible for the wide spread unemployment can be spelt out as under.

1) High level of Population Growth:

It is the leading cause of unemployment in Rural India. In India, particularly in rural areas, the population is increasing rapidly. It has adversely affected the unemployment situation largely in two ways. In the first place, the growth of population directly encouraged the unemployment by making large addition to labor force. It is because the rate of job expansion could never have been as high as population growth would have required.

It is true that the increasing labor force requires the creation of new job opportunities at an increasing rate. But in actual practice employment expansion has not been sufficient to match the growth of the labor force, and to reduce the back leg of unemployment. This leads to unemployment situation secondly; the rapid population growth indirectly affected the unemployment situation by reducing the resources for capital formation. Any rise in population, over a large absolute base as in India, implies a large absolute number.

It means large additional expenditure on their rearing up, maintenance, and education. As a consequence, more resources get used up in private consumption such as food, clothing, shelter and son on in public consumption like drinking water, electricity medical and educational facilities. This has reduced the opportunities of diverting a larger proportion of incomes to saving and investment. Thus, population growth has created obstacles in the way of first growth of the economy and retarded the growth of job opportunities.

2) Limited land for use:

Land is the gift of nature. It is always constant and cannot expand like population growth. Since, India population increasing rapidly, therefore, the land is not sufficient for the growing population. As a result, there is heavy pressure on the land. In rural areas, most of the people depend directly on land for their livelihood. Land is very limited in comparison to population. It creates the unemployment situation for a large number of persons who depend on agriculture in rural areas.

3) Limitations of Agriculture sector:

In Rural Society agriculture is the only means of employment. However, most of the rural people are engaged directly as well as indirectly in agricultural operation. But, agriculture in India is basically a seasonal affair. It provides employment facilities to the rural people only in a particular season of the year. For example, during the sowing and harvesting period, people are fully employed and the period between the post harvest and before the next sowing they remain unemployed. It has adversely affected their standard of living.

4) Fragmentation of land:

In India, due to the heavy pressure on land of large population results the fragmentation of land. It creates a great obstacle in the part of agriculture. As land is fragmented and agricultural work is being hindered the people who depend on agriculture remain unemployed. This has an adverse effect on the employment situation. It also leads to the poverty of villagers.

5) Less technology use in Agriculture:

The method of agriculture in India is very backward. Till now, the rural farmers followed the old farming methods. As a result, the farmer cannot feed properly many people by the produce of his farm and he is unable to provide his children with proper education or to engage them in any profession. It leads to unemployment problem.

6) Failure of Cottage Industries:

In Rural India, village or cottage industries are the only means of employment particularly of the landless people. They depend directly on various cottage industries for their livelihood. But, now-a-days, these are adversely affected by the industrialization process. Actually, it is found that they cannot compete with modern factories in matter or production. As a result of which the village industries suffer a serious loss and gradually closing down. Owing to this, the people who work in there remain unemployed and unable to maintain their livelihood.

7) Poor education system:

The day-to-day education is very defective and is confirmed within the class room only. Its main aim is to acquire degree only. The present educational system is not job oriented, it is degree oriented. It is defective on the ground that is more general then the vocational. Thus, the people who have getting general education are unable to do any work. They are to be called as good for nothing in the ground that they cannot have any job here, they can find the ways of self employment. It leads to unemployment as well as underemployment.

8) Lack of transport and communication facilities:

In India particularly in rural areas, there are no adequate facilities of transport and communication. Owing to this, the village people who are not engaged in agricultural work are remained unemployed. It is because they are unable to start any business for their livelihood and they are confined only within the limited boundary of the village. It is noted that the modern means of transport and communication are the only way to trade and commerce. Since there is lack of transport and communication in rural areas, therefore, it leads to unemployment problem among the villagers.

9) Poor Employment Planning:

The employment planning of the government is not adequate in comparison to population growth. In India near about two lakh people are added yearly to our existing population. But the employment opportunities did not increase according to the proportionate rate of population growth. As a consequence, a great difference is visible between the job opportunities and population growth.

On the other hand it is a very difficult task on the part of the Government to provide adequate job facilities to all the people. Besides this, the government also does not take adequate step in this direction. The faulty employment planning of the Government expedites this problem to a great extent. As a result the problem of unemployment is increasing day by day.

These are the causes of unemployment which are responsible for large youth wasting time effecting low economic growth.

Following diagram discusses the rural employment in 2009-2010

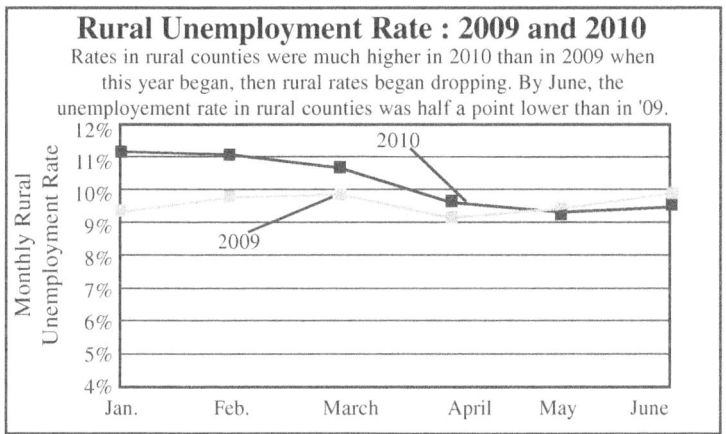

Rural Unemployment Rate : 2009 and 2010

Rates in rural counties were much higher in 2010 than in 2009 when this year began, then rural rates began dropping. By June, the unemployement rate in rural counties was half a point lower than in '09.

Following types of unemployment exists in India:

1) Rural Unemployment:

According to 2001 Census, 72.2 per cent people live in villages. And hence it can be assumed that India is essentially a Rural Economy. Agriculture is their principal means of livelihood and employment is largely available in this major part of economy .

There are **Two** kinds of unemployment exist in rural areas:

a) Seasonal Unemployment:

This is primarily confined to agriculture. Agriculture does not provide employment throughout the year. It is also known as 'perennial unemployment'. Sowing and harvesting season ranges between five and seven months.

For the rest of the period the cultivator remain idle. Experts believe that an Indian cultivator remains unemployed for five to six months. When the next sowing season starts he again goes back to cultivation. Therefore, it is called seasonal unemployment. Seasonal employment is very critical and very difficult to eradicate.

b) Disguised Unemployment:

It is again a feature of the agrarian economy. When more people are engaged than actually required for production, it is a disguised unemployment. If a part of labor force is withdrawn from the farm the total output of the farm will remain unchanged. The withdrawn labor force will be termed as disguisedly employed.

Under this type of unemployment the marginal productivity of labor (i.e., the addition to the total product) over a wide range is zero. Indian agriculture is a self-employing sector. There is absence of alternative occupations in the economy.

The burden of increasing population ultimately; falls on land and there is overcrowding on the farms. Rigid social structure and joint family system encourage this overcrowding. No one appears to be unemployed. But in reality, large part of the labor force is generally underemployed. Seasonal unemployment mixed with this unemployment makes it a fatal problem. Unemployment in rural areas of 4 states of India is given below :

Table-2 : Unemployment in rural areas in some states and India, 2009-10,

State	Labor Force Participation Rate (%)	Unemployment rate (%)
Andhra Pradesh	60.6	7.9
Karnataka	58.2	2.5
Maharashtra	49.0	4.4
Rajasthan	56.2	20.4
India	51.4	9.9

Source : GOI, 2010

2) Urban Unemployment:

According to **2001** Census, **27.8** per cent population lives in urban areas. Therefore, the magnitude of urban unemployment is not as high as that of rural unemployment. Same as in the Rural area, there are **Two kinds** of unemployment in the urban areas:

a) Industrial Unemployment:

The Britishers had demolished the village based industries. The condition of artisans and farmers was not good. They migrated to the urban areas in search of jobs. But they could only increase the number of unemployed persons because of limited number of entrepreneurs..

In recent years many industries have been modernized. New and automation techniques of production have rendered many workers unemployed. It is called 'technological unemployment.

Industrial activities are increasing by leaps and bounds. Fluctuations in the business activities affect the level of employment. Industrial recession of 1966-68 rendered many workers unemployed. Recent power shortage in many states has slackened the industrial activity and increased the number of unemployed persons. It is called 'cyclical unemployment'.

b) Educated Unemployment:

Indian universities and colleges have been producing many graduates every year. Education in India is basically 'job oriented' which ultimately teaches a student to find a particular type of job but the problem is that that student cannot apply his skills elsewhere like for starting an Industry so it is not possible for limited industrial option to cope up with this increasing numbers of students leaving college every year after graduation searching job. Students have been aimlessly studying different courses.

When they come out of college after completing their education, they fail to get suitable jobs. Educated unemployment entails a waste of the country's most valuable resource, the human capital.

Following diagram shows the rate of unemployment in India for a decade:

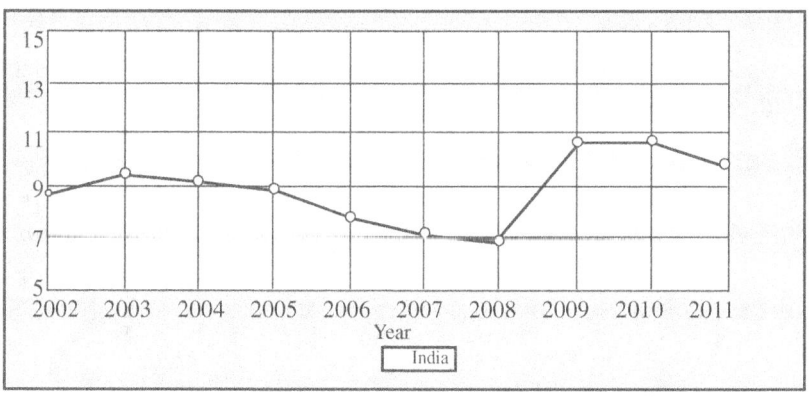

YEAR	2002	2003	2004	2005	2006	2007	2008	2009	2010	2011
RATE	8.8	9.5	9.2	8.9	7.8	7.2	6.8	10.7	10.8	9.8

Rate of unemployment is declining in 2011 and Government should take following measures for overcoming this critical problem.

1) Investment in Primary Industries:
Investment in heavy and basic industries and consumer goods industries should be increased. They provide more employment along with the supply of consumer goods.

2) Development of Cottage and Small-scale Industries:
Development of such cottage and small scale industries provide more employment by adopting labor intensive techniques. Hence its a promising technique of reducing the rate of unemployment for the developing country India.

3) Drastic changes in Educational System:
More emphasis should be given to vocational education rather than theoretical, old knowledge which makes no use of student's brain and make him dependent.

Hence education system must concentrate on overall personality development of a student rather than current job oriented training.

4) Population Explosion:
Population increase at an alarming rate demolish capacity of industry to cope with it results in unemployment. Therefore Rapidly rising population should be checked by adopting family planning and welfare schemes.

5) Agriculture Development:
Modernization of agriculture should be done with a view of attracting more and more youth from villages towards this important sector of economy. This development will keep the employment in villages alive hence urban jobs will be occupied with other people of the country.

6) Rural Works Programs:

Rural works programs should be increased for proper education and development of employment in rural area of a country.

7) Infrastructure development of economy:

Infra-structure of the economy should be developed in order to provoke concrete development of a country from all aspects resulting in a positive environment for employment generation thus reducing unemployment.

8) Subsidies to Private Sector:

Subsidies and other incentives should be given to private sector for assisting other sectors of the economy as well as increasing the rate of employment in that sector..

9) Self-employment Programs:

Young entrepreneurs should be financed for self-employment so as to ensure steady growth of industrial sector. Various programs must be initiated for training as well as education for the new and aspiring entrepreneurs.

Following diagram will show the unemployment rate(per 1000) for persons of age 15 years and above according to usual principal status approach(ps) for each state/ut

Table (5.2) Unemployment Rate (per 1000) for persons of age 15 years & above according to usual principal status approach (ps) for each State/UT

Sl. No.	Name of State/UT/ All India	Rural			Urban			Rural+Urban		
		male	femal	person	male	female	person	male	female	person
1	2	3	4	5	6	7	8	9	10	11
1	Andra Pradesh	21	24	22	46	11	61	27	35	30
2	Arunachal Pradesh	40	86	56	99	252	142	47	101	65
3	Assam	48	128	62	44	206	73	47	138	63
4	Bihar	59	205	85	45	181	64	58	203	83
5	Chhattisgarh	11	6	9	27	59	35	13	11	12
6	Delhi	25	175	45	32	149	49	31	153	48
7	Goa	94	549	231	62	290	109	80	462	179
8	Gujarat	5	13	7	12	42	15	8	18	10
9	Haryana	26	71	30	24	120	36	25	88	32
10	Himachal Pradesh	41	12	28	38	130	63	40	17	31
11	Jammu & Kashmir	33	157	50	44	250	71	36	182	56
12	Jharkhand	37	89	47	50	120	59	39	93	48
13	Karnataka	24	21	23	27	35	29	25	24	25
14	Kerala	32	214	82	40	375	145	34	262	99
15	Madya Pradesh	18	28	20	44	96	51	24	37	27
16	Maharashtra	19	26	21	23	107	42	20	47	28
17	Manipur	25	23	24	87	65	80	39	34	37
18	Meghalaya	24	40	31	42	100	64	27	49	36
19	Mizoram	10	9	10	8	119	43	10	32	19
20	Nagaland	65	48	59	63	72	65	65	52	60
21	Odisha	28	29	28	36	107	43	29	34	30
22	Punjab	13	66	17	13	86	21	13	74	18
23	Rajasthan	12	30	16	16	64	20	13	33	17
24	Sikkim	82	163	113	105	511	229	85	194	126
25	Tamil Nadu	19	24	21	19	41	25	19	29	22
26	Tripura	47	310	115	139	446	236	66	344	141
27	Uttarakhand	35	108	55	21	142	40	32	113	52
28	Uttar Pradesh	22	33	23	32	71	35	24	40	25
29	West Bengal	43	159	61	89	402	139	53	212	78
30	A & N Islands	22	409	108	25	331	119	23	367	113
31	Chandigarh	126	367	161	8	40	12	21	84	28
32	Dadra & Nagar Haveli	12	160	33	-	-	-	10	130	27
33	Daman & Div	9	-	7	3	-	2	7	-	6
34	Lakshadweep	294	240	290	76	356	117	196	314	209
35	Puducherry	5	32	11	43	161	66	30	111	47
	All India	27	56	34	34	125	50	29	69	38

2) Problems of Poverty:

It is a very common problem of developing country like India that more than average population of the country is below poverty line and still facing problem of daily bread and butter.

One thinker brought some insight on this topic and said,

Despite having a poor per capita gross domestic product — about one-thirtieth of what it is in advanced nations — India's growth has collapsed to an ordinary five or six per cent when not supported by foreign inflows. This is down from its peak of nine per cent-plus, which it achieved for four years under Manmohan Singh, and which is now looking unlikely for the near future. Some think, in my opinion wrongly, that this problem can be addressed purely by more reforms. The more India opens itself to foreign money, the more transparent its systems of government are, the more efficient and less corrupt its bureaucracy, the better for its economy. That is the logic. None of this is exceptionable, though all of it assumes that the high growth path is something for which only the government is responsible.

I think we should also look elsewhere to seek an answer to why we cannot grow. I did not write about why this was so in my earlier piece because this brings us into the realm of culture. Economists have little regard for this sort of thing and their work assumes that the environment is everything.

Even if you believe the government's figures, a third of India is poor. The fact is that the government's numbers are based on calorie consumption for immediate sustenance and food. Indians who earn Rs23 a day in villages and Rs29 a day in cities are not poor. A monthly income of Rs674 in villages and Rs860 in cities is thought to be sufficient. This compares with Rs22,000 a month in the United States.
In that sense, the poverty line of India is cruel. It is merciless and doesn't allow the majority of Indians any money for shelter or access to education or health care or sanitation or anything else that civilized nations would consider as essential as food."

From the above elaboration about the current situation of India, it can be very well deduced that India need an overall strategy for reforms and development which will nullifies the effects of poverty, unemployment and other drastic problems.

Report of World Bank:
India now has a greater share of the world's poorest than it did thirty years ago. Then it was home to one fifth of the world's poorest people, but today it accounts for one-third - 400 million.

The study found the number of extremely poor people had declined from half the world's population in 1981 to one fifth in 2010, but voiced concern at its increase in Sub-Saharan Africa and continuing high level in India.

World Bank president Jim Yong Kim said while the overall decline was "remarkable progress", the remaining 1.2 billion people living in extreme poverty was "a stain on our collective conscience." His colleague, World Bank chief economist Kaushik Basu, who until last year was economic advisor to Indian prime minister Dr Manmohan Singh, said the figures called for the world's wealthier countries to do more.

"We have made strides in cutting down poverty, but with nearly one-fifth of the world population still below the poverty line, not enough. Directing investment towards the poor will require coordinated effort by the Bank, our country partners, and the international development community; and will, let's face it, entail sacrifice on the part of those who are fortunate enough to be better off," he said.

The scale of continuing extreme poverty in India, despite its economy nudging growth rates of nine per cent in recent years, highlights what government strategists have called its "ticking time bomb." Its population is expected to reach 1.5 billion and become the world's largest nation by 2026 but its economy is not growing fast enough to create the 20 million new jobs per year they will need to prevent poverty increasing further.

Its problems are compounded by poor health services, child malnutrition and inadequate education and training. Almost half of pupils drop out of school by the age of 13 and only one in ten people have received any form of job training.

The perception of India as a fast-growing economy however has seen developed countries significantly reduce their aid. The United States has announced a 16 per cent reduction while Britain has announced it will end its £280 million per year aid program. Thomas Chandy of Save The Children said 200 million people had been lifted from poverty in the last two decades but the recent economic growth had left one third of the population untouched. "India's status has gone down despite the economic growth, inequality has widened which makes the poor poorer. In child mortality, infant mortality and maternal mortality, India seems to have the largest populations in all these categories. We would like to see focused interventions [because] the most difficult areas remain untouched," he said.

Causes of Poverty In India:
Causes of poverty increase are so obvious because of its nature of increasing each and every other problem along with it.

The economic reforms of 1991, despite spurring a huge growth of the economy, have left the country with terrible inequalities, within cities as well as between urban and rural areas. They were the best opportunity to seriously tackle the causes of poverty in India and more specifically rural poverty. With two thirds of the population living in rural areas and some 500 million poor (or more), even urban poverty stems from the rural migrations to the city.

Yet following causes can be stated as primary causes of Poverty increase:

1) Small Services Sector:
At this stage of development the services and especially IT and finance sector typically don't employ a lot of people. Although the tertiary sector (services) represents 50% of India's GDP, it employs only... 2 million people! So many Indians are quite right to complain that globalization and modernization benefit only the rich.

2) Neglecting the poor:
The manufacturing sector is finally growing, so there are good prospects to reduce the massive unemployment and hence tackle one of the causes of poverty in India. But that leaves the problem of rural poverty. The Chinese government has the merit to have very gradually opened its country and markets to the outside world rather than a "shock therapy". This means that it kept for more than a decade its rural safety nets, giving time to people to adapt to the transition and changes.

On the other hand India just left its rural poor on their own, and their opposition to globalization is in fact very typical: every developing country where social safety nets were quasi-absent has in general a defiant population to the global process.

3) Lack of proper Housing Conditions:
The development of real estate sector, hundreds of millions still

lack a decent home so there should be incentives for the market to cater to the needs of the poor with social housing so that the country gets a chance to solve the problem of its gigantic slums.

4) Market liberalization and globalization:

Many examples now prove that growth and liberalization have contributed to the causes of poverty in India. They have exacerbated inequalities within the population and reduced the role of the state while it was direly needed to develop the country.

In this sense growth itself risks stirring some tensions within a country between those who got rich and those who were left out. There's nothing wrong with market liberalization in itself but in a developing country it can be disastrous because market forces will only invest in profitable areas which leaves plenty excluded in the country. The role of the state here is thus one of empowering citizens and making sure they can participate in the economy and growth of the country.

5) Poor Health:

Many experts have argued that to make the most out of economic growth, the government at all levels should have invested in protecting the people, that is to say invest in public services, for instance in health care. Diseases are one of the main causes of poverty in India, creating a major public safety disaster in India that contributes to keep and make millions fall into poverty. It's estimated that each year, "the cost of health care pushes some 39 million people back into poverty", according to a recent CBS News report.

6) Land inequality and social injustice:

What the government needs is precisely to make sure that the people can also ripe the benefits of the economic growth. So even if the growth in the third sector is impressive, there's still a huge surplus of jobless or underemployed workers at the countryside. And over there, the issue of land inequality is an important bone of contention that if resolved could substantially alleviate poverty.The fact is that for each village, a few land owners have most of the land which they rent to other people to work on, at ridiculously high prices. It's a bit like the rent seekers in feudal societies: they prevent any real growth from happening and just suck up all the money - that they don't reinvest since they don't care all that much about the land itself. Not only is the situation stuck because of this, but land inequalities also reflect the huge imbalance of power carved in the rural society.

7) Minimum Role of women in economic activities:

In many cases the situation of women and their bottom-low participation in the economy among Asian countries counts as one more issue among the causes of poverty in India. Their restricted access to education in rural areas also makes any kind of family planning and educative campaign on child diseases or education quasi ineffective. More women oriented economic programs must be initialized in rural areas so as to make women in rural areas independent resulting in improvement of overall state of economy.

There are still many problems which are not mentioned here because of complex nature of this problem of poverty. Whole book can be dedicated to this single problem which has rooted so deeply in Indian economic system.

The state of Uttar Pradesh alone has 8% of the world's population who live in extreme poverty. However, it's not India's poorest state. With a population of 100 million people, Bihar is poorest. Average income is $294 per year, less than all but two Sub-Saharan African countries. More than half of children under 3 suffer from malnutrition (source).

3) Problem of Inflation:

Rising price is a problem of every nation in world. Developing economy suffers this problem of inflation more than developed countries. It is a fundamental problem and if ignored can cause big damage in the form of poverty, hunger and decrease in overall standard of living of people.

Current Status of India:

Inflation in India has remained high and persistent in the last six years. As the Indian economy grew at an unprecedented rate of almost 8.5 per cent during the period, rising incomes backed up the purchasing power of the population, boosting consumption demand. The rise in demand triggered inflationary pressures, particularly in sectors where supply lagged behind. Gradually, inflation became generalized, as public policy continued to spur growth in consumption demand and wages. Inflation is the increase in the average prices of goods and services, measured by an index. There are three measures of inflation in India: WPI, CPI, and the gross domestic product (GDP) deflator. The third measure is the most comprehensive, as it takes into account all goods and services produced in the economy. All three measures reveal signs of an early pick-up in inflation in 2006-07 and persistence thereafter. WPI inflation consistently surpassed the RBI's comfort threshold of 5 per cent in 51 of the 70 months between April 2006 and January 2012. It averaged 6.6 per cent over 2006-07 to 2010-11, rising from 4.7 per cent during the previous five years. CPI inflation, over the same reference period, rose to 9.0 per cent from 4.1 per cent, and inflation measured by the GDP deflator climbed to 7.4 per cent from 3.9 per cent. During April 2011- January 2012, CPI and WPI inflation averaged 8.8 per cent and 9.1 per cent; inflation measured by the GDP deflator averaged 8.2 per cent in 2011-12. Thus it can be said that inflation in India has become high and persistent.

The past six years, since 2006-07 were passed with a series of adverse supply shocks. The shocks arose from a shortfall in food-grain and non-food grain commodities (vegetables, fruits, protein-based foods - pulses, milk, eggs, meat and fish). Sharp increases in international prices of fuels and commodity too were a trigger. continuity in inflation, however, did not arise from supply shocks. Although supply shocks can trigger sudden and sharp inflationary pressures, the pressures diminish when supplies revive. Persistence in inflation stemmed, instead, from government policies that stimulated consumption demand by increasing wages and salaries but did not do enough to remove supply-side bottlenecks. Under fiscal policies that boosted consumption, the supply shocks had a more lasting effect, reinforcing inflationary pressures.

Inflation was generalized; all the categories of the WPI contributed to inflationary pressures. Food inflation, however, was the most fixed. It averaged 10.2 per cent over 2006-07 to 2010-11, and prevailed at over 15 per cent in the last two years of the period. Manufacturing inflation averaged 5.3 per cent, whereas fuel inflation averaged 10.2

per cent over the five-year period. Although food inflation has declined significantly since December 2011, it is likely to bounce back once the impact of seasonal factors and the effect of high base wear off.

Fiscal policy is the means by which a government adjusts spending and taxation to influence demand and the economy's capacity to produce goods and services. In India, an expansionary fiscal policy has boosted consumption demand in recent years.

Consumption expenditure of the government increased by' 5,300 billion between 2004-05 and 2010-11, in comparison to an increase of ' 1,800 billion in expenditure on capital formation (Figure 1). Of the total direct government consumption expenditure, wages and salaries accounted for almost 50 per cent. Since 2008-09, the government expenditure focused more on boosting consumption demand in the short term.

Inflation is the rapidly rising prices of goods and services caused to the increase in the supply money. Inflation arises when the demand for goods and services in an economy exceeds the supply of same. Inflation is a determinant in functioning of any economy. India is a country with a mixed economy model that comprises both capitalism and socialism hence the challenges faced are vital for its growth model. The recent rise in inflation has been found to consist of several political and economic crisis under the prime ministry of Dr Manmohan Singh. Contesting on the challenges faced, several economists have questioned the method of measuring inflation to be faulty. The present day process being used in India has been The Wholesale Price Index while several other developed countries adopt the Consumer price index to calculate inflation.

Types of Inflation:
Following diagram shows the types of Inflation in detail:

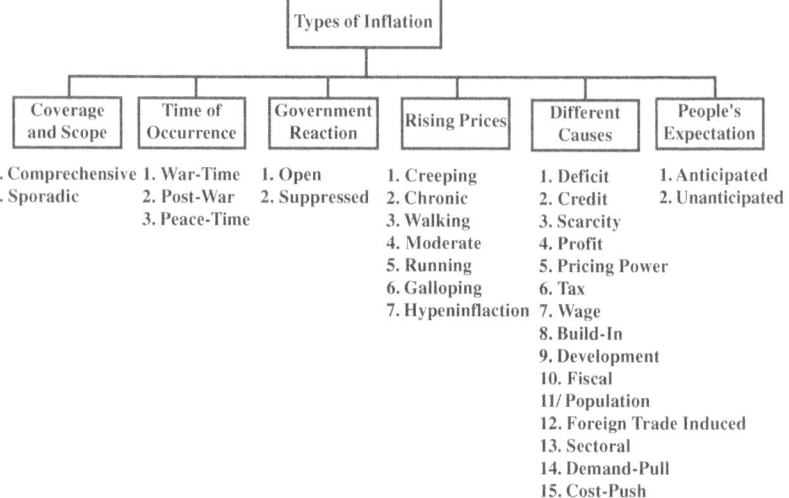

Types of Inflation					
Coverage and Scope	**Time of Occurrence**	**Government Reaction**	**Rising Prices**	**Different Causes**	**People's Expectation**
1. Comprechensive	1. War-Time	1. Open	1. Creeping	1. Deficit	1. Anticipated
2. Sporadic	2. Post-War	2. Suppressed	2. Chronic	2. Credit	2. Unanticipated
	3. Peace-Time		3. Walking	3. Scarcity	
			4. Moderate	4. Profit	
			5. Running	5. Pricing Power	
			6. Galloping	6. Tax	
			7. Hypeninflaction	7. Wage	
				8. Build-In	
				9. Development	
				10. Fiscal	
				11/ Population	
				12. Foreign Trade Induced	
				13. Sectoral	
				14. Demand-Pull	
				15. Cost-Push	

1) Types of Inflation on Scope:
a) Comprehensive Inflation :
When the prices of all commodities rise throughout the economy it is known as Comprehensive Inflation. Another name for comprehensive inflation is Economy Wide Inflation.

b) Sporadic Inflation:
When prices of only few commodities in few regions (areas) rise, it is known as Sporadic Inflation. It is sectional in nature. For example, rise in food prices due to bad monsoon or floods caused due to monsoon can result in the rise in prices.

2) Types of Inflation on Time of Occurrence:
a) War-Time Inflation:
Inflation that takes place during the period of a war-like situation is known as War-Time inflation. During a war, scare productive resources are all diverted and prioritized to produce military goods and equipments. This overall result in very limited supply or extreme shortage (low availability) of resources (raw materials) to produce essential commodities. Production and supply of basic goods slow down and can no longer meet the soaring demand from people.

Consequently, prices of essential goods keep on rising in the market resulting in War-Time Inflation.

b) Post-War Inflation:

Inflation that takes place soon after a war is known as Post-War Inflation. After the war, government controls are relaxed, resulting in a faster hike in prices than what experienced during the war.

c) Peace-Time Inflation:

When prices rise during a normal period of peace, it is known as Peace-Time Inflation. It is due to huge government expenditure or spending on capital projects of a long gestation (development) period.

3) Types of Inflation on Government policies:

a) Open Inflation:

When government does not attempt to restrict inflation, it is known as Open Inflation. In a free market economy, where prices are allowed to take its own course, open inflation occurs.

b) Suppressed Inflation:

When government prevents price rise through price controls, rationing, etc., it is known as Suppressed Inflation. It is also referred as Repressed Inflation. However, when government controls are removed, Suppressed inflation becomes Open Inflation. Suppressed Inflation leads to corruption, black marketing, artificial scarcity, etc.

4) Types of Inflation on Rising Prices:

a) Creeping Inflation:

When prices are gently rising, it is referred as Creeping Inflation. It is the mildest form of inflation and also known as a Mild Inflation or Low Inflation. According to R.P. Kent, when prices rise by not more than (up to) 3% per annum (year), it is called Creeping Inflation.

b) Chronic Inflation:

If creeping inflation persist (continues to increase) for a longer period of time then it is often called as Chronic or Secular Inflation. Chronic Creeping Inflation can be either Continuous (which remains consistent without any downward movement) or Intermittent (which occurs at regular intervals). It is called chronic because if an inflation rate continues to grow for a longer period without any downturn, then it possibly leads to Hyperinflation.

c) Walking Inflation:

When the rate of rising prices is more than the Creeping Inflation, it is known as Walking Inflation. When prices rise by more than 3% but less than 10% per annum (i.e between 3% and 10% per annum), it is called as Walking Inflation. According to some economists, walking inflation must be taken seriously as it gives a cautionary signal for the occurrence of Running inflation. Furthermore, if walking inflation is not checked in due time it can eventually result in Galloping inflation.

d) Moderate Inflation:

Prof. Samuelson clubbed together concept of Creeping and Walking inflation into Moderate Inflation. When prices rise by less than 10% per annum (single digit inflation rate), it is known as Moderate Inflation. According to Prof. Samuelson, it is a stable inflation and not a serious economic problem.

e) Running Inflation:

A rapid acceleration in the rate of rising prices is referred as Running Inflation. When prices rise by more than 10% per annum, running inflation occurs. Though economists have not suggested a fixed range for measuring running inflation, we may consider price rise between 10% to 20% per annum (double digit inflation rate) as a running inflation.

f) Galloping Inflation:

According to Prof. Samuelson, if prices rise by double or triple digit inflation rates like 30% or 400% or 999% per annum, then the situation can be termed as Galloping Inflation. When prices rise by more than 20% but less than 1000% per annum (i.e. between 20% to 1000% per annum), galloping inflation occurs. It is also referred as Jumping inflation. India has been witnessing galloping inflation since the second five year plan period.

g) Hyperinflation:

Hyperinflation refers to a situation where the prices rise at an alarming high rate. The prices rise so fast that it becomes very difficult to measure its magnitude. However, in quantitative terms, when prices rise above 1000% per annum (quadruple or four digit inflation rate), it is termed as Hyperinflation. During a worst case scenario of hyperinflation, value of national currency (money) of an affected country reduces almost to zero. Paper money becomes worthless and people start trading either in gold and silver or sometimes even use the old barter system of commerce. Two worst examples of hyperinflation recorded in world history are of those experienced by Hungary in year 1946 and Zimbabwe during 2004-2009 under Robert Mugabe's regime.

5) Types of Inflation on different Causes:
a) Deficit Inflation:
    Deficit inflation takes place due to deficit financing proposed by government as a part of financial policy.

b) Credit Inflation:
    Credit inflation takes place due to excessive bank credit or money supply in the economy.

c) Scarcity Inflation:
    Scarcity inflation occurs due to hoarding. Hoarding is an excess accumulation of basic commodities by unscrupulous traders and black marketers. It is practiced to create an artificial shortage of essential goods like food grains, kerosene, etc. with an intension to sell them only at higher prices to make huge profits during scarcity inflation. Though hoarding is an unfair trade practice and a punishable criminal offence still some crooked merchants often get themselves engaged in it.

d) Profit Inflation:
    When entrepreneurs are interested in boosting their profit margins, prices rise. This inflation must be monitored by finance department.

e) Pricing Power Inflation:
    It is often referred as Administered Price inflation. It occurs when industries and business houses increase the price of their goods and services with an objective to boost their profit margins. It does not occur during a financial crisis and economic depression, and is not seen when there is a downturn in the economy. As Oligopolies have the ability to

set prices of their goods and services it is also called as Oligopolistic Inflation.

f) Tax Inflation:
Due to rise in indirect taxes, sellers charge high price to the consumers.

g) Wage Inflation:
If the rise in wages in not accompanied by a rise in output, prices rise.

h) Build-In Inflation:
Vicious cycle of Build-in inflation is induced by adaptive expectations of workers or employees who try to keep their wages or salaries high in anticipation of inflation. Employers and Organizations raise the prices of their respective goods and services in anticipation of the workers or employees' demands. This overall builds a vicious cycle of rising wages followed by an increase in general prices of commodities. This cycle, if continues, keeps on accumulating inflation at each round turn and thereby results into what is called as Build-in inflation.

i) Development Inflation:
During the process of development of economy, incomes increases, causing an increase in demand and rise in prices.

j) Fiscal Inflation:
It occurs due to excess government expenditure or spending when there is a budget deficit.

k) Population Inflation:
Prices rise due to a rapid increase in population.

l) Inflation due to Foreign Trade:
It is divided into two categories, viz.,
a) Export-Boom Inflation, and b) Import Price-Hike Inflation.

a) Export-Boom Inflation:
Considerable increase in exports may cause a shortage at home (within exporting country) and results in price rise (within exporting country). This is known as Export-Boom Inflation.

b) Import Price-Hike Inflation:
If a country imports goods from a foreign country, and the prices

of imported goods increases due to inflation abroad, then the prices of domestic products using imported goods also rises. This is known as Import Price-Hike Inflation. For e.g. India imports oil from Iran at $100 per barrel. Oil prices in the international market suddenly increases to $150 per barrel. Now India to continue its oil imports from Iran has to pay $50 more per barrel to get the same amount of crude oil. When the imported expensive oil reaches India, the indian consumers also have to pay more and bear the economic burden. Manufacturing and transportation costs also increase due to hike in oil prices. This, consequently, results in a rise in the prices of domestic goods being manufactured and transported. It is the end-consumer in India, who finally pays and experiences the ultimate pinch of Import Price-Hike Inflation. If the oil prices in the international market fall down then the import price-hike inflation also slows down, and vice-versa.

m) Sectoral Inflation:

It occurs when there is a rise in the prices of goods and services produced by certain sector of the industries. For instance, if prices of crude oil increases then it will also affect all other sectors (like aviation, road transportation, etc.) which are directly related to the oil industry. For e.g. If oil prices are hiked, air ticket fares and road transportation cost will increase.

n) Demand-Pull Inflation:

Inflation which arises due to various factors like rising income, exploding population, etc., leads to aggregate demand and exceeds aggregate supply, and tends to raise prices of goods and services. This is known as Demand-Pull or Excess Demand Inflation.

o) Cost-Push Inflation:

When prices rise due to growing cost of production of goods and services, it is known as Cost-Push (Supply-side) Inflation. For e.g. If wages of workers are raised then the unit cost of production also increases. As a result, the prices of end-products or end-services being produced and supplied are consequently hiked.

6) Types of Inflation on Expectation:
a) Anticipated Inflation:

If the rate of inflation corresponds to what the majority of people are expecting or predicting, then is called Anticipated Inflation. It is also referred as Expected Inflation.

b) Unanticipated Inflation:

If the rate of inflation corresponds to what the majority of people are not expecting or predicting, then is called Unanticipated Inflation. It is also referred as Unexpected Inflation.

Effects Of Inflation:

We have seen types of Inflation in depth, now we shall study effects of **Inflation:**

I.   Inflation if not monitored would move from its initial beneficiary stage to that of a harmful one. For this reason, it is necessary to prevent inflation from gaining strength.

II.   A stronger inflation is more difficult to control than a mild one. And there is no way to control a hyperinflation.

The beneficial effects of inflation are limited to only its initial phase when the price rise is sufficiently mild. During that period, there is a favorable impact upon both output and employment. The increase in prices and distributive inequalities are more than counterbalanced by gains in output and employment.

However, once inflationary process gathers some strength, its ill effects come to dominate the whole economy. These have been only briefly discussed here.

1) Inequality:

Right from the beginning, inflation adds to inequalities of income and wealth. However, in its last phase, it is not longer able to do so because money ceases to bean acceptable store of value. It is a generally agreed statement that inequalities reduce aggregate social welfare and should be avoided provided, in the process, production activity does not suffer.

2) Reduces Savings:

Every economy needs a continuous addition to its productive capacity for which it should encourage capital formation. In a money economy, capital formation takes place when a part of money income is saved and transferred to the investors who, in turn, use it for investment and capital formation. However, inflation, by its very nature, discourages saving activity. It makes consumption more attractive than saving. The adverse impact on saving and capital formation is more serious for a developing country because it needs a higher rate of capital accumulation.

3) Shift of Asset preference:

Inflation leads to a shift in the asset preference of wealth holders. Their preference for tangible assets may be counterbalanced, in the initial phases of inflation, by an increase in interest rate. However, in later stages of inflation, even an upward movement in interest rate fails to neutralize the shift in asset preference.

4) Problems of Balance of Payments:

Inflation leads to balance of payments problems. When domestic prices rise faster than prices in foreign countries, exports tend to lag behind imports. The, rate of exchange also tends to depreciate both on account of falling purchasing power of currency within the country and adverse balance of payments. In some cases, there may also be an outflow of capital. A developed country may be able to handle the problem of adverse balance of payments through structural adjustment, but a developing country is not able to do so easily because they suffer from large institutional and other rigidities.

These and all the problems caused by problem of Inflation must be analyzed and tackled with caution in order to have uninterrupted economic growth.

Some of the key measures of overcoming Inflation problem are given below:

a) Demand Management:

1) Fiscal Measures:

Fiscal consolidation with a focus on increasing investment spending. The government of India has generally insisted on controlling its own expenditure and keeping in check both its revenue and deficit and fiscal deficit.

2) Monetary Measures:

The monetary policy of RBI consists of extensive use of general and selective credit control measures. The main thrust was to restrict bank credit against inflation-sensitive goods and to influence the cost availability and commercial bank credit to industry and trade. Generally, RBI uses its monetary policy to achieve a judicious balance between the growth of production and control of the general price level. It uses CRR and SLR and open market operations to increase bank credit and expansion of business activity in times of recession or to contract bank credit and check business and speculative activity at the time of inflation.

b) Supply Management Measures:
1) Fixation of Maximum prices:

The State Governments are asked to fix the prices of wholesale and retail food grains to control the hoarding and speculative activities. Moreover, the Government also fixes minimum procurement price(MSP) for major crops on the recommendation of Agricultural Prices Commission (APC).

2) Increase in supply of food grain:

Earlier Government used to import food grain and other edible articles as a normal strategy of battling against shortage of food. But after green revolution India become self reliant as far as food is concerned.

3) Removing supply side bottlenecks :

Planning of government spending from consumption to investment to remove supply-side
bottlenecks must be done.

c) Other relevant measures:

1) Productivity improvements in bottleneck areas
2) Implement policies to improve farm productivity
3) Step up efforts at skill development in sectors that face acute skill shortages
4) Install mechanisms to link wages to productivity in the public sector and in government safety-net programs such as the Mahatma Gandhi National Rural Employment Guarantee Scheme (MGNREGS)

5) Reduce shocks from sudden changes in administered prices of petroleum fuels, by aligning them to global prices.
6) Adoption of OGL (Open General License)
7) Substantial reduction of excise duties on a number of items expected to accelerate the pace of industrial revival and raise industrial growth.

Above planned activities must be initiated in order to control the rate of Inflation in country which if ignored, cause disaster in economy.

4) Social Injustice, Parallel Economy, Problem of Black Money:

1) Social Injustice:

The term "social justice" implies several sound and eminently desirable concepts enunciated for the good of society in general, and of course it covers fair play for every section, especially the weaker groups in the population. We may start with certain provisions of the Constitution, which is the fundamental law of the land. The preamble itself says: "We, the people of India, having solemnly resolved to constitute India into a sovereign, socialist and democratic Republic and to secure to all its citizens—Justice, social, economic and political...." Clearly, social justice in all its forms and to all citizens was regarded as fundamental to the set-up which our founding fathers prescribed for the country; it is mentioned on top of the other equally sound concepts, and yet this very concept is being violated by countless people with amazing impunity, without fear. In fact, many would say that it is absurd to talk of social justice in this country, because almost all the traditional and prevalent systems are loaded against social and economic justice. The Preamble provides for "equality of status and of opportunity...." In reality, neither equality of status nor of opportunity is assured. There are distinct classes in society which stick to their privileges and refuse to share their riches and assets with others, even while crore of people live in misery and perpetually groan under the burden of unfair practices, unjust policies and gross inequalities.

The State, according to Article 15(1) of the Constitution, "shall not discriminate against any citizen on grounds only of religion, race, caste, sex, and place of birth or any of them." The State, officially, indeed does not differentiate between man and man on any of these grounds, but at the same time the government and the administrative machinery have proved incapable of enforcing this provision. How else are we to explain the countless cases of social and economic injustice, the increasing inequalities in most spheres of human activity and the endless discrimination against the weaker sections of society, especially Harijans and members of the Scheduled Castes and Tribes? The harassment and the cruelties inflicted on them by landlords in the villages are common knowledge. The lands granted to them have in many cases been grabbed by greedy people; and the equal rights guaranteed to them under the laws of the land are denied to them by selfish people. The reservations in government services, assured to the weaker sections of society, have not benefited the really needy people, because there is virtually no end to impostors who wangle documents, certificates, the fa-cilities and grants given by the government. Chapter III of the Constitution, entitled "Fundamental Rights", enumerates a series of rights which all Indian citizens are supposed to enjoy, and yet the number of people who are able to enjoy these rights in practice is much less than those who are denied their exercise. Their life continues to be one long, tragic and heart-breaking story of deprivation and sufferings through official and public apathy.

Their colossal poverty is a permanent handicap which prevents them from seeking redress from the courts, for grave wrongs done to them month after month by men in privileged positions, and also those who are protected by the men in power; ministers and legislators, in effect their patrons. In other words, they are all partners in the guilt and deserve to be hauled up for violating the Constitution and many other social reform laws passed by the Parliament.

Article 23 of the Constitution specifically prohibits traffic in human beings, "beggar" and other similar forms of forced labor, and any contravention of this provision, it is stated, shall be an offence punishable in ac-cordance with law. But how many people guilty of such defiance have beer, caught and punished? Economic exploitation of labor continues with a vengeance—by capitalists, unscrupulous employers, landlords and others, including senior government officials sand yet no one bothers. There is mere talk and promise, but no concrete action to redress injustices.

There is no discipline, and there are hardly any morals. The absences of these vital traits of character signify the absence of social and economic justice. The argument that the police do not have their heart in the job, because of the relatively low salaries they are paid and the fact that their own senior officials do not assert themselves is hardly convincing. There is no sign of justice or fair play in any sphere of activity. It is injustice and corruption on all over.

Social Injustice is therefore a more complex concept and needs an immediate attention on the part of Government and social service organizations.

2) Parallel Economy:

Parallel economy in India:

Parallel economy means the functioning of an unsanctioned sector in the economy whose objectives run parallel, rather in contradiction with the aroused social objectives. This is variously termed as 'black economy', 'unaccounted economy', 'illegal economy', 'subterranean economy', 'unsanctioned economy' or 'hidden economy'. The National Institute of Public Finance and Policy (NIPFP) defines black money as the aggregate of incomes which are taxable but not reported to the tax authorities.

A hidden economy in its broadest sense may consist of -

a) illegal economy, such as money laundering, smuggling, etc

b) unreported economy including tax evasion

c) unregulated economy, ie economic activities outside regulations.

1) Black money and it effects:

The money laundering is a lack of transparency standards in bilateral and multilateral trade with flourishing offshore banking in tax havens has allowed it to grow unabated in past couple of decades. Experts estimate that around 50 per cent of GDP—or about Rs 33 lakh crore of black money, is generated every year through corruption at various levels. While black money which operates within the country can be productive, what goes overseas is seen as non-productive.

Impact of Black Money:

The circulation of black money has adversely affected the Indian economy in several ways.

1. It leads to the misdirection of precious national resources.
2. It has enormously worsened the income-distribution. The fixed income salary class finds itself ever be the lower rung of the income-ladder as they pay taxes. They are not able to catch up with the people in business, or in professions, or many of those employed who make money by black activities. Many high placed official and honest employees earn much less than an small shopkeeper in big cities like Bombay and Delhi.
3. The existence of a big-sized unreported segment of the economy is a- big handicap in making a correct analysis and formulation of right policies for it.
4. Black money results in transfer of funds from India to foreign countries through clandestine channels. Such transfers are made possible by violations exchange regulations through the device of under – invoicing of exports and over-invoicing of imports etc.
5. Black money requires for its protection, proliferation and expansion of a service organization composed of musclemen, touts and brokers to combat the forces of law and order on the one hand and on the other hand, there are income tax advisers, or chartered accountants in the pay of black money operators
6. Black money has corrupted our political system in a most vicious manner. At various levels, MLAs, MPs, Ministers, party functionaries openly go on collecting funds for party or elections. Ministers dole out favors of crore by accepting black money donations of a few lakh from businessmen National policies are, therefore, being bent in favor of the big business under the pressure of black money.
8. Impact of India's reputation on the world: This Black money and corruptions put a very bad impression in India reputation on the world. Many big businessmen in world are pulling their hand back from India. They are not interested in to do business with India due to this corruption. It's also effect on Indian cconomy. In corruption perceptions index (CPI) India is ranked 87 numbers

out of 178 countries. Due these big scams like 2G scam, commonwealth game scam and the recently coal mines scam..

The politics of black money thus has corroded the moral fiber of Indian polity. Ministers dole out favors of crore by accepting black money donations of a few lakh from businessmen. National policies are, therefore, being bent in favor of the big business under the pressure of black money.

Due to the pernicious impact of black money on the Indian economy and polity that the **Wanchoo Committee** concluded: "It is, therefore, no exaggeration to say that black money is like a cancerous growth in the country's economy which, if not checked in time, is sure to lead to its ruination".

2) Survey on Bribery and Corruption

India lost a staggering $462 billion in illicit financial flows due to tax evasion, crime and corruption post- Independence, according to a report released by Washington-based Global Financial Integrity. The document on the "Survey on Bribery and Corruption" was released at the first annual fraud conference organized by the Association of Certified Fraud Examiners here on June 21, 2011. The report stated that 68% of India's aggregate illicit capital loss occurred after India's economic reforms in 1991, indicating that deregulation and trade liberalization actually contributed to or accelerated the transfer of illicit money abroad. Reports that wealth is stashed in offshore destinations and tax havens also goes to indicate the extent of the problem, the report said.

The KPMG India Fraud Survey 2010 suggested that today India is faced with a different kind of challenge. It is not about petty bribes, popularly known as 'baksheesh' anymore, but scams to the tune of thousands of crore that highlight political and industry nexus which if not checked could have far reaching impact on the economy. India has been facing governance challenges from within at various levels for a long time. "Rigid bureaucracy, complex laws and long-drawn judicial process deter people from considering legal recourse in corruption cases. India has around 35 million court cases pending. Besides lack of manpower and poor infrastructure facilities, other factors hindering the anti-corruption drive include lack of teeth in the legal framework," the study said.

"A large number of respondents stated that organizations pay bribes to win and retain businesses. This is a typical scenario where organizations tend to overlook the implications of encouraging these practices and often look only at short term benefits achieved. They fail to realize that what has worked in their favor could also land into trouble later and lead to adverse consequences for them," the report said.

The study noted that another key area where business is impacted is in the area of mergers and acquisitions. "Nearly 37% respondents opined that the corruption could impact the valuation of a company thereby denying shareholders of a fair price. Moreover, it could also make it difficult for them to find a suitable business partner, thereby seriously impacting the growth prospects of the business," the study said.

3) Some Records of misuse of Money:

The appropriation of public and national wealth through bribes and black money is the third facet of corruption.

2010 was the year of scams — 2G Spectrum, Commonwealth Games, Adarsh Housing Society etc.

2012 was the year of biggest scam of the distribution of coal mines.

Forceful capture of land - 20 police battalions were being used to crush the anti-Posco movement in Odessa and destroy the betel-vine gardens that are the basis of people's prosperous living economy, earning small farmers Rs 400,000 per acre.

The ecology movements and tribal and farmers' movements are fighting against the corruption involved in the massive resource grab and land grab taking place across the country for the mining of bauxite, coal and iron ore, for mega steel plants and power plants, for super highways and luxury townships.

Farmers fighting the land grab along the Yamuna Expressway were killed on May 7. While they received a mere Rs 300 per sq. m. for their land the developers who grab the land in partnership with government using the 1894 colonial land acquisition law sell it for Rs 600,000 per sq. m. This is corporate corruption.

Farmhouses of farmers are burnt and destroyed to create "farmhouses" for the rich. Farms are destroyed to create Formula 1 race tracks and swimming pools for the elite. This obscene, violent, unjust land grab is the cruelest face of corruption in today's India.

4) Role of Government:

The government has empowered its existing institutions and set up new mechanisms and institutions to unearth black money. The antimony laundering law has been strengthened and more entities have been brought under its ambit to create a deterrent. India has joined global efforts to tackle illicit flows and also signed information exchange treaties with many countries. The gradual reduction in income tax rates has also helped improve compliance.

In May 2012, the Government of India published a white paper on black money. It disclosed India's effort at addressing black money and guidelines to prevent black money in the future.

Central Board of Direct Taxes - is a statutory authority functioning across India under the Central Board of Revenue Act of 1963. This organization has Investigation Wings, spread all across India, which are headed by the Director General of Income Tax (Investigation) to find and stop black money. The Director General of Income Tax (International Taxation) is in charge of taxation issues arising from cross-border transactions and transfer pricing. This organization has been in operation for nearly 50 years, is primarily responsible for combating the menace of black money, has offices in more than 740 buildings spread over 510 cities and towns across India and has over 55,000 employees.

Financial Intelligence Unit - has been operating at a separate investigative entity since 2004. This government organization for receiving, processing, analyzing, and disseminating information relating to financial transactions.

Central Board of Excise and Customs and Directorate of Revenue Intelligence - is the apex intelligence organization responsible for detecting cases of evasion of central excise and service tax.

Central Economic Intelligence Bureau - functions under India's Ministry of Finance. It is responsible for coordination, intelligence sharing, and investigations at national as well as regional levels amongst various law enforcement agencies to prevent financial crimes, generation and parking of black money and illegal transfers.

India has Double Tax Avoidance Agreements with 82 nations, including all popular tax haven countries. Of these, India has expanded agreements with 30 countries which requires mutual effort to collect taxes on behalf of each other, if a citizen attempts to hide black money in the other country.

This problem of parallel economy and black money is like a cancer to the body. Its effect can be minimized but it cannot be cured because it is spread to the very root level of economy and eradication of that requires very transparent and accountable Government which can take decisions solely for the improvement of current filthy situation.

3) Lack of Technical Knowledge and Information:

India is developing very rapidly and its power rests in the hands of youth. Youth is biggest asset of India because no other country in the world have such tremendous amount of energetic youth. However today many students are opting for studies in foreign universities because of poor quality of education in India and lack of attentiveness from Government towards education and technical knowledge improvement. The number of Indian students going overseas to study rose a stunning 256% – from 53,266 to 189,629 – in just nine years (2000–2009) according to a study called "Indian student mobility to selected European countries: An overview" by researchers at one of India's top business schools, the Indian Institute of Management–Bangalore.

It is an alarming situation for the country's economic growth as well as social cultural growth too.
Swami Vivekananda said,

Youth, only youth can create miracle for the country and i want youth, energetic, healthy, fearless for the purpose of my Mission. Therefore care must be taken to understand problems of youth and support their moral for better future of the country with positive growth and healthy economic conditions with self reliance.

Chapter 4
The Entrepreneur

Introduction:

The entrepreneur is a key asset of any economy and is responsible for the overall growth of economy because entrepreneur acts like a catalyst in the economic development process.

It is said by one popular entrepreneur that, "progress of any country lies in implementation of economic decisions and only entrepreneurs can perform this task with confidence."

This is the value of entrepreneur that with him the country prosper, without him it is poor. The entrepreneur with his imagination, innovation and vision allow country to prosper. Every entrepreneur is a man of different thinking than ordinary human being because they go deeper in the thinking process. Every entrepreneur in the world rose after facing lot of problems and challenges. Challenges make businessman a great decision maker. Business is about taking decisions and implementation of the same. It might be wrong or right, but true business person only takes decisions very speedily and Rationality. This is the key of success for every entrepreneur. This different thinking and fearless attitude towards challenges make good entrepreneurs. Today, India needs more and more such visionaries like Jamshed Tata who accepted one Idea of constructing an empire as aim for life time and succeeded as we can see today from the success of TATA GROUP.

Definition of an Entrepreneur:

1) An entrepreneur is a person who organizes and operates a business or businesses, taking on financial risk to do so.

2) Howard Stevenson defined this term as, " Entrepreneurship is the

pursuit of opportunity without regard to resources currently controlled."

3) Investopedia defines this concept as, "An individual who, rather than working as an employee, runs a small business and assumes all the risk and reward of a given business venture, idea, or good or service offered for sale. The entrepreneur is commonly seen as a business leader and innovator of new ideas and business processes."

4) The New Encyclopedia Britannica considers an entrepreneur as, " an individual who bears the risk of operating a business in the face of uncertainty about the future conditions."

Leading economists of all schools, including Karl Marx have emphasized the contribution of the entrepreneurs to the development of economies, but the importance of an entrepreneurs was truly advocated by Joseph Schumpeter who said that "The process of development is a deliberate and continuous phenomenon which is actively promoted by the escort service of a change agent who provides economic leadership. This change agent is what is called an **entrepreneur**."

Thus it can be concluded that an entrepreneur is one who innovates, raise money, assembles inputs, chooses managers and sets the organization going with his ability to identify them. Innovation occurs through

1) the introduction of a new quality in a product,

2) a new product,

3) a discovery of a fresh demand and a fresh source of supply and

4) by changes in the organization and management.

Evolution of the term Entrepreneur:

The word Entrepreneur is derived from the French word 'Entrepredre'. which means to 'undertake'. i.e the person who undertakes the risk of new enterprise. The word entrepreneur, hence, first appeared in the French language in the beginning of the sixteenth century. The word was also applied to the leaders of military expedition. But it was Richard Cantillon an Irishman, living in France, who first used the term entrepreneur to refer to economic activities. He defined this concept as, "Entrepreneurs are non-fixed income earners who pay known costs of production but earn uncertain incomes."

Therefore to Cantillon, an entrepreneur is a bearer of risk which is non-insurable. Around 1700 A. D, the term was used for architects and contractors of public works. Bernard Belidor applied it to the function of buying labor and material and uncertain prices and selling the resultant product at contracted rate.

Quesnay regarded the rich farmer as an entrepreneur who manages and make his business profitable by his intelligence, skill and wealth.

As said above the term 'entrepreneur' was applied to business initially by the French economist, Cantillon, in the 18 th century to designate a dealer who purchases the means of production for combining them into marketable products. Another Frenchman, J.B. Say, expanded Cantillon's ideas and conceptualized the entrepreneur as an organizer of a business firm, central to its distributive and production functions. Beyond stressing the entrepreneur's importance to the business. Say did little with his entrepreneurial analysis.

He emphasized the functions of co-ordination organization and supervision.

Some other definitions are given sequentially for better understanding of the evolution of this term:

1) 1734: Richard Cantillon:

"Entrepreneurs are non-fixed income earners who pay known costs of production but earn uncertain incomes."

2) 1803: J.B Say:

"An entrepreneur is an economic agent who unites all means of production- land of one, the labour of another and the capital of yet another and thus produces a product. By selling the product in the market he pays rent of land, wages to labour, interest on capital and what remains is his profit. He shifts economic resources out of an area of lower and into an area of higher productivity and greater yield."

3) 1934: Schumpeter:

"Entrepreneurs are innovators who use a process of shattering the status quo of the existing products and services, to set up new products, new services."

4) 1961: David McClelland:

"An entrepreneur is a person with a high need for achievement. He is energetic and a moderate risk taker."

5) 1964: Peter Drucker:

"An entrepreneur searches for change, responds to it and exploits opportunities. Innovation is a specific tool of an entrepreneur hence an effective entrepreneur converts a source into a resource."

6)1971: Kilby:

"Emphasizes the role of an imitator entrepreneur who does not innovate but imitates technologies innovated by others. Are very important in developing economies."

7) 1975: Albert Shapero:

"Entrepreneurs take initiative, accept risk of failure and have an internal locus of control."

8) 1975: Howard Stevenson:

Entrepreneurship is "the pursuit of opportunity without regard to resources currently controlled."

9) 1983: G. Pinchot:

"Entrepreneur is an entrepreneur within an already established organization."

10) 1985: W.B. Gartner:

"Entrepreneur is a person who started a new business where there was none before."

The concept of entrepreneur and entrepreneurship evolved through the years and now this concept of entrepreneur is a complex phenomenon with many components being included in it.

Thus it can be assumed that this change in the phenomenon is of degree and not of kind. With modernization and globalization every entrepreneur needs to take series of decisions in order to cope with this burden unlike the earlier days when, business was limited in scope.

Following diagram shows the characteristic of an entrepreneur:

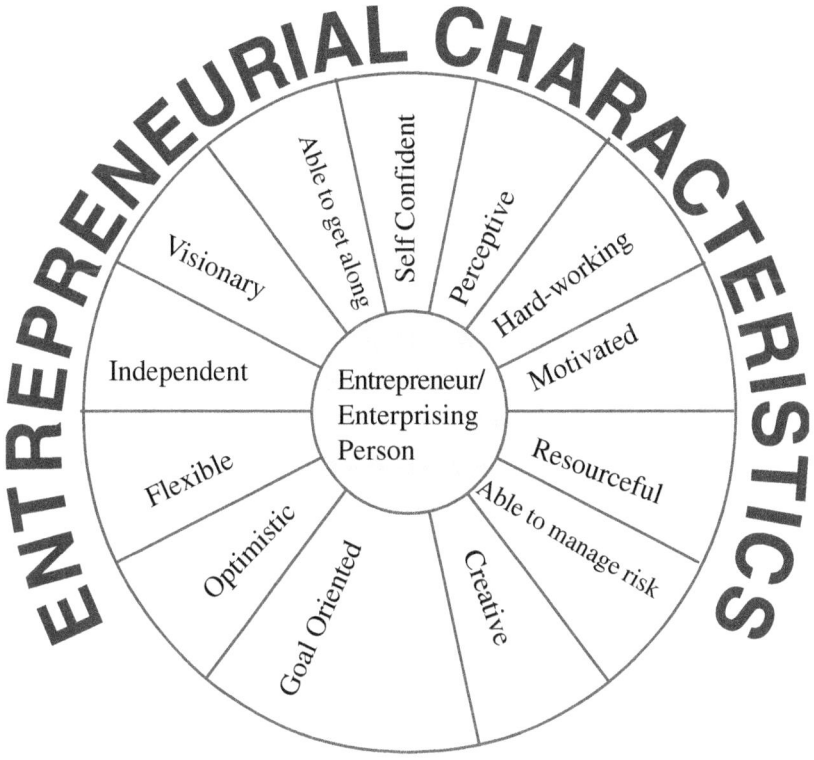

10 Primary Characteristics of an entrepreneur:

1) Pleasure from Work:

What we get out of business in the form of personal satisfaction, financial gain, stability and enjoyment will be the sum of what we put into business. so person must enjoy what he does in business i.e business activity .Success directly connected with the sense of enjoyment from work, so more joy from work, more success from that particular task.

2) Seriousness:

You cannot expect to be effective and successful in business unless you truly believe in your business and in the goods and services that you sell. Far too many home business owners fail to take their own businesses seriously enough, getting easily sidetracked and not staying motivated and keeping their noses to the grindstone. They also fall prey to people who don't take them seriously because they don't work from an office building, office park, storefront, or factory.

3) Planning:

Planning every aspect of your business is not only a must, but also builds habits that every business owner should develop, implement, and maintain. The act of business planning is so important because it requires you to analyze each business situation, research and compile data, and make conclusions based mainly on the facts as revealed through the research. Business planning also serves a second function, which is having your goals and how you will achieve them, on paper. You can use the plan that you create both as map to take you from point A to Z and as a yardstick to measure the success of each individual plan or segment within the plan.

4) Management of Finance:

The lifeblood of any business enterprise is cash flow.. Therefore, all business owners must become wise money managers to ensure that the cash keeps flowing and the bills get paid. There are two aspects to wise money management.

The money you receive from clients in exchange for your goods and services provide (income)

The money spend on inventory, supplies, wages and other items required to keep business operating. (expenses)

5) Positive framework:

Positive framework is very very important characteristic which every entrepreneur must possess because it finally decides the faith of the venture and is responsible element for success or failure.

6) Value of Customer:

One of the biggest features and often the most significant competitive edge the home based entrepreneur has over the larger competitors is the he can offer personalized attention. Call it high-tech backlash if you will, but customers are sick and tired of hearing that their information is somewhere in the computer and must be retrieved, or told to push a dozen digits to finally get to the right department only to end up with voice mail—from which they never receive a return phone call.

7)) Technology usage:

It is not a primary characteristic but is very important in today's environment. This is the environment of technology and it cannot be ignored even if for entrepreneur. Every prospective entrepreneur must look for the technology advancement and must care to appreciate new technology.

8) Entrepreneur Education:

Top entrepreneurs buy and read business and marketing books, magazines, reports, journals, newsletters, websites and industry publications, knowing that these resources will improve their understanding of business and marketing functions and skills. They join business associations and clubs, and they network with other skilled business people to learn their secrets of success and help define their own goals and objectives. Top entrepreneurs attend business and marketing seminars, workshops and training courses, even if they have already mastered the subject matter of the event. They do this because they know that education is an ongoing process. There are usually ways to do things better, in less time, with less effort. In short, top entrepreneurs never stop investing in the most powerful, effective and best business and marketing tool at their immediate disposal—themselves.

9) Be accessible:

We're living in a time when we all expect our fast food lunch at the drive-thru window to be ready in mere minutes, our dry cleaning to be ready for pick-up on the same day, our money to be available at the cash machine and our pizza delivered in 30 minutes or it's free. Hence prospective entrepreneur must be accessible at all time directly or indirectly at the place of service or delivery, thus speedy medium of service providing and material dispatch must be looked for.

10) Follow-up:

Constant contact, follow-up, and follow-through with customers, prospects, and business alliances should be the mantra of every home business owner, new or established. Constant and consistent follow-up enables to turn prospects into customers, increase the value of each sale and buying frequency from existing customers, and build stronger business relationships with suppliers and core business team. Follow-up is especially important with existing customer base, as the real work begins after the sale. It's easy to sell one product or service, but it takes work to retain customers and keep them coming back.

Following table will show the various characteristics of Entrepreneurs for small as well as large scale business:

Characteristics of Entrepreneurs	
Small –Scale Entrepreneurs	
1. Young men	26. Experience
2. Ambitious	27. Meager capital
3. Intelligent	28. Small operation
4. Energetic	29. Employ few people
5. Enthusiastic	30. Small turnover
6. Minimum education	31. Honest
7. Hard working	32. Progressive
8. Confident	33. Patient
9. Passionate	34. Perseverance
10. Dedicated	35. Self-reliant
11. Practical	36. Common sense
12. Goal-oriented	37. Adaptive
13. Mobile	38. Ability to strive
14. Adaptable	39. Compassionate
15. Able	40. Dreamer
16. Aggressive	41. Conscious
17. Innovative	42. Intuitive
18. Well-mannered	43. Practical
19. Self-made person	44. Imaginative
20. Disciplined	45. Achiever
21. Zealous	46. Hopefull
22. Flexible	47. Independent
23. Courageous	48. Self-starter
24. Skilful	49. Individualist
25. Creative	50. Sensitive

51. Perceptive
52. Quality conscious
53. Desire to share experience
54. Ability to change
55. Money oriented
56. Driven by values
57. Intrapreneurial
58. Facilitator
59. Learner
60. Opportunist

61. Ability to strive
62. Task master
63. Striving Richness
64. Gut-Feeler
65. Dictator

Large Scale Entrepreneus

1. Middle aged Professionals
2. Professional Specialists
3. Shareholders contribute venture Capital
4. Energetic
5. Outsourcing
6. Net-workers
7. Ability to get along with people
8. Tolerant
9. Risk Takers
10. Large Assets controlled
11. Engaged in Diversified Activities
12. Diversified products
13. Multiple activities
14. Easy assess to institutional finance
15. Leverages
16. Well connected with Politics Bureacrats
17. Trend setters
18. Demand creators
19. Value driven
20. Corporate Philosophy
21. Ambitious
22. Drive to go ahead
23. Self-confident
24. Innovative/imitative
25. Adaptable
26. Trained
27. Large capital
28. Large operation
29. Skilled manpower
30. Large turnover/scale/profit
31. Honest
32. Progressive
33. Pragmatic
34. Perseverance
35. Self-Reliant
36. Abundant common sense
37. Competitive
38. Versatile
39. Quality conscious
40. Visionaries
41. Focussed

42. Singleness of purpose	55. Contributor
43. Ability to change	56. Knowledgeable
44. Educated	57. Motivator
45. A strong need to achieve	58. Strategist
46. Passionate	59. Goal conscious
47. Analytical	60. Compassionate
48. Optimistic	61. Leader
49. Organisation man	62. Scanner – Looking for
50. Loyal	opportunities
51. Pleasing personality	63. Planner
52. Dynamic	64. Thinker
53. Tolerant	65. People Manager
54. Active	

Competencies of an entrepreneur:

As noted in the introduction, every career draws on the competencies of an individual. Some of these competencies may be general and some peculiar to the chosen career. You may understand competencies to mean abilities and skills. However, we would desist from calling these as personality traits as such a conceptualization only reinforces the mistake and belief that entrepreneurs are born rather than made. We believe that recognition of these competencies as abilities and skills makes entrepreneurship as a teachable and learnable behavior. In this section we orient you towards a set of entrepreneurial competencies developed by the Entrepreneurship Development Institute of India (EDI) Ahmadabad. These competencies were identified by a thorough research procedure based on critical analysis of the case studies of the successful entrepreneurs.

1) Disciplined:

These individuals are focused on making their businesses work, and eliminate any hindrances or distractions to their goals. They have overarching strategies and outline the tactics to accomplish them. Successful entrepreneurs are disciplined enough to take steps every day toward the achievement of their objectives.

2) Confidence:

The entrepreneur does not ask questions about whether they can succeed or whether they are worthy of success. They are confident with the knowledge that they will make their businesses succeed. They exude that confidence in everything they do.

3) Open Minded:

Entrepreneurs realize that every event and situation is a business opportunity. Ideas are constantly being generated about workflows and efficiency, people skills and potential new businesses. They have the ability to look at everything around them and focus it toward their goals.

4) Initiative:

Entrepreneurs know that if something needs to be done, they should start it themselves. They set the parameters and make sure that projects follow that path. They are proactive, not waiting for someone to give them permission. It is an inner urge in an individual to do or initiate something. There is popular saying 'well begun is half done.' It is the entrepreneur who takes or initiates the first move towards setting up of an enterprise. Most of the innovators have got this urge to do something different. Entrepreneur basically is an innovator who carries out new combinations to initiate and accelerate the process of economic development.

5) Competitive:

Many companies are formed because an entrepreneur knows that they can do a job better than another. They need to win at the sports they play and need to win at the businesses that they create. An entrepreneur will highlight their own company's track record of success.

6) Creativity:

One facet of creativity is being able to make connections between seemingly unrelated events or situations. Entrepreneurs often come up with solutions which are the synthesis of other items. They will repurpose products to market them to new industries.

7) Determination:

Entrepreneurs are not pushed back by their defeats. They look at defeat as an opportunity for success. They are determined to make all of their endeavors succeed, so will try and try again until it does. Successful entrepreneurs do not believe that something cannot be done.

8) Strong people skills:

The entrepreneur has strong communication skills to sell the product and motivate employees. Most successful entrepreneurs know how to motivate their employees so the business grows overall. They are very good at highlighting the benefits of any situation and coaching others to their success.

9) Strong work ethic:

The successful entrepreneur will often be the first person to arrive at the office and the last one to leave. They will come in on their days off to make sure that an outcome meets their expectations. Their mind is constantly on their work, whether they are in or out of the workplace.

10) Passion:

Passion is the most important trait of the successful entrepreneur. They genuinely love their work. They are willing to put in those extra hours to make the business succeed because there is a joy their business gives which goes beyond the money. The successful entrepreneur will always be reading and researching ways to make the business better.

Successful entrepreneurs want to see what the view is like at the top of the business mountain. Once they see it, they want to go further. They know how to talk to their employees, and their businesses soar as a result.

11) Information seeker:

Successful entrepreneur always keep his eyes and ear open and is receptive to new ideas which can help him in realizing his goals. He is ready to consult an expert for getting their expert advise.

12) Quality Consciousness:

Successful entrepreneur do not believe in moderate or average performance. They set high standards for themselves and then put in their best for achieving these standards. They strive for excellence and perfection instead of average and general performance.

13) Positive Framework of Mind:

Positive framework of mind is a very important competency of an entrepreneur. Steve Jobs was dismissed from his own company at the age of 30 but in few years he again called back by Apple because of his vision and positive frame of mind.

The above points describing competencies of an entrepreneur is inclusive and not exhaustive. It is said that an entrepreneur is not a different person but he thinks differently than an ordinary person.

Difference between an entrepreneur and Manager:

Generally, an entrepreneur and a manager are considered as synonymous. Even the two terms are used interchangeably. In fact, the two terms differ in their meaning greatly. The major points of distinction between the two are presented as follow:

1) An entrepreneur is the owner of the enterprise but a manager is just an employee in the enterprise of the entrepreneur. Entrepreneur develops an enterprise while manager is just responsible for achieving his particular goal in an organization.

2) The main motive of an entrepreneur is to start a venture by setting up an enterprise. But the main aim of a manager is to render services to an entrepreneur.

3) An entrepreneur, being the owner of the enterprise assumes all risks and uncertainty. But a manager as the servant does not share any risk involved in the enterprise.

4) The reward of an entrepreneur is profit. But the reward of a manager for rendering his services is salary, because he is an employee in company.

5) All the policies and strategic decisions like expansions, diversification, takeovers, mergers, capital budgeting, pricing policies etc. are taken by entrepreneur. But all the managerial and operational decision relating to day-to-day activities of enterprise are taken by manager.

6) An entrepreneur acts as an innovator to maximize the profits. But a manager simply implements the policies prepared by entrepreneur and gives them practical shape.

Thus manager is responsible for managing activities in an

organization while an entrepreneur is responsible for each and every however small aspect of an organization. He is a backbone of that enterprise and without him there will not be any organization.

Distinction between an Entrepreneur and an Enterprise:
Defining entrepreneur and enterprise has always given rise to diverse, often misleading interpretation. In the beginning was the corporation or the entrepreneur?
Are opportunities discovered or enacted?

Every entrepreneur embodies a mental dimension - which revolves around innovating -, an organizational dimension -which is about pressing ahead - and a relational dimension - with an emphasis on leadership traits.

It is safe to say that entrepreneurs act as a balance factor and a catalyst for economic activities.

The problem of self-referentiality appears particularly serious today because an effectively competitive advantage lies in the ability to change. Indeed, any development potential originating with the spread of "entrepreneurial talent" is starting to become increasingly evident.

Entrepreneur is a person who is willing to launch a new venture or enterprise and accept full responsibility for the outcome. While entrepreneurship is one who undertakes innovations, finance and business acumen in an effort to transform innovations into economic goods". This may result in new organizations or may be part of revitalizing mature organizations in response to a perceived opportunity On the other hand an enterprise is a project undertaken, esp. one that is important or difficult or requires boldness or energy or a plan for such a project or it might be a participation or engagement in such projects, a company organized for commercial purposes.

Entrepreneur and Intrapreneur:
The words entrepreneur and intrapreneur have acquired special significance in the content of economic growth in a rapidly changing industrial climate both in developed and developing countries. Entrepreneur is a key person who envisages new opportunities, new techniques, new lines of production, new products and coordinates all other activities. He likes to experiment with new ideas and thus face uncertainty. He works for himself and for profits.

On the other hand, intrapreneurs are entrepreneurs who catch hold of a new idea for product service or process and work to bring this idea to fruition within the framework of the organization. Intrapreneurs with their innovations and dedicated effort are perceived as valuable asset by the organization, inspiring others. They serve as champions to others in that organizations. In America a number of business executives have left their jobs and started their own enterprises because they were not given chance to test and implement their innovative ideas. Later they achieved phenomenal success in their new venture and posed a threat to the companies they left. These executives turned entrepreneurs are known as intrapreneur.

So, in summary we can state the difference as follow:

Entrepreneurs vs. Intrapreneurs:

1) Entrepreneurs provide the spark. Intrapreneurs keep the flame going.
2) Entrepreneurs are found anywhere their vision takes them. Intrapreneurs work within the confines of an organization.
3) Entrepreneurs face many hurdles, and are sometimes ridiculed and riddled with setbacks. Intrapreneurs may sometimes have to deal with conflict within the organization.
4) Entrepreneurs may find it difficult to get resources. Intrapreneurs have their resources readily available to them.
5) Entrepreneurs may lose everything when they fail. Intrapreneurs still have a paycheck to look forward to (at least for now) if they fail.
6) Entrepreneurs know the business on a macro scale. Intrapreneurs are highly skilled and specialized.

What makes entrepreneurs and intrapreneur similar is the passion to see things through to the end and the courage to face failure.

The main disparity between an entrepreneur and an intrapreneur is that an entrepreneur has the freedom to act on his or her whim; whereas, an intrapreneur may need to ask for management's approval to make certain changes in the company's processes, product design or just about any innovation he or she needs to implement. Since an intrapreneur acts on innovative impulses, this may result in conflict within the organization. It is important for organizations who are implementing intrapreneurship, to create an atmosphere of mutual respect among employees.

Difference between entrepreneur and entrepreneurship:

The term entrepreneur is used to describe men and women who establish and manage their own business. The process involved is called entrepreneurship. Entrepreneurship is an abstraction whereas entrepreneurs are tangible people. Entrepreneurship is a process and an entrepreneur is a person. Entrepreneurship is the outcome of complex socio-economic, psychological and other factors.

Entrepreneur is the key individual central to entrepreneurship who makes things happen. Entrepreneur is the actor, entrepreneurship is the act. Entrepreneurship is the most effective way of bridging the gap between science and the market place by creating new enterprises. An entrepreneur is the catalyst who brings about this change.

The distinction between an entrepreneur and an entrepreneurship is given below :

Entrepreneur	Entrepreneurship
PERSON	PROCESS
VISUALIZER	VISUALIZATION
ORGANISER	ORGANISATION
DECISION MAKER	DECISION
PLANNER	PLANNING
TECHINICIAN	TECHNOLOGY
CREATOR	CREATION
RSIK TAKER	RISK TAKING
ADMINISTRATOR	ADMINISTRATION
COORDINATOR	COORDINATION

Chapter 5
Entrepreneurial Behavior

Introduction:

An entrepreneur is an individual who organizes and operates a business or businesses, taking on financial risk to do so. The entrepreneur is commonly seen as a business leader and innovator of new ideas and business processes. An entrepreneur is responsible for various duties and tasks which are very vital for the survival of any organization. He provides oxygen to the activities of an organization.

Management skill and strong team building abilities are often perceived as essential leadership attributes for successful entrepreneurs. Robert B. Reich considers leadership, management ability, and team-building as essential qualities of an entrepreneur. This concept has its origins in the work of Richard Cantillon in his Essai sur la Nature du Commerce en (1755) and Jean-Baptiste Say in his Treatise on Political Economy.

A growing body of work shows that entrepreneurial behavior is dependent on social and economic factors. For example, countries with healthy and diversified labor markets or stronger safety nets show a more favorable ratio of opportunity-driven rather than necessity-driven women entrepreneurs. Empirical studies suggest that male entrepreneurs possess strong negotiating skills and consensus-forming abilities.

Research studies that explore the characteristics and personality traits of, and influences on, the entrepreneur have come to differing conclusions. Most, however, agree on certain consistent entrepreneurial traits and environmental influences. Although certain entrepreneurial traits are required, entrepreneurial behaviors are also dynamic and influenced by environmental factors. In their cornerstone for contemporary entrepreneurship research paper, Shane and Venkataraman (2000) argue that the entrepreneur is solely concerned with opportunity recognition and exploitation, although the opportunity that is recognized depends on the type of entrepreneur; while Ucbasaran et al. (2001) argue there are many different types contingent upon environmental and personal circumstances.

Jesper Sorensen has argued that some of the most significant influences on an individual's decision to become an entrepreneur are workplace peers and the social composition of the workplace. In researching the likelihood of becoming an entrepreneur based upon working with former entrepreneurs, Sorensen discovered a correlation between working with former entrepreneurs and how often these individuals become entrepreneurs themselves, compared to those who did not work with entrepreneurs. The social composition of the workplace can influence entrepreneurism in workplace peers by proving a possibility for success, causing a "He can do it, why can't I?" attitude. As Sorensen stated, "When you meet others who have gone out on their own, it doesn't seem that crazy."

Therefore entrepreneurial behavior have undergone changes over the period and is in an evolving stage. Globalization will cast some demands from entrepreneur which will be adding insights on the definition of entrepreneurial behavior.

In this chapter we are discussing in detail the following points:
1) Entrepreneurial Behavior
2) Comparison between Entrepreneurial and non-entrepreneurial Personality
3) Habits of Entrepreneurs
4) Dynamics of Motivation

5.1) Entrepreneurial Behavior:

a) Entrepreneur:

Broadly, entrepreneurs have two vital roles to play in the economy (1) to introduce new ideas and (2) to energies business processes.

The term entrepreneur, which derives from the French words entre (between) and prendre (to take), referred to someone who acted as an intermediary in undertaking to do something. The term was originally used to describe the activities of what today we might call an impresario, a promoter or a deal maker. The entrepreneur first made an appearance as a distinct economic concept in France, twenty years before the 'father' of economics, Adam Smith published his Wealth of Nations in 1776. Richard Cantillon, an Irishman living in France, suggested in 1756 that the entrepreneur was someone prepared to bear uncertainty in engaging in risky arbitrage buying goods and services at a certain (fixed) price in one market to be sold elsewhere or at another time for uncertain future prices, usually in other market (though, throughout economic history, hoarders or traders who try to 'corner' a market have sought super-profits in the same markets when short supplies send prices rocketing upwards). This concept of entrepreneur as arbitrager is still relevant today but was clearly influenced by the dominance at that time of trade as the chief means for accumulating new wealth and capital. Manufacturing and trade dominated Britain's heyday in Victorian times whereas today, as the case studies show, it is technology, knowledge and services that provide most, though by no means all, new entrepreneurial opportunities.

Here, the role of the entrepreneur is to conceive a business idea in terms of an innovation to be brought successfully to the market and to find the wherewithal to make this happen. The entrepreneur does not necessarily need to have the design, production or delivery skills (this is the function of the firm) nor to shoulder all or most of the risk (this is often assumed by the providers of finance or investors). Indeed, the notion of the entrepreneur as a risk-taking trader, began to be challenged early on by the view of the entrepreneur as an adventurous self-employed manager capable of combining, to personal advantage, capital and labour. It is interesting to note that in France today the entrepreneur is a more generic term mainly referring to small property developers and owners of small construction firms. It would be wrong to state that the element of risk-bearing has completely disappeared from the modern concept of the entrepreneur. The successful management of risk is an important entrepreneurial attribute. However, it does seem true that a swift perception of opportunities and the ability to coordinate the activities of others emerge as the more central economic skills of the modern entrepreneur.

1) An entrepreneur is a person who organizes and operates a business or businesses, taking on financial risk to do so.
2) Howard Stevenson defined this term as, " Entrepreneurship is the pursuit of opportunity without regard to resources currently controlled."
3) Investopedia defines this concept as, "An individual who, rather than working as an employee, runs a small business and assumes all the risk and reward of a given business venture, idea, or good or service offered for sale. The entrepreneur is commonly seen as a business leader and innovator of new ideas and business processes."
4) The New Encyclopedia Britannica considers an entrepreneur as, " an individual who bears the risk of operating a business in the face of uncertainty about the future conditions."

Thus it can be concluded that an entrepreneur is one who innovates, raise money, assembles inputs, chooses managers and sets the organization going with his ability to identify them. Innovation occurs through

1) the introduction of a new quality in a product,
2) a new product,
3) a discovery of a fresh demand and a fresh source of supply and
4) by changes in the organization and management.

b) Entrepreneurship:
1) Entrepreneurship is the act and art of being an entrepreneur or one who undertakes innovations or introducing new things, finance and business acumen in an effort to transform innovations into economic goods
2) Entrepreneurship employs what Schumpeter called "the gale of creative destruction" to replace in whole or in part inferior innovations across markets and industries, simultaneously creating new products including new business models. In this way, creative destruction is largely responsible for the dynamism of industries and long-run economic growth

3) For Frank H. Knight (1921) and Peter Drucker (1970) entrepreneurship is about taking risk. The behavior of the entrepreneur reflects a kind of person willing to put his or her career and financial security on the line and take risks in the name of an idea, spending much time as well as capital on an uncertain venture.

c) Entrepreneurial Behavior:

Formal definition of entrepreneurial behavior is very hard to construct and very complex. An entrepreneurial behavior is a set of activities an individual called an entrepreneur performs for extracting perfect benefit from opportunities to succeed in fulfillment of organizational goals.

1) Entrepreneurial behavior is defined as a set of activities and practices by which individuals at multiple levels autonomously generate and use innovative resource combinations to identify and pursue opportunities.

2) Entrepreneurial behavior has been defined as the study of human behavior involved in identifying and exploiting opportunities through creating and developing new ventures (Ref :Bird & Schjoedt, 2009).

3) Entrepreneurial behavior is a preference for changing the status quo over maintaining it based on relatively greater satisfaction generated by novel information over redundant information. Entrepreneurial behavior underlies the inclination to undertake invention and innovation, including the creation of something new as well as the distribution and adoption of the new throughout society. It is the behavior most likely exhibited by entrepreneurship. An alternative is managerial behavior, which is a preference for maintaining the status quo over changing it.

Thus it can be concluded that an Entrepreneurial behavioral is one of two behavioral alternatives underlying the desire to undertake innovations and to change the status quo. The other is managerial behavior. Entrepreneurial behavior embraces innovation, is motivated to seek changes in the status quo, draws satisfaction from institutional changes. In contrast, managerial behavior is a preference for maintaining the status quo.

The underlying source of entrepreneurial behavior is a relative preference for novel information over redundant information. Both types of information are important to the fight or flight response to a threat. Novel information reveals potential threats that results in automatic physiological responses, which is more satisfying to some than it is to others.

Entrepreneurial behavior is a preference for innovation and a change in existing institutions and the status quo. It can be as simple as the willingness to buy a new electronic gadget or as involved as rebelling against the existing political regime and starting a new nation. It often surfaces in the form of an entrepreneur undertaking the risk of organizing production and launching a new business venture.

Fight or Flight:

An understanding of entrepreneurial behavior requires a look at the very fundamental, physiological response to potential threat, what is called as fight or flight. The human body automatically prepares itself to fight off a potential threat to flee away from it. Respiration increases. Pupils dilate. Brain wave activity increases. Adrenalin is pumped through the body. Heart rate increases. The human body is primed and ready to recognize the threat and to respond.

The key to this automatic response is achieved by distinguishing between what's new and different and what's old and familiar. The old and familiar is less threatening that the new and different. The human brain sorts between two different types of information that comes through the five senses (sight, hearing, touch, taste, and smell), attempting to discern the potential for danger — novel information and redundant information.

Novel: This is new information. An unusual sight. A strange sound. An unexpected touch. A bizarre taste. An uncommon smell. The human brain takes immediate note of this information. Because it is unfamiliar, it might be threatening. This is information that needs to be identified quickly. It needs to stand out from the ordinary and familiar. A self-preservation reaction (fight or flight) might be needed.

Redundant: This is familiar information. A common sight. A routine sound. A ordinary touch. A recognized taste. An everyday smell. The human brain is wired to largely ignore this information. Because it is familiar, it is not threatening. It is the background canvas upon which novel information is displayed.

Redundant and novel information are both intrinsically satisfying. A little bit of excitement is satisfying (think a roller coaster ride). But so too is a little bit of peace and quiet. However, nothing but redundant information is incredibly boring and not particularly satisfying. And nothing but novel information is anxiety inducing, and also not very satisfying. Too much of one or the other is not a pleasant situation. A combination of the two is most enjoyable. It can maximize satisfaction. However, different people have different preferences over the proper mix of novel and redundant information. Some prefer relatively more new and less old. Others prefer relatively more old and less new.

These individual differences give rise to entrepreneurial and managerial behavior. Those who prefer relatively more redundant information and relatively less novel information tend to pursue managerial behavior. Others who prefer relatively more novel information and relatively less redundant information tend to pursue entrepreneurial (and innovative) behavior.

Entrepreneurs exhibit many different personality types; searching for a specific personality pattern is very difficult. There are probably as many personality varieties among entrepreneurs as there are entrepreneurs.

Researcher David McClelland, a noted social psychologist, determined that founders of high-growth companies appear to share a distinct cluster of personal characteristics.

1) Tendency of Achievement:

Growth-oriented entrepreneurs have a high need for achievement. They need to succeed, to achieve, and to accomplish challenging tasks. The strong desire for achievement leads to a desire for independence. The need for achievement may help explain why growth-oriented entrepreneurs are not satisfied with founding or working in one firm; they need to prove themselves again and again.

2) Confidence:

Growth-oriented entrepreneurs listen, but they are able to ignore others' advice. Also, handling skeptics is easy for entrepreneurs. Taking the unpopular course of action, if they consider it best, is the way they do business. Confidence in own view and mind is the primitive quality of an entrepreneur.

3) Persistence:

Growth-oriented entrepreneurs are focused and persistent, constantly doing what is best for the business to succeed. They work hard on the details and relentlessly attempt to find ways to become more profitable. Persistence is a characteristic required for success.

4) High Energy Level:

The capacity for sustained effort requires a high energy level. The necessary work, planning, organizing, directing, creating strategy, and finding funds, can only be accomplished on a demanding schedule

5) Risk-Taking Tendency:

McClelland's findings suggest that people with a high need for achievement tend to take risks. Growth-oriented entrepreneurs believe so strongly in their ability to achieve that they do not see much possibility of failure. Thus they accept risk and find it motivating. These five personal characteristics identified by McClelland can be further condensed into four fundamental behaviors that all successful entrepreneurs exhibit:

5.2) Comparison between Entrepreneurial and non entrepreneurial personality:

What is an entrepreneur? Why are few people successful starting and growing a business and others are not? Is it just luck or being in the right place at the right time? Certainly Bill Gates, with his technical talents, needed the computer revolution in order to make Microsoft the successful company it is. But is it just timing and luck or are other factors involved? Was Steve Jobs had special attributes required for running a business?

Recent research in the field of psychology suggests that personality has a great deal to do with being a successful entrepreneur. In a recent study published in the highly regarded Journal of Applied Psychology (2006, Vol. 91, No. 2, 259-271), Hao Zao of the University of Illinois at Chicago and Scott E. Seibert of the Melbourne Business School analyzed and combined the results of twenty-three independent research studies. A statistical method known as meta-analysis was used which allows research studies to be combined in a way that yields overall trends within a field of research.

So what is the relevance of these research findings? The ability to compare oneself to successful entrepreneurs can help an individual make an important career decision even if they have no previous experience working in an entrepreneurial environment. Avoiding bad career decisions is something all of us desire. Second, these data can help people who support and work with entrepreneurs to make sound decisions.. With tremendous amounts of money at risk, this research allows to make sound decisions about the people involved in addition to market analysis and evaluating the merits of the product/service. As the field of psychology continues to move forward scientifically and further away from the old days of theory and conjecture, the information which results from psychological research can and should be used to support the making of good business decisions. Thus it can be theorized that formal training and education are important for becoming an entrepreneur but foremost attribute require for being an entrepreneur is a staunch belief of oneself and will for success.

Evolution of the concept of entrepreneurial and non entrepreneurial person difference over the years:

Can we reliably differentiate between entrepreneurs and other persons? Although this has been a central question in the field of entrepreneurship (Venkataraman, 1997),

only limited systematic work has attended with this question, and research that focused on personal characteristics and traits has failed to identify consistent differences between entrepreneurs and non-entrepreneurs (cf., Shaver & Scott, 1991).

Pointing to environmental factors, some scholars argued that people become entrepreneurs because of low opportunity costs (Amit & Schoemaker, 1993).

Douglas and Shepherd (1998) hypothesized that individuals choose between entrepreneurial or employment careers (or a combination of the two) based on expected utility such as income, risk, work, and independence. According to a similar view, entrepreneurs react adaptively to various barriers in the labor market. Striving to increase their income, individuals become entrepreneurs when they learn that their prospects of finding a job are slim (Mesch & Czamanski, 1997). Other scholars suggested that entrepreneurship is an antithesis to traditional organizational life where people's aspiration and goals are hindered or blocked. The problem with such views of entrepreneurship is that utility maximization and low opportunity costs do not always lead people to detect opportunities and start a company and many entrepreneurs are not inhibited by high opportunity costs. Likewise, extremely challenging goals frequently lead to a change in goals rather than innovation (Locke & Latham, 1990). This failure to provide satisfactory explanations led some to conclude that differences between entrepreneurs and non-entrepreneurs are largely immaterial to the entrepreneurship phenomenon (Gartner, 1988).

Yet evidence suggests that entrepreneurial success is closely related to the way entrepreneurs perceive information and process knowledge (Baron, 1998). While most research focused on distinguishing between entrepreneurs and other persons emphasized personality, trait, or behavioral constructs and built on limited theoretical work, we focus on cognitive mechanisms as a basis for distinguishing between entrepreneurs and other persons. In stark contrast to the personality or trait approaches, this perspective advises that different people think and process information differently and that such variations may help differentiate people who start companies from people who do not (Baron, 1998, Busenitz & Barney, 1997). Building on the theory of entrepreneurial discovery (cf., Kirzner, 1997) and literature in cognitive psychology, we propose that various cognitive mechanisms as reflected by different information management styles may be associated with founding new businesses. So it is still a question of tremendous importance for psychologists and other academic scholar that Why entrepreneur is the person who is? Different than every other ordinary person? What mental assets he possess? Thus scholars differentiate 6 key aspects by which person becomes an entrepreneur from an ordinary person.

As compared to other persons, entrepreneurs will
(1) be more alert
(2) be more affected by planning failure
(3) less likely to engage in counterfactual thinking
(4) show greater preference for heuristic processing which means imperfect decisions converted into perfect ones like Ratan Tata stated that decisions are not right or wrong. Ability to take decision on time is a key to success.
(5) Confident and not overconfident.
(6) self-efficacy would be a robust variable that is able to differentiate entrepreneurs from non-entrepreneurs.

We argue that such cognitive mechanisms allow some individuals, but not others, to manage and manipulate information, capitalize on knowledge asymmetry, and remain optimistic about probable outcomes who later become an entrepreneur.

5.3) Habits of an entrepreneurs:

It is very hard to point certain habits as habits of entrepreneurs and that of other persons. Every entrepreneur is a person but every person is not an entrepreneur. So what are the habits apart from regular habits of drinking tea and coffee can be summarized here for better understanding of this concept?

It is said that ordinary people often have habits which are not bad but are not good either. Entrepreneur on the other hand have good habits and follows those regularly which results in long term success.

Following habits are generally recognized habits of an entrepreneur:
1) Be Proactive:

Take initiative in life by realizing that your decisions (and how they align with life's principles) are the primary determining factor for effectiveness in your life. Take responsibility for your choices and the consequences that follow. Being proactive requires very much attentiveness towards details and planning. It is often said that "Proper Prior Planning Prevents Poor Performance." Hence care must be taken to consider this habit very seriously and to apply it in regular life.

2) Begin with the End in Mind:

Self-discover and clarify your deeply important character values and life goals. Envision the ideal characteristics for each of your various roles and relationships in life. Create a mission statement.

If we know the end, beginning is not that hard. So end result must be constantly reviewed for achieving the same. Great entrepreneur always look for the good end in mind and start his project.

3) Put First Things First:

Prioritize, plan, and execute your week's tasks based on importance rather than urgency. Evaluate whether your efforts exemplify your desired character values, propel you toward goals, and enrich the roles and relationships that were elaborated in Habit number second. This is another great habit for success.

4) Think Win-Win:

Genuinely strive for mutually beneficial solutions or agreements in your relationships. Value and respect people by understanding a "win" for all is ultimately a better long-term resolution than if only one person in the situation had gotten his way. Positive frame of mind helps in achievement of success even if current scenario is not that good.

5) Seek First to Understand, Then to be Understood:

Use empathic listening to be genuinely influenced by a person, which compels them to reciprocate the listening and take an open mind to being influenced by you. This creates an atmosphere of caring, and positive problem solving.

6) Synergize:

Combine the strengths of people through positive teamwork, so as to achieve goals no one person could have done alone. Unity is strength and proper use of this strength can be very helpful in achievement of organizational goals.

7) Sharpen the Saw:

Balance and renew your resources, energy, and health to create a sustainable, long-term, effective lifestyle. It primarily emphasizes exercise for physical renewal, prayer (meditation, yoga, etc.) and good reading for mental renewal. It also mentions service to society for spiritual renewal.

Good person can be a good entrepreneur. It's a fact and kind of prerequisite for becoming an entrepreneur.

Some other habits based on the observation of scholars and thinkers:

1) Find the Right People:

The first habit you must develop is the habit of hiring the right people to help you achieve your goals. Most of your success as an entrepreneur or executive will be determined by the quality of the people you recruit to work with you or to work on your team. The fact is, the best companies have the best people. The second-best companies have the second-best people. The third-best companies have the average or mediocre people, and they're on their way out of business.

2) Delegation of tasks:

The second habit you need to develop for business success is proper delegation. You must develop the ability to delegate the right task to the right person in the right way. The inability to delegate effectively can be the cause of failure or underperformance of the individual and can even bring about failure of the business.

When people start in business, they usually do everything themselves. As they grow and expand, the job becomes too large for one person, so they hire someone to do part of it. However, if they're not careful, they try to retain control of the task and never fully hand over both authority and responsibility to the other person.

3) Review of expectations:

The third requirement for business success is for you to develop the habit of proper supervision. You must set up a system to monitor the task and make sure it's being done as agreed upon. The rule is, "inspect what you expect." Once you've delegated a task to the right person in the right way, it's essential that you monitor the performance of the task and make sure it's done on schedule and to the required level of quality. Remember, delegation is not abdication. You are still responsible for the ultimate results of the delegated tasks. You must stay on top of it.

When you've delegated a task, set up a system of reporting so that you're always informed as to the status of the work. Be sure the other person knows what is to be done, and when, and to what standard. Checking progress of individual person as well as team is very important and must be looked for.

4) Count what is already achieved:

The fourth practice of successful entrepreneurs and executives is the habit of measuring performance. You must set specific, measurable standards and score cards for the results you require. You have to set specific timelines and deadlines to make sure you "make your numbers" on schedule. Everyone who's expected to carry out a task must know with complete clarity the targets he or she is aiming at, how successful performance will be measured, and when the expected results are due. Tracking what we have already achieved helps in achievement of final goal.

5) People must be informed:

The fifth habit for businesspeople is the habit of reporting results regularly and accurately. People around you need to know what's going on. Your bankers need to know your financial results. Your staff needs to know the status and the situation of your company. Your key people, at all levels, need to know what results are being achieved. The more thoroughly and accurately you report to people the details and situation of your business, the happier they'll be and the better results they will get. So all the external and internal personnel must be informed relevantly about the organization.

We have studied the habits of people who chose to create business organization out of just an idea and get success in their respective field of work.

5.4) Dynamics of Motivation:

Introduction:

Motivation is a mental activity involving creation of a strong desire towards something internal or external which acts as a strong force in human mind. Thus motivation is a very strong psychological force required for success, progress and development.

In this topic we are studying different aspects of motivation, it's impact on the entrepreneur and organization as well.

Sometimes all things are in order yet a person fails in his particular task, this is the perfect example of lack of proper motivation. Proper Motivation brings success and progress because all our energy gets directed towards one objective.

so it is said that, "Motivation is the art of getting people to do what you want them to do because they want to do it."

Definition:

1) Oxford English Dictionary defines motivation as: a reason or reasons for acting or behaving in a particular way or desire or willingness to do something; enthusiasm

2) Motivation is defined as the process that initiates, guides and maintains goal-oriented behaviors. Motivation is what causes us to act, whether it is getting a glass of water to reduce thirst or reading a book to gain knowledge.

3) Harold Koontz defined motivation as, "motivation is a general term applying to the entire class of drives, desires, needs, wishes and similar forces. To say that managers(entrepreneurs) motivate their subordinates is to say that they do those things which they hope will satisfy these drives and desires and induce the subordinates to act in a desired manner."

4) Motivation is the word derived from the word 'motive' which means needs, desires, wants or drives within the individuals. It is the process of stimulating people to actions to accomplish the goals. In the work goal context the psychological factors stimulating the people's behavior can be :
    a) desire for money
    b) success

c) recognition

d) job-satisfaction

e) team work, etc

Thus it can be summed up that Motivation is a psychological feature that arouses an organism to act towards a desired goal and elicits, controls, and sustains certain goal-directed behaviors. It can be considered a driving force; a psychological one that compels or reinforces an action toward a desired goal. For example, hunger is a motivation that elicits a desire to eat. Motivation is the purpose or psychological cause of an action. It involves the biological, emotional, social and cognitive forces that activate behavior. In everyday usage, the term motivation is frequently used to describe why a person does something. For example, you might say that a student is so motivated to get into an engineering program that he spends every night studying.

There are three major components to motivation:

a) Activation,

b) Persistence

c) Intensity.

Activation involves the decision to initiate a behavior, such as enrolling in a medical class. Persistence is the continued effort toward a goal even though obstacles may exist, such as taking more medical courses in order to earn a degree although it requires a significant investment of time, energy and resources. Finally, intensity can be seen in the concentration and vigor that goes into pursuing a goal. For example, one student might coast by without much effort, while another student will study regularly, participate in discussions and take advantage of research opportunities outside of class.

One of the most important functions of management is to create willingness amongst the employees to perform in the best of their abilities. Therefore the role of a leader is to arouse interest in performance of employees in their jobs. The process of motivation consists of three stages:

1) A felt need or drive

2) A stimulus in which needs have to be arouse

3) When needs are satisfied, the satisfaction or accomplishment of goals.

Therefore, we can say that motivation is a psychological phenomenon which means needs and wants of the individuals have to be tackled by framing an incentive plan. Motivation has been shown to have roots in physiological, behavioral, cognitive, and social areas. Motivation may be rooted in a basic impulse to optimize well-being, minimize physical pain and maximize pleasure. It can also originate from specific physical needs such as eating, sleeping or resting.

Motivation is an inner drive to behave or act in a certain manner. "It's the difference between waking up before dawn to pound the pavement and lazing around the house all day." These inner conditions such as wishes, desires, goals, activate to move in a particular direction in behavior.

Types of Motivation:

There are types of motivation according to the sphere of an psychological process of the mind.

Following diagram shows the types of motivation:

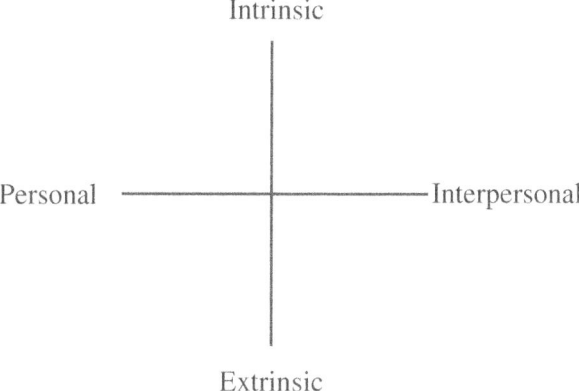

Intrinsic

Personal —————————————— Interpersonal

Extrinsic

Motivation can be divided into two types: intrinsic (internal) motivation and extrinsic (external) motivation.

1) Intrinsic motivation:

Intrinsic motivation refers to motivation that is driven by an interest or enjoyment in the task itself, and exists within the individual rather than relying on external pressures or a desire for reward. Intrinsic motivation has been studied since the early 1970s. Students who are intrinsically motivated are more likely to engage in the task willingly as well as work to improve their skills, which will increase their capabilities. Students are likely to be intrinsically motivated if they, attribute their educational results to factors under their own control, also known as autonomy believe they have the skills to be effective agents in reaching their desired goals, also known as self-efficacy beliefs are interested in mastering a topic, not just in achieving good grades.

Intrinsic motivation is when people engage in an activity, such as a hobby, without obvious external incentives.

Numerous studies have found it to be associated with high educational achievement and enjoyment by students. There is currently no universal theory to explain the origin or elements of intrinsic motivation, and most explanations combine elements of Fritz Heider's attribution theory, Bandura's work on self-efficacy and other studies relating to locus of control and goal orientation. Though it is thought that students are more likely to be intrinsically motivated if they:

Attribute their educational results to internal factors that they can control (e.g. the amount of effort they put in),

Believe they can be effective agents in reaching desired goals (i.e. the results are not determined by luck),

Are interested in mastering a topic, rather than just rote-learning to achieve good grades.

Note that the idea of reward for achievement is absent from this model of intrinsic motivation, since rewards are an extrinsic factor.

In knowledge-sharing communities and organizations, people often give reasons for their participation, including contributing to a common good, a moral obligation to the group, mentorship or 'giving back'. In work environments, money may provide a more powerful extrinsic factor than the intrinsic motivation provided by an enjoyable workplace.

2) Extrinsic motivation:

Extrinsic motivation refers to the performance of an activity in order to attain an outcome, whether or not that activity is also intrinsically motivated. Extrinsic motivation comes from outside of the individual. Common extrinsic motivations are rewards (for example money or grades) for showing the desired behavior, and the threat of punishment following misbehavior. Competition is in an extrinsic motivator because it encourages the performer to win and to beat others, not simply to enjoy the intrinsic rewards of the activity. A cheering crowd and the desire to win a trophy are also extrinsic incentives. So extrinsic motivation is basically advanced as a famous 'carrot and stick' approach in which carrots were final goals and stick represented some strict controlling unit which were responsible for performance of an employee. The 'stick' or fear is a good motivator and when used at the correct times can be very helpful. In that context, fear has always been the 'convenient' choice of Malaysian managers and organisations. When all else fails, the stick approach is somehow most attractive as it usually produces instantaneous compliance and hence immediate results. Fear is also attractive as in the short term, an employee's performance may be improved without any need for incentives or financial remuneration. Fear however has its weaknesses in that an organisation motivated by fear is prone to mutiny. It can also be stressful for employees. It is extrinsic, which means that the motivation only works while the motivator is present. When the motivator goes, the motivation also usually goes.

Importance of Motivation :

Motivation is a very important for an organization because of the following points:

1) Proper use of human resource:

Every concern requires physical, financial and human resources to accomplish the goals. It is through motivation that the human resources can be utilized by making full use of it. This can be done by building willingness in employees to work. This will help the enterprise in securing best possible utilization of resources.

2) Increase in Efficiency of employees:

The level of a subordinate or a employee does not only depend upon his qualifications and abilities. For getting best of his work performance, the gap between ability and willingness has to be filled which helps in improving the level of performance of subordinates. This will result into:

a) Increase in productivity,

b) Reducing cost of operations,

c) Improving overall efficiency.

3) Achievement of Goals:

The goals of an enterprise can be achieved only when the following factors take place :

1) There is best possible utilization of resources,

2) There is a co-operative work environment,

3) The employees are goal-directed and they act in a purposive manner,

Goals can be achieved if co-ordination and co-operation takes place simultaneously which can be effectively done through motivation.

4) Healthy Relationships:

Motivation is an important factor which brings employees satisfaction. This can be done by keeping into mind and framing an incentive plan for the benefit of the employees. This could initiate the following things:

a) Monetary and non-monetary incentives,

b) Promotion opportunities for employees,

c) Disincentives for inefficient employees.

In order to build a cordial, friendly atmosphere in a concern, the above steps should be taken by a manager. This would help in:

5) Cooperation and stability:

Industrial dispute and unrest in employees will reduce. The employees will be adaptable to the changes and there will be no resistance to the change. This will help in providing a smooth and sound concern in which individual interests will coincide with the organizational interests. This will result in profit maximization through increased productivity.

6) Leads to stability of work force:

Stability of workforce is very important from the point of view of reputation and goodwill of a concern. The employees can remain loyal to the enterprise only when they have a feeling of participation in the management. The skills and efficiency of employees will always be of advantage to employees as well as employees. This will lead to a good public image in the market which will attract competent and qualified people into a concern. As it is said, "Old is gold" which suffices with the role of motivation here, the older the people, more the experience and their adjustment into a concern which can be of benefit to the enterprise.

From the above discussion, we can say that motivation is an internal feeling which can be understood only by manager since he is in close contact with the employees. Needs, wants and desires are inter-related and they are the driving force to act. These needs can be understood by the manager and he can frame motivation plans accordingly. We can say that motivation therefore is a continuous process since motivation process is based on needs which are unlimited. The process has to be continued throughout.

Thus motivation is a very important element in the organizational progress and success.

Motivation Theories :

There are various theories of motivation which are developed over the period of time.

Ranging from incentive theory of motivation, Maslow's need hierarchy theory Herzberg's two-factor theory, Alderfer's ERG theory, Self-determination theory, Temporal motivation theory, Achievement motivation, Goal-setting theory, Conscious motivation, Thematic Apperception Test, Intrinsic motivation and the 16 basic desires theory all these theories present motivation, it's effects on the employees and organizational goals.

These all theories are very important for the understanding of the concept of motivation.

However among those theories Abraham Maslow's hierarchy of human needs theory is the most widely discussed theory of motivation.

Need Hierarchy Theory Of Motivation:

Abraham Maslow was born in New York in 1908 and died in 1970, although various publications appear in Maslow's name in later years. Maslow's PhD in psychology in 1934 at the University of Wisconsin formed the basis of his motivational research, initially studying rhesus monkeys. Maslow later moved to New York's Brooklyn College.

Abraham Maslow developed the Hierarchy of Needs model in 1940-50s USA, and the Hierarchy of Needs theory remains valid today for understanding human motivation, management training, and personal development. Indeed, Maslow's ideas surrounding the Hierarchy of Needs concerning the responsibility of employers to provide a workplace environment that encourages and enables employees to fulfil their own unique potential (self-actualization) are today more relevant than ever. Abraham Maslow's book Motivation and Personality, published in 1954 (second edition 1970) introduced the Hierarchy of Needs, and Maslow extended his ideas in other work, notably his later book Toward A Psychology Of Being, a significant and relevant commentary, which has been revised in recent times by Richard Lowry, who is in his own right a leading academic in the field of motivational psychology.

The Maslow's Hierarchy of Needs five-stage model below (structure and terminology - not the precise pyramid diagram itself) is clearly and directly attributable to Maslow; later versions of the theory with added motivational stages are not so clearly attributable to Maslow. These extended models have instead been inferred by others from Maslow's work. Specifically Maslow refers to the needs Cognitive, Aesthetic and Transcendence (subsequently shown as distinct needs levels in some interpretations of his theory) as additional aspects of motivation, but not as distinct levels in the Hierarchy of Needs.

Where Maslow's Hierarchy of Needs is shown with more than five levels these models have been extended through interpretation of Maslow's work by other people. These augmented models and diagrams are shown as the adapted seven and eight-stage Hierarchy of Needs pyramid diagrams and models below.

There have been very many interpretations of Maslow's Hierarchy of Needs in the form of pyramid diagrams. The diagrams below is used as a general interpretations and are not offered as Maslow's original work. Interestingly in Maslow's book Motivation and Personality, which first introduced the Hierarchy of Needs, there is not a pyramid diagram.

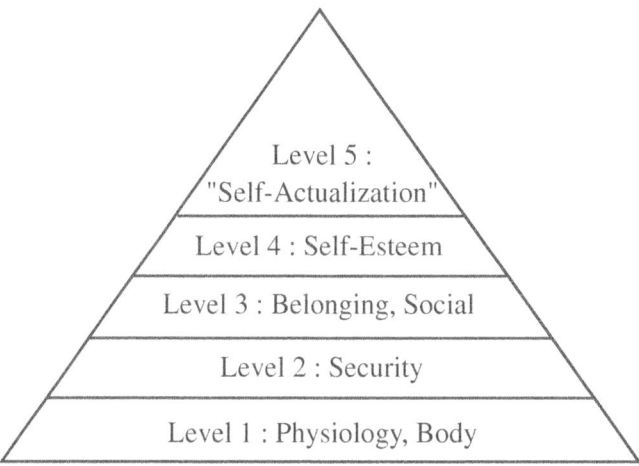

This five stage model can be divided into

1) Basic or physiological needs:

Basic needs of food, clothing and shelter Physiological needs are the physical requirements for human survival. If these requirements are not met, the human body cannot function properly, and will ultimately fail. Physiological needs are thought to be the most important; they should be met first.

Air, water, and food are metabolic requirements for survival in all animals, including humans. Clothing and shelter provide necessary protection from the elements.

2) Security needs:

Fear of losing is covered under these needs. Fear of losing job, property etc.

Safety and Security needs include:

1) Personal security

2)Financial security

3)Health and well-being

4)Safety net against accidents/illness and their adverse impacts

3) Social needs:

Man is a social animal and hence cannot live in isolation. Society is a group of people who are connected or needs to be connected for daily activities.

According to Maslow, humans need to feel a sense of belonging and acceptance among their social groups, regardless if these groups are large or small. For example, some large social groups may include clubs, co-workers, religious groups, professional organizations, sports teams, and gangs. Some examples of small social connections include family members, intimate partners, mentors, colleagues, and confidants. Humans need to love and be loved

4) Self Esteem needs:

Self esteem is a natural phenomenon and these needs covers, status, power, acceptance in a society etc.

Most people have a need for stable self-respect and self-esteem. Maslow noted two versions of esteem needs: a "lower" version and a "higher" version. The "lower" version of esteem is the need for respect from others. This may include a need for status, recognition, fame, prestige, and attention. The "higher" version manifests itself as the need for self-respect. For example, the person may have a need for strength, competence, mastery, self-confidence, independence, and freedom. This "higher" version takes precedence over the "lower" version because it relies on an inner competence established through experience. Deprivation of these needs may lead to an inferiority complex, weakness, and helplessness.

Maslow states that while he originally thought the needs of humans had strict guidelines, the "hierarchies are interrelated rather than sharply separated". This means that esteem and the subsequent levels are not strictly separated; instead, the levels are closely related.

5) Self actualization needs:

This level of need refers to what a person's full potential is and the realization of that potential. Maslow describes this level as the desire to accomplish everything that one can, to become the most that one can be. Individuals may perceive or focus on this need very specifically. For example, one individual may have the strong desire to become an ideal parent. In another, the desire may be expressed athletically. For others, it may be expressed in paintings, pictures, or inventions. As previously mentioned, Maslow believed that to understand this level of need, the person must not only achieve the previous needs, but master them.

One must satisfy lower level basic needs before progressing on to meet higher level growth needs. Once these needs have been reasonably satisfied, one may be able to reach the highest level called self-actualization.

Every person is capable and has the desire to move up the hierarchy toward a level of self-actualization. Unfortunately, progress is often disrupted by failure to meet lower level needs. Life experiences including divorce and loss of job may cause an individual to fluctuate between levels of the hierarchy.

Maslow noted only one in a hundred people become fully self-actualized because our society rewards motivation primarily based on esteem, love and other social needs.

In conclusion we can say that Maslow is obviously most famous for his Hierarchy of Needs theory, rightly so, because it is a wonderfully simple and elegant model for understanding so many aspects of human motivation, especially in an organization.

Chapter 6
Entrepreneurship and Economy

Introduction:

Every economy runs because of a strong and confident leadership. USA is one of the strongest economy of the current world. US government is very good example of leadership. Every entrepreneur is a good leader and must motivate, guide, provokes his subordinates to work recklessly for achievement of a goal. Today US economy is known for entrepreneurs. And it is not coincidence that this world's leading economy is believed to be the most entrepreneurial society in the world. This is the power of entrepreneurs.

Considering our country, Indians have always been entrepreneurs. From the ancient period business was carried in a family which was transferred from father to the son. but recently there has been a shift in the nature of Indian Entrepreneurship. It has come to stand for something that is out of the box and globally oriented. It began with the info tech revolution a decade ago.

Service industry is increasing rapidly so new and different branches are going to be seen by economy in the near future. Indian entrepreneurs are making waves all across the world. Indian business firms are making acquisitions abroad and spreading their tentacles in various corners of the world. Indian Entrepreneurs have proved all doomsday prophecies wrong and on the contrary have flourished under globalization.

Here is a brief profile of some of the famous Indian entrepreneurs:

1) Dhirubhai ambani:
Born: December 28, 1932

Died: July 6, 2002

Achievements:

Dhiru Bhai Ambani built India's largest private sector company. Created an equity cult in the Indian capital market. Reliance is the first Indian company to feature in Forbes 500 list

2) J.R.D Tata:

Born: July 29, 1904

Died: on November 29, 1993

Achievements:

He had the honor of being India's first pilot; was Chairman of Tata & Sons for 50 years; launched Air India International as India's first international airline; received Bharat Ratna in 1992.

JRD Tata was one of the most enterprising Indian entrepreneurs. He was a pioneer aviator and built one of the largest industrial houses of India.

3) Dr. Verghese Kurien:

Born: November 26, 1921

Died: September 9, 2012

Achievements:

Known as the "Father of the White Revolution" in India; Winner of Ramon Magsaysay Award; Awarded with Padma Shri (1965), Padma Bhushan (1966), and Padma Vibhushan (1999)

Dr. Verghese Kurien is better known as the "Father of the White Revolution" in India. He is also called as the Milkman of India. Dr. Varghese Kurien was the architect behind the success of the largest dairy development program in the world, christened as Operation Flood. He was the chairman of the Gujarat Co-operative Milk Marketing Federation Ltd. (GCMMF) and his name was synonymous with the Amul brand.

4) Ratan Tata:

Born: December 28, 1937

Achievement:

Honored with Padma Bhushan, one of the highest civilian awards in 2000.

Ratan Tata was the Chairman of Tata Sons, the holding company of the Tata Group. Ratan Naval Tata is also the Chairman of the major Tata companies such as Tata Steel, Tata Motors, Tata Power, Tata Consultancy Services, Tata Tea, Tata Chemicals, Indian Hotels and Tata Teleservices. He has taken Tata Group to new heights and under his leadership Group's revenues have grown manifold.

5) Kiran Mazumdar Shaw:
Born: March 23, 1953
Achievement:

Chairman & Managing Director of Biocon Ltd; Felicitated with Padmashri (1989) and Padma Bhushan (2005).

Kiran Mazumdar Shaw is the Chairman & Managing Director of Biocon Ltd, India's biggest biotechnology company. In 2004, she became India's richest woman.

In chapter 8 we have discussed biography of 2 famous Indian entrepreneurs namely,

1) Narayan Murthy

2) Cyrus Poonawala

These are just few examples of entrepreneur who have chose different path and succeeded in whatever field they have chosen. Entrepreneurs have capacity to shake the world with their success and progress. Economy is hugely affected by the actions of these entrepreneurs and hence it is very beneficial to study at this level, concept of Entrepreneurship in detail which is a complex phenomenon because though different authors have defined it, no single definition is exhaustive. No one can say with 100 percent accuracy about the characteristics and nature of an entrepreneur. Few of them can be listed but again this list is not full proof. Various additions can be made in that list later on. So who is an entrepreneur? What is an entrepreneurship? Why it affects economy? what is a relation between economy and entrepreneurship?
All the above questions will be answered in this chapter.

Concept of Entrepreneurship:

Entrepreneurship is the act and art of being an entrepreneur or one who undertakes innovations or introducing new things, finance and business in an effort to transform innovations into economic goods. This may result in new organizations or may be part of revitalizing mature organizations in response to a perceived opportunity. The most obvious form of entrepreneurship is that of starting new businesses (referred as startup company); however, in recent years, the term has been extended to include social and political forms of entrepreneurial activity. When entrepreneurship is describing activities within a firm or large organization it is referred to as intrapreneurship and may include corporate venturing, when large entities spin-off organizations. Entrepreneurial activities are substantially different depending on the type of organization and creativity involved. Small scale organization requires different set of activities than the big multinational organization. In economics, entrepreneurship combined with land, labor, natural resources and capital can produce profit. Entrepreneurial spirit is characterized by innovation and risk-taking, and is an essential part of a nation's ability to succeed in an ever changing and increasingly competitive global marketplace.

A complex phenomenon:

Concept of entrepreneurship is a complex phenomenon involving various variables and it basically relates with the entrepreneur who is a human being. Entrepreneurship refers to a process of action an entrepreneur undertakes to establish his enterprise. Entrepreneurship is thus a cycle of actions to further the interests of the entrepreneur. Entrepreneurship is a composite skill, the resultant of a mix of many qualities and traits. This includes imagination , ability to take risks, ability to bring together the factors of production, ability to manage people, ability to understand the technology.

Entrepreneurship is basically dealing with the scarce resources and to put them to maximum advantages. Entrepreneurship today is a product of teamwork and the ability to create, build and work as a team. Entrepreneurship is the propensity of mind to take calculated risks with the confidence to achieve predetermined goal.

Definition of Entrepreneurship:

1) Joseph Alois Schumpeter:

The process to shatter the status quo through new combinations of resources and new methods of commerce.

2) Richard Cantillon:

Entrepreneurship is a matter of foresight and willingness to assume risks, which is not necessarily connected with the employment of labour in some productive process.

3) Entrepreneurship is the act and art of being an entrepreneur or one who undertakes innovations or introducing new things, finance and business acumen in an effort to transform innovations into economic goods.

4) An individual who, rather than working as an employee, runs a small business and assumes all the risk and reward of a given business venture, idea, or good or service offered for sale. The entrepreneur is commonly seen as a business leader and innovator of new ideas and business processes.

5) According to Aldrich, there are four competing definitions of entrepreneurship:

a) The setting up of high-growth and high-capitalization firms (as opposed to low-growth and low-capitalization 'lifestyle' businesses)

b) Innovation and innovativeness leading to new products and new markets (the Schumpeterian tradition);

c) Opportunity recognition (the Kirznerian tradition);

d) The creation of new organisations.

According to Aldrich there are problems with all four of these definitions.

6) Peter Drucker defined this concept as, "Entrepreneurship is a systematic innovation which consists in the purposeful and organized search for changes, and it is the systematic analysis of the opportunities such changes might offer for economic and social innovation."

Entrepreneurship is neither a science nor an art. It is a practice. It has knowledge base. Knowledge in entrepreneurship is a means to an end. It is not just about making money. It is about imagination. flexibility, creativity, willingness to think conceptually, readiness to take risks, ability to mobilize agents of production and capacity to see changes as an opportunity. It is also about marrying passion and process with a good dose of perseverance.

7) In the words of A. H. Cole, "entrepreneurship is the purposeful activity of an individual or a group of associated individuals, undertaken to initiate, maintain or organize a profit oriented business unit for the production or distribution of economic goods and services."

8) McClelland described the innovative characteristics of entrepreneurial role. Entrepreneurial role by definition involves doing things in a new and better way. A businessman who simply behaves in a traditional way is not entrepreneur. Moreover, entrepreneur role calls for decision making under uncertainty. If there is no significant uncertainty and the action involves applying known and predictable results, then entrepreneurship is not at all involved.

McClelland identified two characteristics of entrepreneurship.

1) Doing things in a new and better way. This is similar with the innovative characteristic given by Schumpeter and,

2) decision making under uncertainty i.e risk as identified by Centillon.

McClelland more explicitly emphasised the need for achievement or achievement orientation as the most directly relevant factor for explaining economic behavior. This motive is defined as a tendency to strive for success in situations involved and of one's performance in relation to the same standard of excellence. So basically entrepreneurship is the function of creation of something innovative and involves organizing and staffing , undertaking risks and dealing with economic uncertainty.

9) Everett E. Higgins defined entrepreneurship as the function of seeking investment and production opportunity, organizing and enterprise to undertake a new production process, raising capital, hiring labour, arranging the supply of raw materials, finding site, introducing a new technique and commodities, discovering new sources of raw materials and selecting top managers of day to day operations of the enterprise.

Chart showing various definitions of entrepreneurship is given on the last page of this chapter.

Characteristics of entrepreneurship:

Entrepreneurs have many of the same character traits as leaders, similar to the early great man theories of leadership; however trait-based theories of entrepreneurship are increasingly being called into question. Entrepreneurs are often contrasted with managers and administrators who are said to be more methodical and less prone to risk-taking. Such person-centric models of entrepreneurship have shown to be of questionable validity, not least as many real-life entrepreneurs operate in teams rather than as single individuals.

Entrepreneurship is a process of creating something new, and organizing and coordinating and undertaking risk and handling economic uncertainty.

Following diagram will show the characteristics of entrepreneurship :

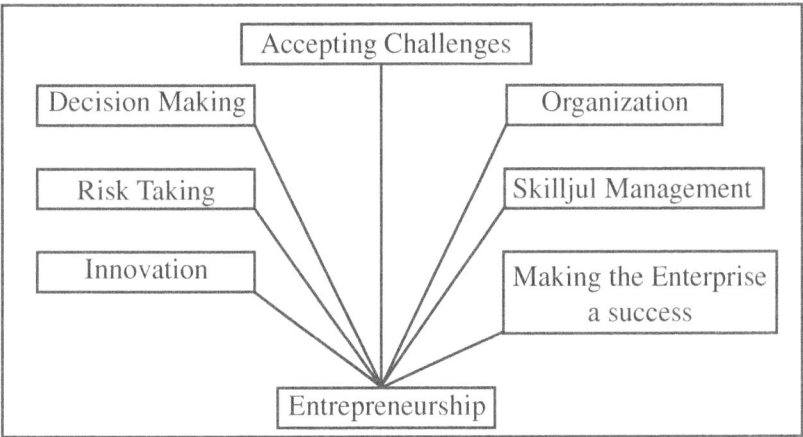

Evolution of the entrepreneurship in India:

Entrepreneurship in India was developed from ancient period when barter system was established and people used to trade with the goods from place to place. Entrepreneurship was existed even during vedic period and sources have discovered that many people went to different locations of the India just to start a new and innovative venture. Kautilya have mentioned qualities of an entrepreneur using different terminology.

Growth of India's entrepreneurship must be bifurcated in two time periods namely

1) Entrepreneurship during pre- independence period
2) Entrepreneurship during post independence period

1) Entrepreneurship during pre- independence period:

The evolution of the Indian entrepreneurship can be traced back to even as early as Rig-Veda, when metal handicrafts existed in the society. This would bring the point home that handicrafts entrepreneurship in India was as old as the human civilization itself, and was nurtured by the craftsman as a part of their duty towards the society.

Before India came into contact with west, people were organized in a particular type of economic and social system of the village community. Then, the village community featured the economic scene in India. The Indian towns were mostly religious and aloof from the general life of country. The elaborated cast based diversion of workers consisted of farmers, artisans and religious priests. The majority of the artisans were treated as village servants. Such compact system of village community effectively protect in village artisans from the onslaughts of external competition was one of the important contributing factors to the absence of localization of industry in ancient India. Evidently, organized industrial activity was observable among the India artisans in a few recognizable products in the cities of Banaras, Allahabad, Gaya, Puri & Mirzapur which were established on their river basins. Very possibly this was because the rivers served as a means of transportation facilities. These artisan industries flourished over the period because the Royal patronage was to them to support them. The workshops called 'khar khanas' came into existence. The craftsmen were brought into an association pronounced as 'guild system'. On the whole, perfection in art, durability beyond doubt and appeal to the eye of the individual were the distinguishing qualities inherent in the Indian craftsmanship that brought much everlasting laurels of name and fame of the illustrious India in the past. To quote, Bengal enjoyed worldwide celebrity for Corah, Lucknow for chintzes, Ahmadabad for dupttas, and dhotis, Nagpur for silk boarded cloth, Kashmir for shawls and Banaras for metal wares. Thus, form the immemorial till the earlier years of the 18th century, India enjoyed the prestigious status of the queen of the international trade with the help of its handicrafts. Unfortunately, so much prestigious Indian handicraft industry, which was basically a cottage and small sector, declined at the end of the 18th century for various reasons.

These may be listed as:

1. Disappearance of the Indian royal courts who patronized the crafts earlier.
2. The lukewarm attitude of the British colonial government towards the Indian crafts.
3. Imposition of heavy duties on the imports of the Indian goods in England.
4. Low priced British made goods.
5. Development of transport in Indian facilitating the easy access of British product
6. Lack of transportation and communication facilities:
7. Not encouraged the establishment of heavy industries:
8. Political turmoil : Political turmoil and abolition of princely courts

The story of the Indian entrepreneurship is replete with paradoxes and surprises. During the precolonial and colonial era, the entrepreneur was seen more as a trader-money lender merchant, bound rigidly by caste affiliations and religious, cultural and social forces ranging from the philosophy of Karma to the system of joint family. Entrepreneurship as we understand it today was definitely not forthcoming from this social segment. A number of political, economic factors too had an inhibiting effect on the spirit of enterprise among Indians. Lack of political unity and stability, absence of effective communication systems, existence of custom barriers and oppressive tax policies, prevalence of innumerable currency system – all these combined together to restrict the growth of native entrepreneurship until around the third decade of the 19th century. The religious system of education and the low social esteem accorded to business were the other potent forces that discourage the emergence of large scale commercial ventures in the pre independence India.

The first half of the present century witnessed a gradual change in the scenario. During this period, there was a visible tendency among the natives to take to business. The spread of secular education, rising nationalist feelings and social reform movements must have given a fillip to this initial phase of the emergence of entrepreneurship. Further, the two world wars and the enormous opportunities they created for the growth of Indian industrial ventures brought about a radical change in the societal attitudes in favor of industrial entrepreneurship and broadened the vision of Indian businessmen. The independent India thus could claim to have created a conductive climate for spread of entrepreneurship. It is in this broad backdrop that the later evolution and growth of Indian entrepreneurship has to be located. We shall discuss evolution of entrepreneurship after post independence period in the following part.

2) Entrepreneurship during post independence period:

After taking a long sign of political relief in 1947, the Government of India tried to spell out the priorities to devise a scheme for achieving balanced growth. For this purpose, the Government came forward with the first Industrial Policy, 1948 which was revised from time to time. The Government in her various industrial policy statements identified the responsibility of the State to promote, assist and develop industries in the national interest. It also explicitly recognized the vital role of the private sector in accelerating industrial development and, for this, enough field was reserved for the private sector. The Government took three important measures in her industrial resolutions:

(i) to maintain a proper distribution of economic power between private and public sector;

(ii) to encourage the tempo of industrialization by spreading entrepreneurship from the existing centers to other cities, towns and villages, and

(iii) to disseminate the entrepreneurship acumen concentrated in a few dominant communities to a large number of industrially potential people of varied social strata. To achieve these adumbrated objectives, the Government accorded emphasis on the development of small-scale industries in the country.

Particularly since the Third Five Year Plan, the Government started to provide various incentives and concessions in the form of capital, technical know-how, markets and land to the potential entrepreneurs to establish industries in the industrially potential areas to remove the regional imbalances in development. This was, indeed, a major step taken by the Government to initiate interested people of varied social strata to enter the small-scale manufacturing field. Several institutions like Directorate of Industries, Financial Corporations, Small-Scale Industries Corporations and Small Industries Service Institute were also established by the Government to facilitate the new entrepreneurs in setting up their enterprises. Expectedly, the small-scale units emerged very rapidly in India witnessing a tremendous increase in their number from 121,619 in 1966 to 190,727 in 1970 registering an increase of 17,000 units per year during the period under reference. The recapitulation of review of literature regarding entrepreneurial growth in India, thus, leads us to conclude that prior to 1850, the manufacturing entrepreneurship was negligible lying dormant in artisans. The artisan entrepreneurship could not develop mainly due to inadequate infrastructure and lukewarm attitude of the colonial political structure to the entrepreneurial function. The East India Company, the Managing Agency Houses and various socio-political movements like Swadeshi campaign provided, one way or the other, proper seedbed for the emergence of the manufacturing entrepreneurship from 1850 onwards. The wave of entrepreneurial growth gained sufficient momentum after the Second World War. Since then the entrepreneurs have increased rapidly in numbers in the country. Particularly, since the Third Five Year Plan, small entrepreneurs have experienced tremendous increase in their numbers. But, they lacked entrepreneurial ability, however. The fact remains that even the small entrepreneurship continued to be dominated by business communities though at some places new groups of entrepreneurs too emerged. Also, there are examples that some entrepreneurs grew from small to medium-scale and from medium to large-scale manufacturing units during the period. The family entrepreneurship units like Tata, Birla, Mafatlal, Dalmia, Kirloskar and others grew beyond the normally expected size and also established new frontiers in business in this period. Notwithstanding, all this happened without the diversification of the entrepreneurial base so far as its socio -economic ramification is concerned.

Knowledge-intensive entrepreneurship in sectors such as IT and biotechnology has also increased since the economic liberalization process started in1991. The number of new companies formed during the 1980-2006 period points to a possible growth in entrepreneurship.

Figures from the Ministry of Corporate Affairs show that from 1980 to 1991, the average number of companies formed each year was14,379, while from 1992 to 2006, the average number of companies formed per year was 33,835. According to the paper, liberalization itself kick-started the growth of entrepreneurship in India for it presented businesses in the country with new market opportunities. Liberalization also reduced entry barriers for new entrepreneurs as it dispensed with or reduced regulatory measures such as industrial licensing. Similarly, improved availability of financial support from both official and private sources boosted the growth of entrepreneurship. However, entrepreneurship in India could have grown much faster if the capital market had been strengthened to support the system.

Even today, the capital market is not a major source of finance for enterprises, which mostly rely on internal sources of funding or debt. A study of 588 start-ups that participated in a competition conducted recently by National Entrepreneurship Network revealed that 70 per cent relied on personal savings for initial funding. Government-supported and public-private partnership ventures such as the National Science and Technology Entrepreneurship Development Board, Technopreneur Promotion Program and business incubators in colleges and technology parks also facilitated the growth of entrepreneurship in India. Simultaneously, private sector initiatives such as The Indus Entrepreneurs and National Entrepreneurship Network also supported India's knowledge-intensive enterprises. The increased availability of technically trained people and programs that offered formal training in entrepreneurship also bolstered the growth of entrepreneurship.

The changing economic scenario domestically and globally warrants that this exercise is done in right earnest without losing much time. The goals of economic policy in the nineties and beyond appear now to be twofold:

a) developing a viable, efficient and internationally competitive small industry and
b) creating an innovative, socially responsible and liberated class of entrepreneurs who can take on the challenges that spring up as the process of liberalization and reform progress.

With liberalization setting in, it was bound to be sooner, rather than later, that a new business class would emerge. Never could we have predicted that Azim Premji, who inherited a vegetable oil company, could beat traditional industrialists in becoming the richest Indian. And that a school teacher's son, Narayana Murthy, would own the most valued company in the country, Infosys. Such twists of fate, possible only in today's India, were impossible for decade ago.

The Four Types of Entrepreneurship:

1. Small Business Entrepreneurship:

Today, the overwhelming number of entrepreneurs and startups in the United States are still small businesses. There are 5.7 million small businesses in the U.S. They make up 99.7% of all companies and employ 50% of all non-governmental workers. Travel agents, internet commerce storefronts, carpenters, plumbers, electricians, etc. They are anyone who runs his/her own business. They hire local employees or family. Most are barely profitable. Their definition of success is to feed the family and make a profit, not to take over an industry or build a $100 million business. As they can't provide the scale to attract venture capital, they fund their businesses via friends/family or small business loans. In India there are more than 70 percent small business owners and the number is still rising.

2. Startup Entrepreneurship:

Unlike small businesses, scalable startups are what Silicon Valley entrepreneurs and their venture investors do. These entrepreneurs start a company knowing from day one that their vision could change the world. They attract investment from equally crazy financial investors – venture capitalists. They hire the best and the brightest. Their job is to search for a repeatable and scalable business model. When they find it, their focus on scale requires even more venture capital to fuel rapid expansion. Narayan Murthy, Steve jobs, Sergey Brin and Larry Page are some of the examples of this type of business who expanded their business later.

3. Large Company Entrepreneurship:

Large companies have finite life cycles. Most grow through

sustaining innovation, offering new products that are variants around their core products. Changes in customer tastes, new technologies, legislation, new competitors, etc. can create pressure for more disruptive innovation – requiring large companies to create entirely new products sold into new customers in new markets. Existing companies do this by either acquiring innovative companies or attempting to build a disruptive product inside. Ironically, large company size and culture make disruptive innovation extremely difficult to execute.

4. Social Entrepreneurship:

Social entrepreneurs are innovators focus on creating products and services that solve social needs and problems. But unlike scalable startups their goal is to make the world a better place, not to take market share or to create to wealth for the founders. They may be nonprofit, for-profit, or hybrid. Many NGO's in India are working for the society up liftment or for solving various problems.

Importance of Entrepreneurship:

A very vital and fundamental role is played by entrepreneurship in any economy and the reasons why it holds such a dominant role in the economy is discussed predominantly in the given topic. The constructive impact of entrepreneurs on the society is also quite evident in the given paragraphs. When a 2 year and 10 nation survey was conducted the impact of entrepreneurship stood up evidently saying that the countries have high levels of entrepreneurial activities when compared to countries having lower levels of the same shoed drastic differences in factual data of growth rate. As seen in the beginning of this chapter world's strongest economy USA is also known for its entrepreneurial growth. Now let us go in depth of the reasons why entrepreneurship holds a dominant position in the economy?

The following reasons can be mentioned:

1) Creation of employment:

people often hold a view that all those who do not get employed anywhere jump into entrepreneurship, a real contrast to this is that 76% of establishments of new business in the year 2003 were due to an aspiration to chase openings. This emphasizes the fact that entrepreneurship is not at all an encumbrance to an economy. What more is that approximately 34 million of fresh employment opportunities were created by entrepreneurs from the period of 1980. This data makes it clear that entrepreneurship heads nation towards better opportunities, which is a significant input to an economy.

2) Increase in technology usage:
Almost 2/3% of all innovations are due to the entrepreneurs. Without the boom of inventions the world would have been a much dry place to live in. Inventions provide an easier way of getting things done through better and standardized technology. Example of Apple can be stated here with rapidly improving the technology bringing it to a new level.

3) Increase in wealth of a nation and person as well:
All individuals who search business opportunities usually, create wealth by entering into entrepreneurship. The wealth created by the same play a considerable role in the development of nation. The business as well as the entrepreneur contributes in some or other way to the economy, may be in the form of products or services or boosting the GDP rates or tax contributions. Their ideas, thoughts, and inventions are also a great help to the nation.

4) Individual prospects gets increased:
The individual gets maximum scope for growth and opportunity if he enters into entrepreneurship. He not only earns, the right term would be he learns while he earns. This is a real motivating factor for any entrepreneur as the knowledge and skills he develops while owning his enterprise are his assets for life time which usually, lacks when a person is under employment. The individual goes through a grooming process when he becomes an entrepreneur. In this way it not only benefits him but also the economy as a whole.

5) Opportunity for people:
Although entrepreneurship is a challenging task but in most of the cases the rewards it gives are much more than what one anticipates. It does not only reward an entrepreneur at financial levels but also on individual level. It provides self satisfaction to the entrepreneur.

6) Entrepreneurship provides self sufficiency:

The entrepreneur not only become self sufficient but also provide great standards of living to its employees. It provides opportunity to a number of people working in the organization. The basic factors which become a cause of happiness may be liberty, monetary rewards, and the feeling of contentment that one gets after doing the job. Therefore the contribution of entrepreneurs makes the economy an improved place to live in.

7) Increase in per capita income of a person:

It increases sale and purchase movement along with increase in job opportunities so as to have a better standard of living and overall growth of economy.

8) Reducing Poverty:

Entrepreneur creates jobs and so develops the progressive environment in an economy so as to marginally reduce the percentage of poverty and therefore increasing the development of a country.

Now as we are through with the importance of entrepreneurship let us become a bit more specific and enter into individual country details. The importance of entrepreneurship for some countries is given as under; -

a) Importance of entrepreneurship in America:

US economy is known for entrepreneurs. And it is not coincidence that this world's leading economy is believed to be the most entrepreneurial society in the world. This is the power of entrepreneurs. American economy is well known for its flexibility, adaptability, and grasping of opportunity and it is all because of prevalence of entrepreneurial culture in the economy. The above statement can be well supported with the help of factual data given; taking into account the period 2003 to 2007 the generation of employment has reached 7.2 million which is more than the total jobs being generated in Japan and Europe. For this the economy had to work upon the same for 41 months without any postponement. For these jobs the American workforces are taking back home hefty amounts. Post tax earnings have gone up by 9.6% that is $2,840 from the time when the president has taken oven the charge. The growth of America is in leaps and bounds and that is all because of the insistence and efficiency of American entrepreneurs.

b) Importance of entrepreneurship in European economy:

The importance of entrepreneurial activities was realized by the European economy in the year 1980. Recently a number of fresh opportunities for entrepreneurial proposals are being dug up in European economy. The entrepreneurs are today seen as the catalyst which speeds up the process of creating wealth for the economy, providing jobs, and providing an assorted range of goods and services to the consumers. Entrepreneurial undertakings are now being introduced to college going students which could give them an idea of creating and managing firms, relevance of entrepreneurship firms to European financial system, uniqueness of monetary ventures, managing human resources, pecuniary transactions, legality in dealings, and learning entrepreneurial skills.

c) Importance of entrepreneurship for India:

Entrepreneurs are driving the growth of the Indian economy. For the first time in 200 years, India is getting back its position as an economic power. With GDP growing at 8+ percent, experts are expecting the Indian economy to overtake developed countries in the decades to come.

The Indian entrepreneur is thinking big and aiming high. The recent spate of global acquisitions by Indian industry leaders has forced the business community the world over to sit up and take notice of Indian economic power. The Tata-Corus deal set the tone for the year and was followed by Birla's acquisition of Novelis. With the Indian rupee up against the dollar and the global economy as playing field, we can expect to see more such deals in the future.

Entrepreneurship and Economic development:

In terms of how entrepreneurship has been a stimulant in economic growth, there exist enormous discussions and debates but it is however eminent to realize the importance of constant innovations and rivalry enhancement (Todtling & Wanzanbock, 2003). There has been a problem in defining and measuring entrepreneurial factors and this has further complicated the exact contributions to economic growth. According to Carree and Thurik (2002), the concept of entrepreneurship is multidimensional and largely ill-defined. Understanding the role of entrepreneurship in the process of economic growth will therefore require a framework because of the nature of intermediate variables and connections which exist (Bygrave & Minniti, 2000). The best examples of these intermediate variables include innovation, competition mainly characterized by exit and entry of firms, variety of supply and particular energy and efforts of invested by entrepreneurs. Other conditions of entrepreneurship also add up when it comes to their contributions to economic growth (Robbins, Pantuosso, Parker & Fuller, 2000). These conditions include personal traits, cultural and institutional factors as shown in diagram below.

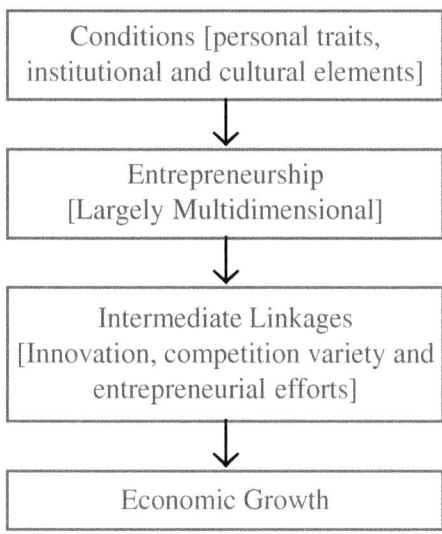

Extended definition of Entrepreneurship:

This implies that linking entrepreneurship to economic growth will be to amalgamate individual to aggregate levels. Considering this linkage however requires revisiting the definition of entrepreneurship, whereby entrepreneurs, either as individuals or a team, manifest their willingness and abilities to create new opportunities in economy (Todtling & Wanzanbock, 2003). In this manner, novel products, production modalities, organizational schemes and product-market combinations are created. The entrepreneurs seek to introduce their newly crafted ideas in the existing market in the face of obstacles and uncertainties. They also make critical decisions in terms of business location, forms and the utilization of available resources and institutions (Acs & Armington, 2004). In a nutshell, entrepreneurship refers to the behavioral attributes of individuals and should not be confused with well-defined professional persons (Lloyd-Ellis & Bernhardt, 2000). Entrepreneurship play a critical role in the development of the economy as this is the key contributor to innovativeness and product improvement. It is one of the important ingredients to the creation of new employments and in the building of communities in ways of offering them jobs. By contributing to local charities, taking part in local business, investing in projects in communities and creating and participating in different networks in entrepreneurship, they buildup robust communities which contribute to the community development. Governments should develop policies which will enhance entrepreneurship by understanding the critical difference existing between small business owners and entrepreneurship. At the same time, a misconception about entrepreneurs and where entrepreneurs can be found can also help the local people to create the right picture of entrepreneurship and thus become aggressive and contribute to economic development.

The entrepreneur who is a business leader looks for ideas and puts them into effect in fostering economic growth and development. Entrepreneurship is one of the most important input in the economic development of a country. The entrepreneur acts as a trigger head to give spark to economic activities by his entrepreneurial decisions. He plays a pivotal role not only in the development of industrial sector of a country but also in the development of farm and service sector. The major roles played by an entrepreneur in the economic development of an economy is discussed in a systematic and orderly manner as follows.

1) Balanced Regional Development:

Entrepreneurs help to remove regional disparities through setting up of industries in less developed and backward areas. The growth of industries and business in these areas lead to a large number of public benefits like road transport, health, education, entertainment, etc. Setting up of more industries lead to more development of backward regions and thereby promotes balanced regional development.

2) Entrepreneurship reduces the Concentration of Economic Power:
Economic power is the natural outcome of industrial and business activity. Industrial development normally lead to concentration of economic power in the hands of a few individuals which results in the growth of monopolies. In order to redress this problem a large number of entrepreneurs need to be developed, which will help reduce the concentration of economic power amongst the population.

3) Capital Formation:
Entrepreneurs promote capital formation by mobilizing the idle savings of public. They employ their own as well as borrowed resources for setting up their enterprises. Such type of entrepreneurial activities lead to value addition and creation of wealth, which is very essential for the industrial and economic development of the country.

4) Creation of Large-Scale Employment Opportunities:
Entrepreneurs provide immediate large-scale employment to the unemployed which is a chronic problem of underdeveloped nations. With the setting up. of more and more units by entrepreneurs, both on small and large-scale numerous job opportunities are created for others. As time passes, these enterprises grow, providing direct and indirect employment opportunities to many more. In this way, entrepreneurs play an effective role in reducing the problem of unemployment in the country which in turn clears the path towards economic development of the nation.

5) Wealth Creation and Distribution:
It stimulates equitable redistribution of wealth and income in the interest of the country to more people and geographic areas, thus giving benefit to larger sections of the society. Entrepreneurial activities also generate more activities and give a multiplier effect in the economy.

6) Better standard of living:
Increase in the standard of living of the people is a characteristic feature of economic development of the country. Entrepreneurs play a key role in increasing the standard of living of the people by adopting latest innovations in the production of wide variety of goods and services in large scale that too at a lower cost. This enables the people to avail

better quality goods at lower prices which results in the improvement of their standard of living.

6) Increase in per capita income and national product as well:
Entrepreneurs are always on the lookout for opportunities. They explore and exploit opportunities,, encourage effective resource mobilization of capital and skill, bring in new products and services and develops markets for growth of the economy. In this way, they help increasing gross national product as well as per capita income of the people in a country. Increase in gross national product and per capita income of the people in a country, is a sign of economic growth.

7) Link between forward and backward:
Entrepreneurs like to work in an environment of change and try to maximize profits by innovation. When an enterprise is established in accordance with the changing technology, it induces backward and forward linkages which stimulate the process of economic development in the country.

8) Promotes Country's Export Trade:
Entrepreneurs help in promoting a country's export-trade, which is an important ingredient of economic development. They produce goods and services in large scale for the purpose earning huge amount of foreign exchange from export in order to combat the import dues requirement. Hence import substitution and export promotion ensure economic independence and development.

9) Helps in Overall Development:
Entrepreneurs act as catalytic agent for change which results in chain reaction. Once an enterprise is established, the process of industrialization is set in motion. This unit will generate demand for various types of units required by it and there will be so many other units which require the output of this unit. This leads to overall development of an area due to increase in demand and setting up of more and more units. In this way, the entrepreneurs multiply their entrepreneurial activities, thus creating an environment of enthusiasm and conveying an impetus for overall development of the area.

Thus entrepreneurship is a very strong motivator for the overall development of an economy. Without improvement of entrepreneur the development of economy will be a baseless dream.

Entrepreneurship and Industrialization :

Industrialization refers to the process in which a society or country (or world) transforms itself from a primarily agricultural society into one based on the manufacturing of goods and services. Individual manual labor is often replaced by mechanized mass production and craftsmen are replaced by assembly lines. Characteristics of industrialization include the use of technological innovation to solve problems as opposed to superstition or dependency upon conditions outside human control such as the weather, as well as more efficient division of labor and economic growth.

Basically Industrialization is most commonly associated with the European Industrial Revolution of the late eighteenth and early nineteenth centuries. The onset of the second World War also led to a great deal of industrialization which resulted in the growth and development of large urban centers and as well as suburbs. Industrialization is an outgrowth of capitalism and its effects on society are still undetermined to some extent, however it has resulted in a lower birthrate and a higher average income.

Entrepreneurship on the other hand is the act and art of being an entrepreneur or one who undertakes innovations or introducing new things, finance and business in an effort to transform innovations into economic goods.

Thus entrepreneurship motivates industrial growth. Industrial sector is thus significantly important for an overall progress of the economy. Industrialization acts as a bridge between entrepreneurship and economic development.

Economic development is a very complex process and requires large scale movement of human resource to an entrepreneurship. This process of shift is affected by industrialization.

Entrepreneurship development is a priority level task of any economy along with industrialization because of obvious features of an entrepreneurship and positive effects it brings on the economy.

The industrial policy of free India was first announced in 1948. This policy envisaged a mixed economy with an overall responsibility of the Government for the planned development of industries and their regulations in national interest. It stated the right of the state to acquire an undertaking. The public interest, and reserved an appropriate sphere for private enterprise. According to this policy Indian industries were classified into three groups.

1. The first category included arms and ammunitions, atomic energy, river valley projects, and the railways. There were to be directly under the management of the state.

2. The second category included coal, iron and steel, aircraft, telephones, telegraphs, wireless, shipbuilding and mineral oils which were also to be the responsibility of the state. The private undertaking in these industries were to, however, continue for at least ten years.

3. The third category included the remaining industries, which were to be developed by private enterprise.

Evaluation of Industrialization in India:

1) Growth of national income:

Growth of national income in GNP per capita in India was about 1.4% in the years from 1960 to 1980. The effects of the reforms of the 1980s are reflected in growth figures: the average GNP per capita growth increased to 3.25%. And with further opening up in the 1990s, the GNP per capita reaches new heights with 3.8% average growth in the period from 1987 to 1997.

2) Poverty Reduction:

In the early 1950s, about half of India's population was living in poverty. Since then, poverty has been declining slowly. The poverty reduction was given new impetus by the reforms: falling from around 55% in 1974 to just under 35% in 1994 by a headcount index. In the 1980s and 1990s, poverty reached historically low levels. Still, because of India's rapid population growth rate, the relative reduction of poverty has not been sufficient to reduce the absolute number of poor which increased from about 164 million in 1951 to 312 million in 1993-94.

3) Reduction of income inequalities:

The reduction of income inequalities has only made slight advances. The biggest advances were made mostly before the reforms. On the other hand, one of the biggest increases in inequality happened in the late 1970s, and the developments for the late 1980s / early 1990s in Figure 1 look promising. Compared to other low-income economies, the inequality is relatively low.

4) Education:

From 1960 to 1977 the reduction of illiteracy was only 11%. From 1978 to 1995, it was 25%, thus much higher. Of course, there are also long-term developments involved here, so that the higher reduction in the second period might be partially due to actions taken in the first period.

5) Health:

Life expectancy, used as an indicator of health, has increased constantly since independence. During the period from 1960 to 1980, it increased from 43 years to 52 years, which is an increase of 21% in 20 years. From 1980 to 1995 it grew to 62 years, which is a 19% increase in only 15 years. This means that the growth of this indicator has increased by a rate of 24% compared to the previous period.

Even clearer is the improvement in the reduction of infant mortality. This was reduced by 25% in the period 1960 to 1995 and a further reduction of 45% took place from 1980 to 1995. This is partially due to better education of mothers, as well as to an improved economic situation of parents.

Still, economic growth alone is not enough. Amartya Sen emphasizes that growth must be "high and participatory". But even today, India's "have-nots are treated virtually as are-not " due to the caste-system and are neglected. Sen toured India in January 1999 to communicate his message that Indians are woefully underfed, undereducated and sickly, even by the standards of poor countries.

Entrepreneur as a Catalyst:

We have seen earlier that entrepreneur acts as a prime force for the development of economy.

Leader is responsible for the progress of the nation, he takes the nation with his strong motivation on a new level. Entrepreneur is a leader who works for a purpose and achieves economic objectives which ultimately results in a tremendous economic progress of a country. Catalyst is a term used here to show the effects of actions of an entrepreneur on the growth, development of the country.

Catalysts are substances that increase the rate of a reaction by providing a low energy "shortcut" from reactants to products. In some cases, reactions occur so slowly that without a catalyst, they are of little value. So it is not a case that country will progress without an entrepreneur with agriculture sector and small business people. But entrepreneurs boost this process therefore they are referred as a catalyst. so basically a catalyst lowers the activation energy required for the reaction.

Hence high economic development often comes hand in hand with increase in entrepreneurship rate for a particular period.

Entrepreneur as a catalyst to Economic Progress:
Following diagram will show the factors proving the above fact that entrepreneur acts as a catalyst to economic progress:

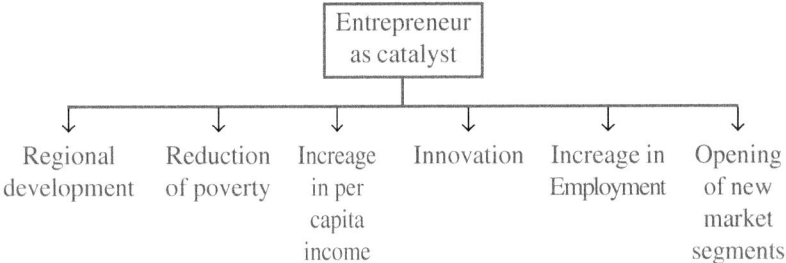

1) Regional development:
Because of new job opportunities and expansion of business activities, entrepreneur becomes responsible for balance regional development. Gujarat is a state where newer entrepreneurship skills are being developed because of good governance as compared to other states of the country. Gujarat will dominate the industrial sector in the future because of its stable growth rate and valuable economic policies attracting many businessman including TATA group.

2) Reduction of poverty:

In India before the industrialization agriculture sector was prominent and hence poverty existed in rural parts of the country. After increase in the service sector and other industrial avenues, per capita income and employment increased resulting in reduction of poverty. Still poverty exist in rural part of a country with tremendous rate which will be vanished with a growth of entrepreneurial activities.

3) Increase in per capita income :

Increase in per capita income is an obvious effect of increase in entrepreneurship in the country. India witnessed huge increase in per capita income of the country with the booming of service industry and other industrial sector.

4) Innovation :

Entrepreneurship and innovation are generally used as synonym because entrepreneurship without innovative idea is impossible. Entrepreneurship suggests innovative ways of business different from that of ordinary business.

5) Increase in employment:

It is also obvious factor showing effects of entrepreneur on the economic development of a country.

Tata group is one of the largest group in India. There are more than 450,000 employees across the country as on 2013. Infosys , Tcs, Wipro have thousands of employees working all over the country.

6) Creation of new market segments:

Reliance is a best example for showing how the entrepreneurship can create new market segments which ultimately results in a growth of the organization. currently Reliance is present in literally every sector of business from perishable food items to digital set top boxes.

Hence economic development is the outcome of the activities of entrepreneurs who put chemicals together and crystallization follows with the laws of nature.

Entrepreneurship : Some Important Definitions

Table showing various definitions of Entrepreneurship is given below

Joseph Alosis Schumpeter : (1883-1950)	Schumpeter described entrepreneurship as a process to shatter the status quo through new combinations of resources and new methods of commerce.
Richard Cantillon :	Entrepreneurship is a matter of foresight and willingness to assume risks, which is not necessarily connected with the employment of labour in some productive process.
Leon Walrus :	Entrepreneurship is not itself a factor of production, but rather a function that can be carried on by an agent.
William Diamond :	Entrepreneurship is equivalent to 'enterprise' which involves the willingness to assume risks in undertaking an economic activity particularly a new one.
Jaffrey A. Timmons :	Entrepreneurship is the ability to create and build something from practically nothing. A human creative activity.
Janil and Howard Stevenson :	Entrepreneurship is a process by which individuals – either on their own or inside organisation – persue opportunities without regard to the sources they currently control.
Isrel Kirzner :	Entrepreneurship means alertness towards profit opportunities.
Arthur H. Cole :	Entrepreneurship is the purposeful activity of an individual or a group of associated individuals, undertaken to initiate, maintain or aggrandize profit by production or distribution of goods and services.
Everett E. Heggins :	Entrepreneurship is meant the function of seeking investment and production opportunity,

	organizing an enterprise to undertake a new production process, raising capital, hiring labour, arranging the supply of raw materials, finding site, introducing a new technique and commodities, discovering new sources of raw materials and selecting top managers of day-to-day operations of the enterprise.
Peter F. Drucker : (1909 – 2005)	Entrepreneurship is neither a science nor an art. It is a practice. It has knowledge base. Knowledge in entrepreneurship is a means to an end. It is not just about making money. It is about imagination, flexibility, creativity, willingness to think conceptually, readiness to take risks, ability to mobilize agents of production and capacity to see change as an opportunity. It is also about marrying passion and process with a good dose of perseverance.
M. Low and J. MacMIllan :	Entrepreneurship is the creation of a privative economic organisation (or network or organizations) for the purpose of gain or growth under conditions of risk and uncertainty.
H. Aldrich and C. Zimmer :	The definition of entrepreneurship includes more than the mere creation of a business, it also includes the generation and implementation of an idea.
Robert Ronstadt :	Entrepreneurship is the dynamic process of creating incremental wealth. The wealth is created by individuals who assume the major risks in terms of equity, time, and/or career commitment or provide value for some product or service.
Robert D. Hisrich :	Entrepreneurship is the process of creating something new with value by devoting the necessary time and effort, assuming the accompanying financial, psychic and social risks and receiving the resulting rewards of

	monetary and personal satisfaction and independence.
John J. Kao :	Entrepreneurship is the attempt to create value through regulation of business opportunity, the management of risk-taking appropriate to the opportunity, and through the communicative and management skills to mobilize human, finanacial, and material resources necessary to bring a project to fruitition.
Robert K. Lamb :	Entrepreneurship is that form of social decision which is performed by economic innovators.
V. R. Gaikwad :	Entrepreneurship connotes innovativeness, an urge to take risk in face of uncertainties and an intuition.
Musscleman and Jackson :	Entrepreneurship is the investing and risking of time, money and effort to start a business and make it successful.
H. N. Pathak :	Entrepreneurship involves (i) perception of an opportunity (ii) organising an industrial unit, and (iii) running the industrial unit as a profitable, going and growing concern.
The Global Entrepreneurship Monitor :	Entrepreneurship, the process of planning, organising, operating and assuming the risk of a business venture, is now a mainstream activity.

The culture of entrepreneurship is deeply rooted: Entrepreneurs are celebrated role models, failure is seen as a learning experience and the entrepreneurial career option is regarded as attractive. In today's economic environment, entrepreneurship is a key component of globalization.

Chapter 7
Organizations and Institutions Promoting Entrepreneurship

Introduction:

Entrepreneurship refers to a process of action an entrepreneur undertakes to establish his enterprise. Entrepreneurship is thus a cycle of actions to further the interests of the entrepreneur. Entrepreneurship is a composite skill, the resultant of a mix of many qualities and traits. This includes imagination , ability to take risks, ability to bring together the factors of production, ability to manage people, ability to understand the technology.

Entrepreneurship is basically dealing with the scarce resources and to put them to maximum advantages.

It is prominently visible in recent years that economic growth in terms of balance regional development, reduction in poverty, increase in standard of living of people is achieved by economy, passively. In other words this significant progress have achieved irrespective of the government policies. So entrepreneurship is acting as a backbone of growth as stated in the previous chapter. So we can deduce that role of government towards the problems of growth is shared by the leadership of talented and dynamic team of entrepreneurs.

Since the success of entrepreneurship activities, government changed its perspectives towards entrepreneurship development and introduced various organizations and institutions involving in promotion and development of entrepreneurial talent in the country.

In this chapter we are dealing with such institutions engage in training, development and finance related issues for entrepreneurs.

Narayan Murthy, Founder of INFOSYS have very good thought on the government role in the process of economic development.

He said that, " India's growth potential has been affected by the inaction and lack of urgency by its bureaucrats.

The government's role to get economic growth back in order has been quite clear for the last many years. For one, they will need to create infrastructure quickly—power, roads, ports, and airports. Second, we have to raise the confidence of investors—domestic and foreign, so that they can be sure that we won't go back on our word. We have to create policies that will enhance productivity, and we will need to make our environment much more welcoming for foreigners. In addition, we will need to improve the efficiency of our bureaucracy and ensure that state governments are much more enthusiastic about investments in their states. Needless to say, we need to create an environment of peace, harmony and stability in the country.

And as far as entrepreneurs are concerned he said that,

" Entrepreneurs need to benchmark themselves with the global best in terms of quality, productivity, and customer focus. The country is open today. Imports come in from all over the world, especially China, which is known for improving quality, productivity and bringing down their price. So we need to become very competitive. Entrepreneurship is a journey that requires significant sacrifice, and therefore it requires entrepreneurs to hold a good value system. We still have many issues in basic healthcare, nutrition, education, and shelter which mean that opportunities exist everywhere.

Information of Institutions and organizations:

Policies pursued by the government over the years have resulted in the growth of small scale sector to a considerable extent. To accelerate the pace of industrialization in the country and also to support economic development, Government at central as well as at state level has made good efforts by way of implementing various measures. Government have set up number of agencies and institutions to assist and support emerging and established entrepreneurs to set up and develop their business at two levels-small and medium. Starting a business or an industrial unit requires various resources and facilities. Finance has been an important resource to start and run an enterprise because it facilitates the entrepreneur to procure land, labour, material, machines to run an enterprise. Hence finance is the most important requirement of the business. Considering this, the government has come forward to help small entrepreneurs through the financial institutions and nationalized banks. But the finance alone is not sufficient to start a business. A minimum level of prior built up of infrastructural facilities is also needed. This is one of the reasons for lack of industrial development in backward areas. Creation of infrastructure involves huge funds. In view of this various central and state government institutions have come forward to help small entrepreneurs in this regard by providing them various kinds of support and facilities. Institutional support makes the economic environment more conducive for the growth of the business. These institutions are supporting the entrepreneurs in various aspects of the business such as education, training, finance, marketing etc.

Support system for the development of entrepreneurship exists in the form of following institutions.

1) Educational institutions providing professional and non-professional or traditional courses
2) Financing institutions
3) Promoting institutions
4) Non-government organizations
5) Government's support
6) Support from family members, relatives and friends

1) Educational Institutions providing Professional and Non-Professional courses:

Even though education is not pre condition for entrepreneurship development, the education which is suitable for a particular type of business definitely fosters the entrepreneurship. There were examples of big businessmen in the past who successfully started and expanded their business without having any formal degree. But they were born entrepreneurs. Today the availability of different institutions providing education, training and guidance to the emerging entrepreneurs has proved that entrepreneurs are not born, but they can be made. The number of educational institutions grew substantially in the last four decades, especially in the last two decades there has been a phenomenal growth in the number of private self-financing institutions. The growth of professional and non-professional colleges has helped the young generation to acquire qualification necessary for choosing a particular type of career.

A survey of entrepreneurs engaged in the manufacturing of Ayurvedic medicines in Thane district shows two categories of qualification acquired by entrepreneurs, suitable and not-suitable. The qualification of entrepreneurs having degree in Ayurveda or Ayurvedic Pharmacy or a diploma in Ayurveda or graduation in Pharmacy or Pharmaceutical Chemistry, Chemistry and Botany of a recognized University is directly related to their business, so they are grouped in the category of entrepreneurs having suitable qualification. A quite few number of entrepreneurs are either Arts or Commerce graduates. They are grouped in the category of entrepreneurs not having suitable qualification. As far as the theme of the present research is concerned the professional colleges means the colleges offering full-time graduate and post-graduate courses in Ayurveda and Pharmacy.

Non-professional colleges are Arts; Science and Commerce colleges offering traditional courses. According to 2001 data Ayurvedic colleges in Maharashtra offering graduate degree are 57 and those offering post-graduate degree are 19 in number with the capacity of admitting 2640 and 260 students respectively. Pharmacy colleges offering degree course are 51 and post-graduate courses are 9 in number with the capacity of admitting 2500 and 148 students respectively.

According to 2003 data total number of Arts, Science and Commerce colleges in Maharashtra are 1319 having the capacity of admitting 8 lacs students. Out of these colleges 873 colleges are grantable, 222 colleges are partially grantable and 224 colleges are permanently Nongrantable (Pradhan) Following training institutions are currently active in this area of entrepreneurship development:

1) Entrepreneurship Development Institute of India (EDII)
2) Small Industries Service Institute (SISI)
3) Council for Advancement of People's Actions and Rural Technology (CAPART)

Of the above institutions we are going to discuss the first one that is Entrepreneurship Development Institute of India (EDII) and detailed discussion about the MCED, DIC and Maratha Chamber of Commerce and their role have been done in later part of this chapter.

a) Entrepreneurship Development Institute of India (EDII):

Entrepreneurship Development Institute of India (EDII), Ahmadabad, is an autonomous non-profit institution, set up in 1983, sponsored by following financial institutions:

a) Industrial Development Bank Of India (IDBI)
b) Industrial Finance Corporation Of India (IFCI)
c) Industrial Credit and Investment Corporation Of India (ICICI)
d) State Bank Of India (SBI)

The government of Gujarat has also provided assistance for the setting up of EDII.

Entrepreneurship Development Institute of India (EDII) has been spearheading an entrepreneurship movement throughout the nation with a belief that entrepreneurs need not necessarily be born, they can be developed through well conceived and well directed activities.

EDI has helped set up twelve state-level exclusive entrepreneurship development centers and institutes. Entrepreneurship has been taken to schools, colleges, science and technology institutions and management schools in the water performance sector by including entrepreneurship in their curricula. The University Grants Commission appointed the EDI as an expert agency to develop a curriculum on Entrepreneurship.

In the international arena, the development of entrepreneurship by sharing resources and organizing training programs, have helped the EDI earn support from the World Bank, Commonwealth Secretariat, UNIDO, ILO, FNSt, British Council, Ford Foundation, European Union and other agencies.

Objectives of Entrepreneurship Development Institute of India (EDII) are following:

1) Augment the supply of trained entrepreneurs through training
2) Generate opportunities for the development of small scale businesses

3) Generate a multiplier effect on opportunities for self employment
4) Improve managerial capabilities of small scale industries
5) Promote Micro- enterprise at the rural level
6) collaborate with similar organizations in India and other developing countries to accomplish the above objectives
7) Motivate the support environment to facilitate potential as well as existing entrepreneurs to establish and manage their enterprises
8) augment the supply of trainer motivators for entrepreneurship development
9) contribute to the dispersal of business ownership of new knowledge and thus expand the social base of Indian Entrepreneurial class
10) Contribute the creation and dissemination of new knowledge and insight into entrepreneurial theory and practice through research.
11) participate in institution building efforts.
12) Provoke the spirit of ENTREPRENEURSHIP among youth of the country

Entrepreneurship Development Institute of India (EDII) has supported the creation of Centers for Entrepreneurship Development and Institute of Entrepreneurship Development in various states of the country to achieve institutionalization of ED activities.

Training Programs of Entrepreneurship Development Institute of India (EDII):

The training programs of the Institute are grouped under four heads:

1) Entrepreneurship in education
2) Micro-finance and micro-enterprise development
3) Performance and growth of existing entrepreneurs and
4) Performance improvement of ED institutions and ED programs.

The educational environment and policy framework offer opportunities for sustainable self- employment to ensure the contribution of the workforce to the industrial economy. Entrepreneurship, self employment and enterprise creation thus provides solution to the crisis of both unemployment and disguised unemployment. With this in view, the Entrepreneurship Development Institute of India (EDII) has designed and successfully implemented several national and international training programs and workshops for the academic community and for the youth.

Entrepreneurship Development Institute of India (EDII) organizes training programs on Informal Micro Credit Delivery Systems (IMCDS) and management for strengthening the participating NGOs in the area of informal credit. To strength NGOs through building their managerial capabilities, the EDII has launched a program on the sustainability of NGOs through better management. It also provides a platform to NGOs and bankers with the objective of facilitating the access of the poor to credit.

The small industry sector is required to boost up to face the challenges of liberalization and globalization. The Entrepreneurship Development Institute of India (EDII) in 1984 initiated Performance Improvement Program in anticipation of the need of management strategy and growth-oriented awareness and competencies. These programs focus on functional management inputs and strategy techniques, thereby channelizing entrepreneurial competencies to motivate enterprise

b) State level training organizations in promoting Entrepreneurship:

1) Maharashtra Centre for Entrepreneurship Development (MCED)

Area of Entrepreneurship Development:

MCED has been a pioneer in espousing social and economic entrepreneurship since 1988. It is a training institute in the core area of entrepreneurship development. It works as a facilitator and guide for the creation and cultivation of the entrepreneurial spirit and the concept of 'self-employment' in a nation that is largely driven by third party employment.

At MCED, there is always the hummable buzz of people discussing, brainstorming, making plans and revamping shelved ideas. The thrum of work and the exciting buzz of activity is an indelible part of the work culture. MCED is also an incredibly technology savvy organization which, not surprisingly, is amongst the few offices to enforce the paperless office concept.

Related to other organizations:

which, not surprisingly, is amongst the few offices to enforce the paperless office concept. This relaxed and fertile office environment has been nurtured by the lack of a formal overseer as is the case in other organizations. The Governing Council is the final authority for this stalwart organization. Governing Council The council makes the guidepost decisions but the driving force of the organization has always been the sheer determination of the employees.

Training Committee Works:

The training that has to delivered across a wide range of core specializations must have the business angle and the necessary macros in place to ensure sustainable quality and uniformity. This work is overseen by the Executive Committee. The Executive Committee does the pulse checking of the organization and trickles down the macro perspective to the root level, as is part and parcel of any organization. The Executive Committee is answerable to the Governing Council and is headed by the Executive Director of the company. For more details on the persons who constitute this body, please click the related link on the left panel.

Growth and Expansion of MCED:

From the time that MCED first maneuvered uncharted territory in the state where 'entrepreneurship training' was unheard of, even less known was this nascent organization that was christened as Maharashtra Centre for Entrepreneurship Development' in short, MCED. MCED is phonetically pronounced as 'em-ced'. With a handful of employees, trained at the Entrepreneurship Development Institute of India (EDI-I) Ahmedabad, the eventual fate and destiny of the organization was, at that time, unknown and could only be guessed at. The organization restructured and played on the opportunities that the country's tumultuous political and social scenario threw up and in its 'opportunist' plan of growth and expansion, it has grown into the leviathan giant in entrepreneurship training that it is now.

Entrepreneurship Training:

Every employee has been empowered and has a sense of pride and ownership in the stakes of the institution. MCED's product and sole selling point is the niche 'entrepreneurship training' that has been hailed and recognized across the country as being on par with international standards. So, where the policies are decided by the Governing Council, the Executive Committee keeps its ear to the ground to have a real time perspective of the business as a whole.

MCED is a training institute where is the product 'entrepreneurship training' is intangible. Thereby, the main assets of the organization are the human resources that are an invaluable asset.

APPRECIATION FROM ENTREPRENEURSHIP DEVELOPMENT INSTITUTE (INDIA):

"MCED is the best entrepreneurship development institute in the country. It has become self-reliant and proves its entrepreneurial capability." It further certifies that the percentage of trainees who start their own business after training from MCED is creditable. 90% of the trainees pay their loans in time with full honesty.

The findings of EDI – I are –

a) 90% of the trained borrowers are regular in the repayment of loans

b) Rs. 1/- spent on training earns investment of Rs. 1,509/-.

c) Investment of Rs. 6530/- on training creates one permanent employment.

What this means is that we have a higher conversion ration of successful and sustained entrepreneurs who have been trained as per the philosophy propounded by David McClelland. To read comprehensive literature on entrepreneurship online, please visit our 'Publication' section on the homepage. If you would want to take the exciting leap into being the master of your own future, contact any of our offices listed in the left panel and find out what you can do for yourself with our help.

2) District Industries Centre (DIC):

These centers were established in the year 1978 with a focus to provide integrated administrative support for promotion of small scale industries in rural areas. These centers act as a chief coordinator in respect of various government departments and other agencies. DICs provide a single window interacting agency to the budding entrepreneurs at district level.

The organizational structure of DIC's consists of one general manager four functional managers and three project managers to provide Technical Services.

Role of DICs:
1) Technical support for preparation of project report
2) Information on machinery and equipment
3) Promotion of new industrial estate
4) Approval of project reports of special types
5) Training through Entrepreneurship development programme
6) Allotment of raw materials
7) Financial assistance under self-employment schemes
8) Assistance under Equipment Leasing Scheme through NSIC
9) Assistance in marketing linkage with central government
10) Assistance in ancillary industry tie-up with government undertakings
11) Marketing assistance through participation in exhibition / Trade fairs / Buyers-sellers meet
12) Attending problems related to SSI registration/ Bank loan/ marketing of production
13) Financial assistance for modernization of unit
14) Export assistance
15) Assistance in sick unit revitalization
16) Promoting entrepreneurship through National level awards for innovative products
17) Promotion of products under non-conventional energy sources
18) Assistance in standardization of products
19) Assistance in design and product development for handicrafts

3) Maratha Chamber of Commerce Industries and Agriculture (MCCIA):

MCCIA has been playing a significant role in accelerating the industrial and economic development of Pune region for more than seven decades now. It is one of the most active chambers of Commerce in India and has been instrumental in promoting number of institutions in Pune. MCCIA has continuously driven to make Pune a global business destination and has been catalyst for economic development of the region.

Following part will explain the role of MCCIA in state development.

1) Functioning of the Chamber:

The Chamber renders services to the industry through its 30 committees consisting of reputed experts, professionals and entrepreneurs through strategic planning, sending memorandum to Government on policies and regulations and organizing educative events and symposiums for members.

2) The History :

Maratha Chamber of Commerce and Industries (MCCI) was founded by Late Mr. A. R. Bhat in 1934 to accelerate the industrial growth in and around Pune. Mr. Bhat was a journalist and an economist and was the General Manager of the famous Marathi newspaper 'Kesari'. Thus the first office of the MCCI was established in 'Kesari' premises. In 1947 the Chamber moved to their own premises on Tilak Road, Pune. In 1998 agricultural activities were also included in the scope of the Chamber's activities and MCCI became MCCIA. In July 2006 most of the offices shifted to the modern office at the MCCIA trade Tower on Senapati Bapat Road, Pune.

3) Vision:

To facilitate the transformation of Maharashtra as the premier destination globally for Industry, Trade, Commerce and Agriculture.

4) Mission:

1) To make a beginning by developing Pune into a world class centre by improving its physical and social infrastructure.

2) To promote Information Technology, Biotechnology as focal industries by leveraging the existing educational, industrial and agricultural resources in Maharashtra.

3) To be effective voice of Trade, Commerce, Industry and Agriculture by :

   a) Recommending appropriate policy guidelines to the concerned authorities.

   b) Forging a common platform with affiliated bodies with a view to project a unified voice for all associations active in commerce, industry and agriculture.

c) Providing a platform for networking and knowledge sharing especially to enhance the abilities of the members to forge ahead in the competitive world.

d) Increasing our membership.

e) Recognizing the services of individuals and organizations for their outstanding contribution to social and economic development in Maharashtra.

5) Activities:

1) Making representations at the concerned Government Departments.

2) Partnership with the Government for different projects.

3) Branding for Pune to attract investments.

4) Infrastructure Development.

5) Promoting international Trade and Business.

6) Guidance and assistance to SMEs.

7) Spreading awareness on the current issues and latest Technology and Tools.

8) Events : Seminars, Workshops and Exhibitions.

9) Database Creation.

10) Economics Research activity

6) Committees:

1) Agriculture & Agri-Business

2) Animation and Gaming

3) Auto Component

4) Central Excise

5) Civil Aviation

6) Corporate Legislation

7) Corporate Social Responsibility

8) Defense

9) Direct Taxation

10) Education

11) Electronics

12) Energy

13) Finance Sector & Insurance

14) Foreign Trade Regulations

15) Health Care
16) Hospitality
17) HRD
18) Industrial Relations
19) Information Technology
20) Infrastructure Facility & Real Estate
21) Innovation and R & D
22) International Business and Relations
23) Polymer & Rubber
24) Quality and Productivity Excellence
25) Road & Traffic Management
26) Senior Executive's Forum
27) Small & Medium Enterprises
28) State Level Taxation
29) Tourism
30) Women Entrepreneurs' Committee

Thus MCCIA is a very strong institution for the development of entrepreneurship in the state of Maharashtra

2) Financial Institutions:

Finance is one of the essential requirements of an enterprise. Without adequate funds, no business can be developed. In India, Central and state governments are promoting number of financial institutions to bring in the industrial development in the country. Some of the important financial institutions are:

1) Industrial development bank of India (IDBI)
2) National bank for agriculture and rural development (NABARD)
3) Export import bank of India
4) Small industrial development bank of India (SIDBI)
5) Industrial investment bank of India
6) Industrial finance corporation of India (IFCI)
7) Industrial Credit and Investment Corporation of India (ICICI)
8) Industrial Reconstruction Bank of India
9) Indian banking system and commercial banks
10) State Financial Corporations

11) Life Insurance corporation of India (LIC)

12) Unit Trust of India (UTI)

3) Promoting institutions:

Government at state and central level has introduced lot of measures to support the growth and development of entrepreneurs. Government has set up number of promoting agencies and institutions to help emerging and established entrepreneurs, especially small and medium entrepreneurs. These institutions support the entrepreneurs in respect of training, finance and marketing. Some of such institutions are:

1) District Industries centers (DICs)

2) Small Industries Development Organization(SIDO)

3) The National Small Industries Corporation Ltd.(NSIC)

4) Small Scale Industries Board (SSIB)

5) Small industries Service Institutes (SISIs)

6) Industrial estates

7) Khadi and Village Industries Corporation(KVIC)

8) Technical Consultancy Organizations

Of these detailed information about DIC have been given in previous topic.

4) Non Government Organizations supporting entrepreneurship:

Non-governmental organizations (NGOs) are legally constituted corporations created by natural or legal people that operate independently from any form of government. The term originated from the United Nations, and normally refers to organizations that are not a part of a government and are not conventional for-profit businesses. In the cases in which NGOs are funded totally or partially by governments, the NGO maintains its non-governmental status by excluding government representatives from membership in the organization. In the United States, NGOs are typically non-profit organizations. The term is usually applied only to organizations that pursue wider social aims that have political aspects, but are not openly political organizations such as political parties.

NGOs are difficult to define and classify, and the term 'NGO' is not used consistently. As a result, there are many different classifications in use. The most common NGOs use a framework that includes orientation and level of operation. An NGO's orientation refers to the type of activities it takes on. These activities might include human rights, environmental, or development work. An NGO's level of operation indicates the scale at which an organization works, such as local, regional, international or national.

We are concerned about the role of NGOs in the entrepreneurship development and thus we shall discuss some of the leading NGOs in this particular area in the following part.

1)Wadhwani foundation:
Wadhwani foundation is a non-profit organization founded by Dr. Ramesh Wadhwani, an IT entrepreneur in Silicon Valley, California (Hattangadi, 2007).The foundation's strategy is to inspire, educate and nurture new entrepreneurs, to develop and fund non-profit programs and organizations that create entrepreneurial education, build networks, raise awareness, perform research and help develop a supportive policy environment. In addition, certain sections of the population need extra support due to their physical or economic constraints. Such people receive the benefits from such foundation.

2) National Entrepreneurial Network (NEN):
The National Entrepreneurship Network is a network of academic institutions across India performing research and developing and providing world-class education, skill building programs, networking activities. The goal of this network is to launch 2,500 entrepreneurs who will create a minimum of 500,000 jobs by 2014. This will create as much value for the Indian economy over the next ten years as the IT industry has over the past fifteen years. This network will inspire thousands of talented individuals to choose entrepreneurship, and equip them to build companies that are more successful, on a larger scale, creating 100,000 new jobs. Every participating institution will be able to leverage the resources created by other NEN partners. Participation in joint activities creates opportunities for larger networks and continued sharing of ideas. The NEN interaction will significantly enhance the effectiveness, quality, scale and reach of each individual participant in

the network. The research performed by NEN partners will increase the understanding of the needs, contributions and characteristics of entrepreneurs and their ventures.

3) Ashoka Foundation:

This foundation is trying to develop social entrepreneurial culture all over the world. Ashoka fellows inspire others to adopt and spread their innovations. Ashoka develops models for collaboration and designs infrastructure needed for this growth. Ashoka fellows are leading social entrepreneurs who can provide innovative solutions to social problems. Ashoka fellows work in over sixty countries around the world. They are remodeling systems of resource allocation, infrastructure and value-chains.

4) Dr. Reddy's Micro Entrepreneurship development Cell (MEDC):

This NGO works for developing small scale livelihood options for youth from marginalized communities in agriculture, animal husbandry and vending. MEDC encourages, nurtures and supports youth for entrepreneurship. MEDC also helps them in the matters of business plan, banking and market linkages. MEDC provides the youth with the required life skills, technical skills, soft skills and career skills to perform well to establish their own small scale units as their livelihoods options (Hattangadi, 2007: 209).

6) Government Support:

The Ministry of Small Scale Industries designs policies, programs, projects and schemes in consultation with its organizations and various stakeholders and monitors their implementation with a view to assisting the promotion and growth of micro and small enterprises. The role of ministry of small scale industries is thus to mainly assist the states in their efforts to promote the growth and development of the SSI, enhance their competitiveness in an increasingly marketed economy and generating additional employment opportunities.

The specific schemes/ programs undertaken by the organizations of the Ministry try to provide one or more of the following:
a) Adequate credit from financial institutions/ banks;
b) Funds for technology upgradation and modernization;

c) Integrated infrastructure facilities;

d) Modern testing facilities and quality certification laboratories;

e) Access to modern management practices and skill upgradation through appropriate training facilities; assistance for better access to domestic and export markets.

f) Cluster-wide measures to promote capacity building and empowerment of the units and their collectives, in addition to all or some of the above-mentioned supports.

g) Implementation of the policies and programs/ schemes for providing various support services to SSIs is undertaken through its attached office, namely, the Office of Development Commissioner (SSI) also known as Small Industries Development Organization (SIDO) and the National Small Industries Corporation (NSIC).

5) Support from family members:

Family members including spouse, children and parents create a strong support system for the budding entrepreneurs. This support can be emotional, financial, administrative or technical. Any businessperson has to face various problems like ups and downs in the business, payment recovery problem and financial crunch resulting from it, worker's non-co-operation and industrial unrest. Spouse can extend support during all such types of crises. In some communities like Marwari, there is a provision of community funds which can be used to help the needy entrepreneurs. Maharashtrians generally prefer service to business which usually involves risks. This risk aversion tendency keeps them away from the business. Friends and relatives also avoid those entrepreneurs who are in need of financial help. Now this picture is changing fast. Mental set up of Maharashtrians is also changing and it is reflected in the preference of young and talented Maharashtrians for business. Their inclination for business facilitated the setting up of different associations through which they solve their mutual problems by way of organizational efforts.

Conclusion:

In a concluding part we can say that these training and supplementary institutions are very important in participating entrepreneurial development and success in provoking more and more people for changing their role in the economy and to become successful entrepreneur.

Emerging entrepreneurs are just like babies. They cannot stand on their own feet, at least in the initial stage of their business, without the support of strong support system. The support system helps them knowingly and unknowingly in various forms. It can be in the form of educational and training institutes from where they acquire qualification, necessary for their business. These institutes play an important role in grooming and nurturing the budding entrepreneurs in the right direction. It is the inspiration taken from the biographies of great industrialists and the efforts taken by the educational institutions these days to develop interests among the students to select entrepreneurship as a career option, that slowly help in transforming the personality of an ordinary individual into the personality of an entrepreneur.

It is true that a true leader is not born but made. Just like that true entrepreneur is not born but he becomes.

Chapter 8
Biographical Study of Entrepreneurs

An entrepreneur is a person who have something special than an ordinary person because of that speciality he runs an organization taking each and every important decision crucial for the survival, progress and development of the same. Every entrepreneur is responsible for the progress of economy which is the resulting outcome of the success of his individual organization. An entrepreneur becomes a role model for the generations to come and therefore it becomes necessary to understand life and nature of such entrepreneurs who managed an organization with whooping success.

In India many business role models can be selected for study but as per the syllabus we are discussing following three business personalities who have excelled in their particular scope of work.

1) Narayan R. Murthy:

Personal Life:

Nagavara Ramarao Narayana Murthy is the full name of the Mr. Narayana Murthy. He was born on Aug 20, 1946 at Mysore, Karnataka to Sri R H Kulkarni and Vimala Kulkarni. His father was a high school teacher and an avid reader of English Literature. He was very good in studies, especially in Physics and Mathematics. He joined National Institute of Engineering, then affiliated to University of Mysore and graduated in 1967 with a degree in Electrical Engineering. Two years later, in 1969 he received his master's degree from Indian Institute of Technology, Kanpur.

His wife, Sudha Murthy (Kulkarni), is a social worker and author. She does philanthropic work through the Infosys Foundation. He has two children, a son Rohan Murty and a daughter Akshata Murthy. Rohan Murty is a Junior Fellow in the Society of Fellows at Harvard University. He has a Ph.D. in Computer Science from Harvard University and a Bachelor's degree in Computer Science from Cornell University and has held fellowships at MIT, Caltech, and Microsoft Research. He has authored several papers and patents as part of his research on wireless and mobile computing. On 1 June, he joined Infosys as an executive assistant to his father. Rohan Murty is married to Lakshmi Venu, daughter of TVS Motor Company Chairman Venu Srinivasan. Akshata Murthy completed her MBA from Stanford Business School and is married to Rishi Sunak.

Professional Life:

Murthy started his career at IIM Ahmedabad as chief systems programmer. There he worked on India's first time-sharing computer system and designed and implemented a BASIC interpreter for Electronics Corporation of India Limited. He started a company named Softronics. When that company failed after about a year and a half, he joined Patni Computer Systems in Pune.

Murthy along with other six software professionals founded Infosys in 1981 with an initial capital injection of Rs 10,000, which was invested by his wife Sudha Murthy. Murthy served as the CEO of Infosys for 21 years from 1981 to 2002 and was succeeded by co-founder Nandan Nilekani in 2002. At Infosys he articulated, designed and implemented the Global Delivery Model for IT services outsourcing from India. He held the executive position of Chairman of the Board from 2002 to 2006, when he became the "non-executive" Chairman of the Board and Chief Mentor. In August 2011, he retired completely from the company and taking the title Chairman Emeritus.

Murthy serves as an independent director on the corporate boards of HSBC(The Hongkong and Shanghai Banking Corporation) and has served as a director on the boards of DBS Bank(The Development Bank of Singapore Limited), Unilever, ICICI and NDTV. He also serves as a member of the advisory boards and councils of several educational and philanthropic institutions, including Cornell University, INSEAD (European Institute of Business Administration), ESSEC(*École Supérieure des Sciences Économiques et Commerciales* is one of the foremost business schools in France), Ford Foundation, the UN Foundation, the Indo-British Partnership, Asian Institute of Management, a trustee of the Infosys Prize, and as a trustee of the Rhodes Trust that manages the Rhodes Scholarship. He is also the Chairman of the Governing board of Public Health Foundation of India He also serves on the Asia Pacific Advisory Board of British Telecommunications. In 2005 he co-chaired the World Economic Forum in Davos. He also received an honorary degree from Lancaster University.

On 1 June 2013, Murthy returned to Infosys as Executive Chairman and Additional Director.

Success Story:

Founder of Infosys, Mr. Narayan Murthy is legendary person who brought Indian company in the listing of NASDAQ. He brought up the IT sector in India and created lot of employment opportunity in India. He dreamt of forming IT company with his six friends and his wife Sudha assisted in accomplishing dream. In the year 1981 when he was dreaming to have his company but somewhere was lacking behind in generating funds. The unknown savings of his wife Rs. 10, 000 helped him to take the first step which brought turning point in his life. According to him people who strive to achieve their dream, people who work hard are not backward people, instead they are forward. Apart from giving new route to IT industry in India he is also known for his simplicity. He believes in sharing wealth with needy people. The more he gets, the more he shares. In the year 1991 when Indian doors for liberalization where left open, he got hold of this opportunity and then never turned back. However huge his company may be but his way of living life is still simple. This small town Mysore boy has still not changed his life style and this can be known because still he does not know to drive a car. During Saturdays when drivers have off, Mr. and Mrs. Murthy prefer to travel by company's bus. They are continuing to maintain low profile, even though they earn a good the amount of money. Narayan Murthy was offered for security of Z category when Dr Rajkumar was kidnapped by Veerappan. This gentlemen did not accept the security offer as he did not want people near to him to get disturbed because of security.

In 2012, NR Narayana Murthy was named among the 12 "greatest entrepreneurs of our time" according to a Fortune magazine list that is topped by Apple's late chief Steve Jobs. It includes Microsoft founder Bill Gates and Facebook CEO Mark Zuckerberg for turning "concepts into companies" and changing the "face of business".

2) Cyrus Poonawala:

Dr. **Cyrus S. Poonawalla** is the Chairman of Poonawalla Group which includes Serum Institute of India, which is an Indian biotech company that manufactures pediatric vaccines.

He did his schooling from The Bishop's School in Pune, and later graduated from Brihan Maharashtra College of commerce, in 1966. He was awarded a Ph.D. by the Pune University in 1988 for his thesis entitled "Improved Technology in the manufacture of specific Anti-toxins and its socio-economic impact on the Society".

Dr. Poonawalla was married to the late Mrs. Villoo Poonawalla and have a son Adar who is the Executive Director (Operations) at the Serum Institute and is leading Serum's charge into new drugs and markets.

Dr. Poonawalla has a passion for collecting cars and has fascinating collection of sports cars and custom-built limousines. He owns a Cessna 560XL Citation Excel jet, Bell 407 helicopter and recently acquired a new Falcon 900EX business jet. As per Forbes Mar 2013 rankings, Cyrus Poonawalla's net worth is $3.9 Billion and is ranked 14th richest person in India & 346th richest in the world. Cyrus Poonawalla is the founder of Serum Institute. Serum Institute of India Ltd. is the world's largest producer of Measles and DTP group of vaccines. It is estimated that two out of every three children immunized in the world is vaccinated by a vaccine manufactured by Serum Institute. The company's range of products has been used in 140 countries across the globe. The Poonawalla Group of Companies has grown and diversified into a multi-faceted organization with a nationwide network of offices, extensive manufacturing facilities, and fully fledged research and development capabilities with a total annual turnover exceeding Rs. 12 billion. The Group is professionally managed and engaged in a wide array of activities ranging from Horse Racing and Breeding, Biotech, Engineering and Hotels. Prime factors in the Group's growth and success have been its emphasis on quality, innovation, dedication and customer support. The Group is committed to preparing for the future by operating its existing divisions to their full potential through market opportunities that may present themselves in the service of the nation's core capabilities. Its current endeavors have a direct bearing in matters of consequence in the nation's physical well being and the efficient operations of its infrastructural economy.

Early Career:

In 1966 Dr.Poonawalla and his brother Zavaray launched Serum Institute of India which launched its first therapeutic anti-tetanus serum within two years, and began producing the anti-tetanus vaccines.

Born into a family whose decades-old ties to India's horse racing circuit through the family's owned Poonawalla Stud Farms, by age 20, Dr. Poonawalla realized that horse racing had "no future in the socialist India of the time." And first experimented with cars. Along with his school friend he built a $120 prototype sports car modeled on the D-type Jaguar. But producing it on a commercial basis required more money than they had. Dr. Poonawalla abandoned the idea, realizing that making a product for the masses, rather than India's elite, would be a smart move. A chance conversation with a vet at the farm led Dr. Poonawalla into vaccines. At the time, the farm's retired horses were donated to government-owned Haffkine Institute in Mumbai, which made vaccines from horse serum.

Dr. Poonawalla figured he could take up the challenge of meeting the demand for vaccines in the country by extracting the serum from horses himself and producing cheaper vaccines. He and his brother Zavaray, who partnered with him early on, raised $12,000 by selling horses and persuaded their father to put up the rest. They set up the venture in 1966 on a 12-acre lot and began producing vaccines.

In 1966 Dr.Poonawalla and his brother Zavaray launched Serum Institute of India which launched its first therapeutic anti-tetanus serum within two years, and began producing the anti-tetanus vaccines.

By 1974 they introduced the DTP vaccine, which protects children from diphtheria, tetanus and pertussis, followed by an anti-snake-venom serum for snakebites in 1981.

In 1989 Serum Institute began the production of its Measles Vaccine M-Vac and within a year Serum Institute became the country's largest vaccine manufacturer. In the 80s India was made self-sufficient for Tetanus, Diphtheria and Whooping Cough vaccines thanks to the production from Serum Institute.

In 1994, Serum Institute got accredited by the World Health Organization (WHO) to export vaccines from India and started supplying high quality vaccines to U.N. Agencies such as UNICEF (United Nations Children's Fund), PAHO (Pan American Health Organization).

From the inception, Dr. Poonawalla's primary concept was not only to make life-saving drugs and vaccines, which were in shortage in the country, but also to see that every child was protected. At that time his dictum was "Health for all by 2000 AD". The resultant effort was the National Program of Immunization, which is largely dependent on the vaccines manufactured by Serum Institute and now that philosophy has proliferated worldwide to International U.N. Agencies.

By 1998 Serum Institute was exporting vaccines to over a 100 countries and by 2000 one out of every two children in the world was vaccinated by a vaccine of Serum Institute of India.

Dr. Poonawalla's strong belief in "No Compromise with Quality" and willfull commitment in "Health for All with affordable Vaccines" has today lead Serum Institute to become India's leading biotech company producing over a billion doses a year that sell in more than 140 countries around the world.

Horse Racing:

Dr. Poonawalla has strong ties with India's horse racing and breeding Industry through the family's Poonawalla Stud Farms, started by his late father and now run by him and his younger brother Zavaray. He was the sole representative of India at the International Federation of Horseracing Authorities (IFHA) and was a member of the Asian Racing Federation (ARF) for more than a decade.

He was also elected Vice Chairman of the Asian Racing Federation and also held various esteemed posts in the Horseracing field that include Chairman, Turf Authorities of India, Royal Western India Turf Club, Stud Book Authority of India and Pattern Races Committee.

3) Milind Kamble:

Milind Kamble chairman of Dalit Indian Chambers of Commerce and Industry (DICCI) is an activist and working for dalit empowerment through forming business activities and promoting business mind among dalits. He is owner of a construction company

Milind Kamble said that, "Ultimately, we would aspire to see a Tata or Birla from among the Dalits,"

The spark for setting up Dicci has come from the industry lobby group, Federation of Indian Chambers of Commerce and Industry (Ficci). Dalits consist of castes and tribes, scheduled or listed in India's Constitution as the under-privileged sections of society.

The Dalit Chamber came into being in 2005 as a lobbying platform for the ambitious Dalit entrepreneurs. It also plans to support education and training, entrepreneurship and mentoring in the community. It mandates at least 50 per cent of the jobs in the firms of its members for Dalits.

"With this, we also want to break the general perception that Dalits are always dependent and cannot do anything on their own. They need reservation for jobs, scholarship for education, BPL card for mid-day meals, etc, is the perception," Kamble said.

Milind Kamble is a son of a school teacher from Latur district of Maharashtra.At the vanguard of the capitalist movement of Dalits, Kamble said, "Our aim is to be a job-giver and not a job-seeker." Kamble himself is a job- giver, being the managing director of the Rs.101-crore Fortune Construction Company.

He was among the few Dalit engineers who spurned the easy way of getting into a government job using reservation. Instead, Kamble worked with a private firm as a civil engineer for five years before floating his own firm - FCC. He also serves as director on the boards of two more firms.

Dicci was formed by members who have established themselves as industrialists without taking advantage of government sops. From five chapters and 500 members, Kamble wants to grow it 10 fold in the next 12 months.

"Quality and cost are what matters to a client, and nothing else.

That way after globalization, caste does not matter much," said Kamble, who has been inducted as an invitee member of the National Advisory Committee (NAC) of the UPA government.

"Dicci wants to take advantage of reservations and grow as part of the system to build capital and remain job givers. That way we seek inclusive growth as against exclusive growth others advocate," Kamble said.

Thus after reading short biography of Milind Kamble we can deduce that he is an active inspiration for many young and aspirant youth striving for starting a new project and wants to become an entrepreneur.

References

Recommended Books
1. A complete guide to successful Entrepreneurship – Pandya G. N. – Vikas Publishing House
2. Business Environment - Francis Cherunilam – Himalaya Publishing House.
3. Business Environment - Tandon B C.
4. Crusade - ShirkeB.G. - Ameya Prakashan
5. Dynamics of Entrepreneurship Development and Management - Desai Vasant – Himalaya Publishing House
6. Entrepreneurial Development – Khanka - S. Chand.
7. Entrepreneurial Development – Gupta, Shrinivasan - S. Chand.
8. Entrepreneurship - Robert D. Histrith - Tata McGraw Hill Publishing Co.
9. Environmental Pollution & Health – U. K. Ahluwalia
10. Environmental Studies basic concepts – U. K. Ahluwalia
11. Environment Protection Act (1986) Bare Act.
12. Essentials of Business Environment - K. Aswathappa - Himalaya Publishing House
13. Indian Economy - Dutta Sundaram –
14. Trainers Manuals - NIESBUD, New Delhi.
15. Trainers Manuals - NIMID, Mumbai,
16. Udyog - Udyog Sanchalaya, Mumbai.

Questions for Self Study

Essay Questions

1) **Chapter 1:**

1) Define the term Business Environment. Describe in detail the factors of Business Environment. **[Oct 2011, April 2011, Oct 2012]**
2) Distinguish Inter-relationship between Entrepreneur and Environment.**[Oct 2010]**
3) State Concept of Business Environment. Explain in detail the types of Business Environments **[April 2011]**
4) Define the term Business Environment. Describe in detail the types of Business Environment.**[April 2012]**

2) **Chapter 2**

1) Define Natural Environment. Explain in detail the ways of protecting natural environment.
2) Elaborate the concept of Pollution and state ways of overcoming pollution problem.
3) State types of Natural resources. Explain the concept of depletion of natural resources.
4) Define Natural resources. What are the ways of conservation of natural resources.

3) **Chapter 3**

1) Explain in details about Problems of Growth.
2) What is Poverty ? Explain causes and remedies of Poverty **[Oct 2011]**

3) Explain Causes and Remedies of Unemployment [Oct **2010, April 2011, April 2012**]
4) What is Parallel Economy ? Explain Causes of Parallel Economy. [Oct **2010**]
5) What is Inflation ? Describe the causes and remedies of Inflation **[Oct 2012]**

4) Chapter 4

1) What do you mean by Entrepreneur ? Describe in detail the qualities of a successful entrepreneur. **[Oct 2011, Oct 2010, April 2011, April 2012, Oct 2012]**

5) Chapter 5

1) Describe in detail Habits of Entrepreneurs.**[Oct 2010, April 2011, April 2012]**
2) Explain in detail Dynamics of Motivation. **[April 2011]**

6) Chapter 6

1) Define Entrepreneurship. Elaborate evolution of Entrepreneurship in India.
2) Explain the concept of Entrepreneurship. How entrepreneur acts as a catalyst for economic growth?
3) Evolution of the definition of entrepreneurship. Explain types of entrepreneurship.

7) Chapter 7

1) Write essay on Support systems for the development of entrepreneurship.

Short Notes:

1) Chapter 1

1) What is 'Educational Environment' **[Oct 2010]**
2) Write a note on Natural Environment **[Oct 2010]**
3) State Concept of 'Business Environment'**[Oct 2010]**
4) Cultural Environment

6) Chapter 6

1) Explain importance of Entrepreneurship).[**Oct 2010**]
2) Define the term entrepreneurship[**Oct 2010**]
3) State any two names of Entrepreneurship in Economic Theory [**Oct 2010**]
4) Explain Concept of 'Entrepreneurial as a Catalyst'[**Oct 2010**]

7) Chapter 7

1) Economic Development and Industrialization [**Oct 2011**]
2) Maharashtra Centre for Entrepreneurship Development (MCED) [**Oct 2011**]
3) Write a detail note on Entrepreneurship Development Institute of India (EDI). [**Oct 2011**]
4) What is 'MCED' ? [**Oct 2010**]
5) What is 'D.I.C.' ? [**Oct 2010**]
6) Write a detail note on Non-Government Organisations (NGOs).[**April 2012**]

8) Chapter 8

Write Short Notes on the following
1) Narayan Murthy
2) Cyrus Poonawala
3) Milind Kamble

पुणे विद्यापीठाच्या प्रथम वर्ष कला व वाणिज्य शाखेच्या सुधारित अभ्यासक्रमानुसार (२०१३-१४) नामवंत लेखकांनी लिहिलेली उपयुक्त क्रमिक पुस्तके. तसेच महाराष्ट्रातील इतर सर्व विद्यापीठांना उपयुक्त.

(एफ.वाय.बी.कॉम.)

१) व्यावसायिक अर्थशास्त्र — डॉ. एस. व्ही. ढमढेरे
   डॉ. एस. जी. शिंदे

२) विपणनशास्त्र आणि विक्रयकला — डॉ. एस. व्ही. कडवेकर
   (विपणनशास्त्राची मूलतत्त्वे)

३) व्यावसायिक पर्यावरण व उद्योजकता — प्रा. रवींद्र कोठावदे

४) कार्यालयीन संघटन-कौशल्ये — डॉ. जगदीश लांजेकर

५) ग्राहक संरक्षण व व्यावसायिक नीतिमूल्ये — डॉ. जगदीश लांजेकर

6) Financial Accounting — Prof. Vaishali Apte
   Prof. Suresh Bhirud
   Prof. Bhaskar Naphade

7) Business Economics — Prof. Vaishali Apte

8) Marketing and Salesmanship — Dr. S. V. Kadavekar
   (Fundamentals of Marketing)

9) Business Environment & Entrepreneurship — Prof. Ravindra Kothavade

10) Business Mathematics and Statistics

(एफ.वाय.बी.ए.)

१) भारतीय अर्थव्यवस्था : समस्या व भवितव्य — प्रा. डॉ. सतीश श्रीवास्तव
   (Indian Economy : Problems and Prospects)

२) भारतीय शासन व राजकारण — प्रा. नितीन बिरमल
   (Indian Government and Politics) — प्रा. वैशाली पवार

३) सामान्य मानसशास्त्र — प्रा. मुकुंद इनामदार
   (General Psychology) — प्रा. केशव गाडेकर
   डॉ. अनिता पाटील

४) समाजशास्त्र परिचय — प्रा. पी. के. कुलकर्णी
   (Introduction to Sociology)

५) छत्रपती शिवाजी महाराज आणि शिवकाल : (सन १६३०-१७०७) डॉ. गणेश राऊत
   (Chhatrapati Shivaji Maharaj and his times : 1630 - 1707)

६) भूरूपशास्त्राची मूलतत्त्वे — श्रीकांत कार्लेकर, अ. वि. भागवत
   (Elements Of Geomorphology)

७) आधुनिक भारतीय राजकीय विचार — डॉ. प्रकाश पवार
   (Modern Indian Political Thought)

टिपा

टिपा